WITCHY SOUR

THE MAGIC IN MIXOLOGY SERIES BOOK TWO

GINA LAMANNA

For updates on new releases, please sign up for my newsletter at www.ginalamanna.com.

Feel free to get in touch anytime via email at gina.m.lamanna@gmail.com!

SYNOPSIS

A *DARK STRANGER. A DEADLY POTION. A school for scoundrels...*

Lily Locke has barely had time to sink into her role as The Isle's newest Mixologist when a series of events sends her world spiraling out of control. Her vampire cousin is overtaken by a serious bout of blood intolerance issues, and the key ingredient for the antidote is missing.

Meanwhile, Zin is training day and night under the watchful eye of Grandma Hettie to break into the elite, male-dominated world of the Ranger security force, but it's a constant uphill battle. Then Ranger X turns Lily's world upside down when he breaks the longstanding rules of the island and throws both her heart and her head into a tailspin.

Hooded strangers, dangerous potions, and a budding romance threaten to ruin all that Lily's worked to achieve. Add in a stolen spellbook, and Lily's barely able to hold her head above water.

When a body turns up on the beach, Lily must catch the murderer before a true battle begins...

Welcome back, Islanders.

ACKNOWLEDGEMENTS

Dear Readers,

Thank you for continuing on with the next story from The Isle! Without you, *Witchy Sour* couldn't exist. I read every email, comment, and message I receive, and it always brightens my day. Thank you!

Book Helpers:

I appreciate each and every one of you who helped with this book in some shape or form!

Joy – For making quotes sound good with your graphics!

Stacia – Thank you for your patience, and for being more organized than I ever could.

To Connie – For the cast of beautiful dolls – I can't wait to show them off!

Kim – For making me laugh!

Dianne & Barb for your advance reading, and for your support.

SMO'7 – For the most perfect palm tree on The Isle.

To Mom & Dad—For letting me believe in magic

To Alex—For believing in The Isle. я тебя люблю!

To Meg & Kristi—For being as good of sisters as Poppy and Zin

To my Oceans Apart ladies—To the best book friends a girl could ask for

To Sprinkles On Top Studios—my awesome cover designer. Photo Courtesy of Deposit Photos

And last but not least, to all my family and friends, thanks for making me laugh.

CHAPTER 1

"**Y**OU HAVE *GOT* TO GET some sleep."

I looked up, forcing a half smile at the surprise visitor lounging against the doorframe.

"Watching that safe is not going to bring your spellbook back, Lily," Ranger X said, sliding into the storeroom like a whiff of smoke. Despite his large frame, he moved like the wind, bringing with him the crisp, pleasant scent of the outdoors mixed with something else, something sharper. Peppermint, maybe. "Can I help you?"

"No," I sighed, letting my hands fall to the table and my head slump onto them. "I know your Rangers are looking for it, but... *The Magic of Mixology* is my future."

"It's not so bad." Ranger X clunked something on the table next to me, and a quick peek through my folded arms told me it was a bottle of wine. "They say the true Mixologist rarely needs to look up spells. It comes from—"

"In here, I know," I said, thumbing toward my chest. I had gone over this a thousand times in my own head. "But '*in here*' is a little confused right now since I didn't even know I was a witch until a few weeks ago."

Instead of responding with words, his hands carefully, cautiously came to rest on my shoulders. He let his fingers linger on my bare skin, waiting for an argument. I gave him none.

With painstaking precision, he began to rub my shoulders, the skin exposed around my simple, spaghetti-strapped sundress. I groaned, a happy groan—the sound of stress audibly slipping from my muscles—before collapsing onto my arms once more, dipping my head onto a pillow of my own limbs.

"You are wound tighter than a spring," he said, kneading each individual knot with care before moving on to the next. "Not healthy, Lily."

"Tell me something I don't know," I mumbled, trapped somewhere between a state of bliss and shock. Ranger X had never touched me like this, and even if I'd wanted him to stop, I couldn't have spoken the words. There was a magic in his touch, a tenderness that had nothing to do with spells or potions. "You don't have to be here, you know. It's late."

"I was heading home and saw your light on, so I decided to stop."

"You just happened to be patrolling The Isle with a bottle of wine?"

His pause was fleeting, his fingers tensing on my shoulders until he sensed the joke, and laughed. "You'd be surprised at some of my terrible ideas."

For some reason, the awkwardness of his response made me snort with laughter, and I straightened up, even though letting his hands slip from my shoulders was a sin. "I don't think it's a bad idea at all."

"No?"

I shook my head, finally taking a moment to tear my eyes from the empty safe where my spellbook once lived. This time I focused, taking a hard look at the man who flipped my stomach in somersaults. X must have come straight from the office because he was wearing a suit—and that man could *wear* a suit.

Unfortunately, he was missing a few pieces. Somewhere along the way, he must have lost a tie, along with a few buttons from the top of his white shirt, leaving it open a bit lower than it should be, his tan skin exposed. The black mop of hair on his head was ruffled, and if I wasn't mistaken, there was a tiny twig poking out of his messy locks.

"Had some business to take care of before I came here," he said with an apologetic shrug. "Sorry about my appearance."

I swallowed in lieu of a response. To me, he looked perfect. The scar over his eye decorated his expression, making him appear both tough and vulnerable.

I raised a hand to his cheek where a small scratch gleamed red. "You're hurt. Let me get you a bandage."

Ranger X wrinkled his nose like someone had unleashed foul egg odor. "For this scratch? No." He gave a devilish wink. "Think this is bad? You should see the other guy."

My eyes widened with a mixture of disbelief and horror. "What did you *do?*"

"Nothing. Nothing *bad*, I promise."

I narrowed my eyes at him. "Are you lying to me?"

"No?" He pursed his lips, his eyes searching for a way out of my interrogation. "Want some wine?"

I gave him a slow roll of my eyes that showed I knew he was changing the conversation. However, I didn't have the strength to argue with him. "Only if you'll join me for a glass. I'm already depressed enough without drinking alone."

That got a smile out of him, and from somewhere in his suit he pulled a bottle opener and went to work on the wine.

"You didn't plan this at all," I teased as he handed me a glass. I took a long sip of the deep, red wine, the rich taste warm and comforting. Between the backrub and the wine, I'd be counting sheep in no time. "What do you think about this?"

Ranger X followed my nod toward the empty safe. He strode around the room, his brown eyes soaking up every detail of the place. When he finally returned to my side, he set those eyes on me.

He said something, a mixture of words that probably made sense, but since I was too busy soaking up his presence, I missed all of them. Those eyes of his were so dark they walked a fine line between good and evil.

"What do you think?" he asked, startling me so thoroughly that I sloshed half my wine out of the glass.

"Um, yes?" I quickly grabbed a rag and wiped up the spill.

"You weren't listening." It was a statement, one that curved the corner of his lips upward. "I was asking if you had any theories about who might have had access to the spellbook before it was stolen."

"Oh, well," I paused in thought. "Gus, of course. The previous Mixologists. I'm sure there are others who have seen it. Gus doesn't hide the manuscript. During the day, it's almost always out on the table in plain sight. He'll yell at people if they touch it, but I know for a fact that Mimsey and Poppy and Zin have flipped through it when he's not looking."

"So, anyone who's visited the bungalow could've seen it."

I wrinkled my nose. "I suppose. We rarely locked it away. The night it was stolen was the first night we'd put it in the safe since my arrival on the island. Usually Gus is here so late, and back so early, he'll either take it with him, or leave it out for a few hours."

"So whoever stole it had to know it wouldn't be guarded—at least, not by you or Gus—on that very night."

"I don't like the sound of that," I said. "That would mean it's someone close enough to know our schedule."

Ranger X merely raised an eyebrow.

"It couldn't have been," I said. "With the exception of Harpin, I *like* everyone I've met on this island. Why would they steal from me?"

"Does Harpin have a motive to steal the book?"

I bit the edge of my lip. "Maybe. He's been angling for my job for a long time. If he had the potions book, maybe he'd try to take over. Use it in his tea shop to cook up something deadly, I don't know."

Ranger X seemed distracted, and it took me a moment to realize he was staring at my lips instead of listening to what I was saying.

"Hey, you," I said, reaching out and snapping a finger in his direction. "I'm talking to you."

He recovered as gracefully as possible, blinking and dragging his gaze up to my eyes. "I was… reading your lips."

"Yeah, yeah. Anyway, there's a spell system guarding this book. It's extremely thorough, according to Gus."

"I know the system, I've studied it." Ranger X shook his head as my mouth opened. "Don't worry, I have no use for your light reading. If I wanted your Mixology book, I'd already have it. Lily, believe me when I say—it's not the *book* that I want."

The way his eyes played over my face, I sensed there was something else he wanted entirely. However, now was not the time to deal with our personal history. "You've studied the spell system?"

He nodded. "I use it as an example when training new Rangers. It's one of the most complicated security systems out there."

"Can you walk me through it?" I asked. "I've seen Gus's rough sketch, but I don't understand it. He's not the most patient teacher in the world."

X's eyes gleamed. "You don't say. Where is he, by the way?"

"Went home for the night. Even Gus needs sleep, you know."

"I'll help, but then you must promise to get some rest, too. You were practically snoring when I rubbed your back."

"I don't snore."

"That's what they all say."

"*All?*" I raised an eyebrow. "Who does *all* include?"

"Figure of speech!" Ranger X grimaced, a slight red adding to the tanned color of his face. "Lily, I don't—I'd never—"

"I know, I know, I'm kidding." I reached over and squeezed his arm. I might as well have squeezed a brick. "Now, how does this system work?"

❧

Hours later, well past midnight, Ranger X and I stepped back.

"I think that's everything," he said slowly.

"Isn't that enough?" I surveyed our creation—a series of ribbons,

threads of yarn, pieces of rope, all crisscrossing in organized chaos—
and my eyebrows raised. "All these spells, and somebody still stole
the book?" I asked, my voice colored with shades of disbelief and
awe. "How?"

"That's the million coin question," X said. "Don't forget, there
was also a spell on the safe itself. If someone who had never touched
the book tried to remove it from the safe, an alarm would sound
both here, and at Ranger HQ. It never went off."

"So that means someone found a way around the spell."

"That, or it's someone who has handled the book previously.
Someone who understands the intricacies of the spell system, and
someone smart enough to fool them."

I sighed, not liking the list of names that were left for me to
ponder. "I can't think anymore."

"I have to get going, but it'd be a shame not to finish this wine."
He held up the bottle, a hopeful look in his eye. "Will you help me
polish it off?"

I held up my glass. "Can't hurt."

"It's good for you. Loosens you up."

I crooked an eyebrow in his direction. "You're trying to loosen
me up?"

"Not you—everyone. I mean, not everyone, I mean wine
loosens everyone up." Ranger X closed his mouth, and then started
over. "Do you want me to top off your glass or not?"

I laughed, this unsure, awkward side of him was one I rarely
saw. When he was around his team of Rangers, he was all boss, all
the time. I liked this side for a change. "Come join me."

Before he sat down on the couch, he bent over a never-used
fireplace, muttered a few words, and a fire began to roar. "Ambiance,"
he said briskly as he joined me on the couch.

We lounged next to each other, both of us sipping our wine in
silence, pondering the maze of spells. To me, it looked all *Beautiful
Mind* with a twist of chaos theory, and I was mostly glad there were
people smarter than me to understand it.

The only thing I knew for certain, however, was that whoever had stolen the spellbook was somebody I knew. Somebody who knew me, knew my schedule, knew the security system.

That was a short list of people, and a list I didn't like to consider under the circumstances.

Instead of running over that list of names, it was easier to close my eyes and snuggle up on Ranger X's shoulder. He worked nicely as a pillow. I curled my legs under my body and told myself I was only resting my eyes.

The next thing I knew, my wine glass was lifted from my fingers, and a set of arms thick as tree trunks lifted me, cradled me, and carried me upstairs. I struggled to open my eyes through the haze, but sleep called louder than consciousness, and my body fell limp against Ranger X's chest.

He deposited me as gently as he might a kitten on my bed, the fluffy comforter enveloping me as he tucked the edges in snug around my shoulders.

"Goodnight, Lily Locke," he said, brushing strands of flyaway hair off my forehead. "Sleep tight."

I might have mumbled something back, but already, I was well on my way to slumber.

When I woke in the morning, I found it impossible to remember if the brush of his lips against my forehead had been a sweet piece of reality, or nothing but a dream.

⚬⚬⚬

An orangish glow peered over the horizon and turned the sky a beautiful watercolor of cotton candy pink and Easter-egg purple. Taking a seat on one of the bar stools, I cupped a warm concoction both stronger and tastier than human coffee. Here on the Isle, it was known as a Caffeine Cup.

I woke early this morning, despite my late evening with Ranger X. The memories of last night had me humming as I awaited the arrival of the regulars. The bungalow, as I'd so fondly nicknamed the beach house and bar combination, served as my home, workshop, and storefront. It was a cute place with purple and pink paint, and large windows hugged by rickety white shutters.

I greedily stole the last few minutes of peaceful quiet for myself. The palm leaves rustled, the gentle lake waves lapped against the white sand shores, and the sky grew powder blue and free of clouds. The beautiful climate, one of sunshine and balmy temperatures, was controlled by a nifty little charm that allowed the islanders to live under tropical blue skies year round, despite our location in the middle of Lake Superior.

The relaxing morning sounds were shattered by two bubbly voices carrying across the open sand. With a smile, I hopped to my feet and turned up the fire under the teakettle. I waved at my cousins and set two more coffee cups out, along with a fancy beaker that looked like a chemistry set to brew my infamous new recipe.

"You're all ready for us? What gets you up before noon?" My plump, sunny cousin named Poppy bounced up the stairs to the bar and gave me a squeeze. "That smells delicious."

I grinned and placed a filter on top of the beaker. Dumping a finely mixed potion the consistency of coffee grounds into the contraption, I winked. "And that's just the smell. Wait until you get a taste."

"If that tastes as good as it smells, I might never leave," Poppy groaned. "You said you're looking for roommates, right? I'm ready to get out of my mom's abode. I mean, I love Chunk, but I think he can take care of himself."

I winked. "The offer never expires."

I'd only known my cousins for a few weeks, but already I'd mentioned the possibility of them moving in with me. The bungalow had plenty of space for all of us, and it'd give them the opportunity to move out of their childhood homes. Unfortunately, we'd been so busy with the hunt for the missing spellbook that the subject hadn't come up again.

Resting a hand on my hip, I shut the burner off and poured the boiling water over the powder. The instant the water hit the mixture, the tiny grains bloomed up to three times their size, reminding me of a marshmallow heated in the microwave. The water dripped through slowly, and Poppy deeply inhaled the rich scent.

"Is she okay?" I waved a hand in front of my other cousin's face. "Earth to Zin! Want some?"

Zin was the exact opposite of Poppy. While Poppy was blond and bubbly and over-the-top in every way, Zin was all sharp angles, jet black hair, and edgy attitude.

"You're interrupting her concentration," Poppy said with an eye roll. "She's been trying to see if she's telepathic."

Zin's eyes were closed. At the sound of her name, she took a few steps forward, feeling her way around blindly. She tried to sit down, but her hands grasped at air until finally, she gave up and peeked. Climbing onto a stool, she pouted. "I can hear you rolling your eyes, Poppy, and you should stop. I think I'm getting the hang of it."

"You just opened your eyes to find the chair," Poppy said. "Forget it, Zin. You're not telepathic!"

Zin grumbled something then swiveled the bar stool to face the counter. She closed her eyes and raised both hands to the side of her head with her thumb and middle fingers touching in circles. She could pass for a far more feminine, and far more petite, version of Buddha.

"Are you meditating?" I asked.

"I'm telepath-ating."

"You look like you're meditating," Poppy said. "That's how meditators sit."

"Have you ever seen a telepathic person sit?" Zin opened one eyelid. "Maybe this is how they sit."

Poppy rolled her eyes and looked at me. "The Rangers have an open enrollment period in a month and Zin's training hard for it."

"I didn't know they had open enrollment," I said, pouring the concoction from the beaker into cups. I pushed the mugs over to them and then filled another one for myself. "I thought that was more of a recruitment thing."

"It is, in a sense. This is the first time they're letting folks volunteer to be Candidates," Poppy said with a smug smile. "I suggested it. She has to be chosen to participate of course, but it's a small step forward."

"That's great! I'm surprised they went for it," I said cautiously. "The Rangers seem... strict."

The Rangers were the darkest, the most dangerous wizards on The Isle. They walked the line between good and evil to protect the rest of us—a never-seen, never-heard sort of bunch.

"Your boyfriend was a big reason that the program started." Poppy gave me the side-eye as she took a sip from the mug. "You should tell him thanks."

My cheeks flamed red. "He's not my boyfriend!"

"What is he?" Zin peeked through the other eyelid. Now both her eyes were open, and the only thing meditative about her position was the crossing of her legs and the circles of her hands.

"Well, Ms. Telepathy, shouldn't you be able to tell me?"

"Telepathy is a fine art. I don't just go reading each and every one of your thoughts," Zin said crossly. "It takes time, energy, and practice, and I don't have the patience to be focusing on your love life. I'm working on bigger and better things."

"The only thing you need to focus on is not spilling your coffee all over the counter." Poppy nodded toward the cup in Zin's hand, which was balanced at a precarious angle. Foregoing all signs of telepathy, Zin groaned and swung her legs down from the stool, setting the cup on the counter. Poppy shook her head. "I'm telling you that telepathy is not a requirement to become a Ranger."

"What are the requirements?" Zin asked. "If you'd just tell me, I wouldn't have to keep bothering you."

"She's been asking me this question every day since the trials have been announced, and she knows I can't say," Poppy said, turning back to me. She raised her mug. "This is good, by the way."

"Why can't you say? The requirements aren't public?"

Zin shook her head. "It's considered a 'natural fit' process. What the Rangers look for in a Candidate is largely a mystery. They say the true signs of a Ranger will emerge naturally, and if they give off hints, people will game the system."

"That makes training difficult," I said with a sympathetic look to Zin. "I'm sure you'll do fine."

"Hold on, don't you wiggle out of this one," Poppy said, pointing to me. "Even though Zin's not telepathic, she's got a point. What is Ranger X to you? You can't keep secrets from us, you know. We're your cousins and your friends, so that's a double no-no. Spill the beans, Lily."

"There are no beans to spill!" I shrugged, stalling with a huge gulp of coffee. I took my time swallowing, but even so, both pairs of eyes bored into my skull until I relented. "Fine, you want the truth? There's nothing between us... anymore. We're just working together to find *The Magic of Mixology*, that's all. Nothing more than that."

"Why don't I believe you?" Poppy narrowed her eyes at me. "I think there's more to it than that."

"You're a skeptic, and you're as bad as Hettie trying to set me up on a date. I've hardly been here two months and you all are acting like I'm turning 'spinster' on my next birthday."

"Well, you aren't getting any younger," Zin pointed out. "No offense."

"You can't talk." Poppy jabbed a finger at Zin. "You're more interested in learning how to fight people than love them."

"There are more important things than getting married." Zin

pointed her nose up and sniffed. "I'd say becoming a Ranger is one of them."

"So?" Poppy asked sharply. "Where is X now? Has he bought you dinner yet or something?"

"I told you! We're just working on the case. Come here, I'll show you the map we made last night." Turning from the bar, I led the girls into the storeroom.

"Last night, huh?" Poppy followed me inside, surveying the hectic display in the room. "Did he stay over?"

Off to one side of the storeroom was the semi-hidden staircase that led a few floors up through a twisty, turny passageway. At the top was the attic—I warmed thinking of my trip upstairs with X just hours before.

"No, of course not," I said. "We were working. That's it. We have a working relationship."

"Your relationship is a piece of work," Poppy grumbled. "Get over it and just make out with him already."

I waited a moment, praying my ears would stop burning red. "Look. Do you see the ropes? That's what we were doing all night. Believe me, it wasn't romantic."

"What am I looking at?" Zin stomped in a few moments later, her leather pants making slight squishing noises as she strode across the bar with thick, intimidating boots that somehow looked stylish. The whole vibe matched with her leather jacket and heavy eyeliner, complemented by the straight-edged bob falling just below her chin; the style a little longer in the front and shorter in the back.

"I thought you were telepathic," I said, unable to help myself. "Why don't you tell me?"

Zin crossed her arms. "Maybe I'm not telepathic, okay? I'm still working on finding my Uniqueness."

"Your uniqueness?"

"Every Ranger has some quality that makes them a unique asset to the business," Poppy explained. As the part-time dispatcher for

Ranger HQ, Poppy often had surprising insight into the top secret agency. "For some, it's a learned skill. You know, like the ability to kill someone with a pinky nail or tie five hundred different styles of knots or speak six languages."

"That's a lot to learn," I said. "What's the other option?"

"Some have natural tendencies that make their Uniqueness easier to learn. For example, there's one Ranger who can sniff out a poisonous potion from miles away. He's got a natural skill, but he's trained himself to be the 'go-to-guy' when mysterious potions show up on The Isle."

"Those are the only options?" I asked. "Where does telepathy come in?"

"There's one last group," Poppy explained. "Those born with an advantage. You know, the shape shifters and what not—those who can add a unique twist to the agency."

"It's difficult to find a Uniqueness that hasn't been taken already," Zin said. "I thought about knife throwing, but there's already an expert. Same with archery. There's nothing left!"

"Why can't you have two people with the same thing?" I asked. "It doesn't seem like it'd hurt to double up."

Poppy and Zin swiveled their gazes to me like I'd grown eight heads.

"That's why it's called a Uniqueness," Zin said eventually. "It has to be unique."

"But why?"

"Think of it this way," Poppy said. "Each Ranger is a snowflake. This is not one massively trained army, it's a small group of swift, deadly men. The more people who know the secrets they do, the less private those secrets become, and sometimes, those secrets need to remain buried. Each Ranger has one specialty, and once that specialty is covered—that's it."

"In the event one of them can't continue to do their job for any reason..." Zin started, but trailed off. "Let's just say, I'd be waiting a long time for an opening. That is why I need to make my own."

"I'll help you," I said. "So will Poppy. What are you good at?"

Zin shrugged. "I can shoot arrows. I can handle a knife, and I can smell a potion about fifty percent of the time."

Poppy snorted. "No way are you becoming the poison tester. Those aren't great odds at survival, so I won't let you."

"That's what I'm saying! Nothing stands out," Zin said, her shoulders sinking. "I'm never going to make it."

"That's not true." I moved to her side, squeezing her in a one-armed hug. "We'll figure it out. Maybe it'll just take some time for the right idea to hit you. You're a shifter, what about that?"

Zin stiffened under my arm. "No."

"She's sensitive about that subject," Poppy whispered, leaning in. "Still can't figure out her final form. The Rangers won't let her in until she can shift consistently, so she's got a month to figure it out. That's probably why she's tense. Do you have a potion for that? Some sort of Stress Relief beverage?"

"I don't need it," Zin argued. "I don't want to talk about it anymore. What are these ropes all about, anyway? Is this about your missing spellbook?"

I nodded, wishing I could help her feel better, but I didn't know the first thing about shape shifting. Or Rangers. Or really, much of anything magical except for the few simple potions I'd been learning with Gus.

Zin raised her eyebrows at the ropes strewn across the room. "How is this supposed to help you find a thief?"

I stepped over a piece of wire to stand in the center of the room. "Each one of these yarn strings represents a protective spell that'd been actively guarding the spellbook. They act like an alarm system, and in theory, one or more of the alarms should have gone off before the book could have been stolen."

"No alarm went off?" Poppy asked.

"That's the problem," I said. "Whoever stole the book

maneuvered past one of the most complicated spell systems on the island."

"Do you think it's someone with insider knowledge on the setup?" There was a hint of caution in Poppy's voice that caught me by surprise.

"That's the puzzle," I said. "I don't know. Gus and I have been over every last inch of this place, and neither he nor I have any guesses as to how a person could get away so cleanly. I worked it out with X last night, and he didn't have a clue, either."

"Gus is a smart guy," Zin said. "He knows his way around this place?"

"Better than anyone," I said, starting to nod. Then I caught the meaning behind Zin's words and stopped mid-head-bob. "You're not suggesting that Gus had something to do with this?"

Zin raised her shoulders. "I mean... the person must be familiar with the spellbook. They must have had access to the book before. They must've picked it up, and probably looked through the layout of the spell system protecting it. The person would likely have to know this space very well."

"They'd also have to know you," Poppy said, chiming in. "What time you go to sleep, how you work, your systems."

"No!" I shook my head violently. "Gus loves this place more than anyone else. There's no way he'd sabotage it, or steal the book. He's worried sick about it; we both are!"

"Where is he now?" Zin gave a pointed stare around the room. "What's he up to?"

"I don't have to babysit him every minute of the day," I said more crossly than I intended. Like it or not, my feathers were ruffling. Plus, Gus should've been here by now, and Gus was never late. "He can come and go as he pleases."

"Don't be blind to the facts," Zin said. "You have to consider every option. Even those closest to you."

"He'd never—"

"I'd never what?" Gus spoke from across the room, catching us all off guard as the door banged open against the wall. "I heard my name. I'd never what?"

I swallowed hard. My assistant and mentor stood hunched over a cane, his white hair a bit windblown, and his blue eyes creased in something resembling amusement. "Nothing."

"Don't say nothin', I ain't an idiot." Gus smacked his cane against the ground. When he tired of whacking the floor, he crossed his arms and nearly knocked Poppy's head off with the wrong end of the stick. Gus didn't need the cane to walk—he needed it to make a racket when he was upset. The man looked like an octogenarian, but he had the strength of someone half his age, and the sassiness of someone double his age. "Go on. Be honest, now. I can tell when yer lyin'."

I glared at Zin. "Nothing. We were just talking about—"

"—potions," Poppy interrupted. "Lily is working on the Menu. We were trying to help her come up with a new drink name."

"I think I've got it," I said with a nod. Quickly running through a list of drinks in my head, I picked the first one that came to mind. "Whiskey... er, sour. Witchy Sour!"

Gus rolled his eyes. "I think yer'all lyin' to me."

Poppy shook her head. "Lying is such a strong word."

"But it's the accurate one," Gus shot back. "You two are tryin' to convince Lily that she's gotta examine the one person who had access to the spellbook. The one person on The Isle who logically could've pulled this heist off. Am I right?"

An awkward silence descended on the room.

"Not really," I hedged. "I was just explaining the spell system to them. About how unlikely it was that someone could've pulled off the theft at all."

"They've got a point." Gus tossed his cane onto the long, wooden table in the center of the room. "A darn good point."

We usually used the table top to chop leaves, examine

ingredients, and mix up new potions, but for now, Gus ignored its purpose and used it as a cane-rack. Walking without any trace of a limp, he crossed the room with ease and stopped in front of the open safe. The girls and I glanced at one another as he examined the empty space.

"Gus?" I asked eventually. He hadn't moved for a few minutes, and I worried he'd taken a nap standing up. "What are you thinking?"

Gus turned around with a wild grin on his face. "I'm thinkin' you've got yourself a good set of friends, Lily. These two ain't afraid to point blame at anyone, including myself, and I can appreciate that."

I slid a sideways gaze at Poppy, who shrugged back at me.

"Takes guts," Gus said with a laugh. "But that's who you need around you. These ladies don't trust anyone. I like 'em."

Offering a hesitant smile, I spoke cautiously. "I like them too."

"Good." Gus's amused expression vanished in an instant. "So tell them to scram because we've got work to do."

CHAPTER 2

TWO HOURS LATER, I FLEXED my fingers and pushed back my chair. After hunching over a table for the last few hours, I was ready to be done working for the month, let alone the day.

I'd been tasked with the intense process of documenting hundreds of jars from the most recent supply shipment. Gus wasn't a patient man on a good day, and today wasn't a good day. He worked like an assembly line, passing one bag of supplies to me before I was done with the previous five.

"I need a break." I stood up. "My fingers are going to freeze up like this."

Gus raised his eyebrow as I made gnarly claws in his direction. "Then freeze up they will. We're not done yet."

"Maybe not," I said, peering over his shoulder. "But unfortunately, we've got a visitor. You've always said that customers come first!"

Grumbling, he didn't bother to look up from his work. "Come right back once you serve'm."

With a sigh of relief, I slipped out of the apron I always used while sorting supplies. I was still so new to this Mixology business that I didn't trust myself to properly identify all of the ingredients, and if one particle of Moonstone dropped on my shirt, it'd burn straight through like acid. Luckily, the apron had been enchanted to repel harmful particles. It was the magical version of a Hazmat suit.

I bounced out the door, which led from the storeroom to the

outdoor bar appropriately named Magic & Mixology. "Hey there, how can I help…" My sentence trailed off as I laid eyes on the man before me. "You?"

The visitor grinned, the smile one that could shine down from magazine covers. He had sandy-brown hair and dark-brown eyes—the rich sort of brown found in the depths of the best cup of coffee—that sucked me into their world. "Hi."

That one simple word was enough to make me forget a proper response. Something about this guy, something in the air, or something in his aura, was enchanting. His very presence had the ability to scramble my thoughts. "Hi," I said again. "I'm Lily, the resident Mixologist. Are you new around here?"

"Fresh off the boat. I've been here before, but it's been a while." He thumbed behind him toward the dock, never once taking his eyes off of me. "I'm visiting, and I was told you have the best beverages around. Do you by chance have food, too?"

I gave an idiotic sort of grin. "Um… yes?"

"Is that a question?" The man winked then slipped onto a bar stool. "I'd love to see a menu if you have one."

Muttering furiously to myself, I turned my back to him so he couldn't see the embarrassed blush climbing up my cheeks. After a few deep breaths, I twirled back around with a gracious smile and handed over the menu. "I'm sorry if I seem a bit disoriented. I was working all morning and just pulled my head out of it, so I might still be in La La land."

"La La land? Sounds like a fun place." He pulled the menu toward him and pursed his lips as he glanced over it. "This looks great. I'll take whatever you recommend."

He handed the menu back, looking up just in time to catch me staring at him. I mumbled a thank-you while giving myself a mental head slap. I wasn't looking to date anyone, and I certainly wasn't looking for a relationship… but something about this man was captivating.

"How about eggs and toast?" I asked once I'd gathered my voice. "I'll pair it with a Caffeine Cup. Simple, but it's the most popular option."

"That sounds lovely."

I made a few notes on my pad of paper because if I didn't, I was afraid I'd forget everything. Meanwhile, the visitor looked around the bar with curiosity.

"We don't get strangers around here all that often," I blurted out of the blue. Closing my eyes, I breathed out. "I'm sorry," I said, opening my eyes again. "I meant to ask where you are from, and it came out wrong."

The man turned twinkling eyes on me. "Call me Liam. I come from the same place you do."

"St. Paul?" I gaped. "Minnesota?"

He laughed. "No, I just meant the mainland. America."

"Oh, wow." I held a hand over my heart. "I was gonna say, that's a huge coincidence. What brings you out this way?"

"Business," he said with a small smile.

"What sort of business are you in?" I leaned on the counter, realizing all at once that I hadn't started preparing his food. "I'm sorry, you don't have to answer. I'm just being nosy. You're probably in a rush, and here I am chatting your ear off. I'll get your food ready now."

"I'm here for a few days at least," he said. "Don't worry, I'm in no rush. I just arrived, and I don't have a single meeting until tomorrow. In fact, I thought it'd be fun to get to know the new Mixologist."

"You've been here before?"

He nodded. "Many times."

"Are you…" I cleared my throat. "Are you from here?"

"I'm a wizard, if that's what you're asking," he said with a broad smile. "No, I was not born here, but both of my parents were. My father was a shifter, my mom a witch. They moved over to the mainland when they found out she was pregnant."

"This seems like a great place to grow up," I said, filling the tea kettle with water. "Why would they move away?"

"You didn't like growing up in St. Paul?"

I thought back to my younger days. It'd been only my father and me, and he hadn't been a particularly "active" parent, to put things nicely. Most of the time, I'd entertained myself. Friends had been few and far between. "It wasn't bad. Although, I have family here, and it would've been fun to grow up with my cousins."

"We're similar, you know."

"What do you mean?"

"According to her friends, my mother wanted to raise me without the knowledge of magic," he said. "The rumors say your mother might have felt similarly to mine."

I set the tea kettle on the stove, not sure if I should be flattered or nervous that I was considered important enough to spur rumors. Reaching above the cupboard, I removed a small vial of Liquid Lighter. After adding a few drops onto the burner, a perfectly blue flame sprouted up and began to boil the kettle. "If both your parents were magic, why would they want to keep it a secret from you?"

"I'm not sure, exactly. My parents were killed when I was young, so I only have hearsay to piece their stories together, and I've heard conflicting facts. It doesn't help that I didn't hear these stories until my adult years. As a child, I was placed in an orphanage. I never did get to ask them why they wanted to raise me away from here, and by the time I reconnected with the magical society, so much time had passed that it was hard to track down friends of my parents to find out information."

"Oh my gosh, I am so sorry." I dropped the piece of bread I was holding, missing the toaster by a mile. "I shouldn't have asked. I had no idea."

"How could you? We just met." With a tight smile, Liam reached over and picked up the bread from the counter. He dropped it into the toaster and pushed the lever down. "It was a long time ago. I really don't mind talking about it."

"How did you find out about this place?"

"Well, things started to happen when I turned sixteen. As you can imagine, growing up in an orphanage wasn't easy. Things didn't get any easier when I entered the foster care system."

"I can't even imagine."

"I think that maybe you can." Liam's eyes turned knowingly in my direction. "Some of the families I had were... well, they didn't like me much, and they didn't hesitate to let me know it. Then there were the other ones. The ones where it wasn't what they said, but what they didn't say. Sometimes indifference stings more than outright meanness. Never having someone at a school event. Never having a parent who cared enough to stop by for career day. Never having someone to ask why I was upset, or sad, or angry. That can hurt more than sharp words."

I opened the fridge behind the bar. I was grateful he couldn't see my ears as they turned a bright shade of red. His words hit home more than I cared to admit, though how he could've guessed was another question entirely. I kept my head stuck in the fridge for a bit longer than necessary.

"I'm sorry about that," I said, pulling the eggs out and setting them next to the stove. "I wouldn't wish that sort of life on anyone."

"I survived. Even so, I was an emotional kid. When I turned sixteen, things changed. I'd get angry. The others would say something hurtful, and then shortly after, something bad would happen to them. Once, one of my 'brothers' blamed me for taking the family car and going for a joyride. Of course I didn't do it, but his parents didn't believe me. They punished me and gave their kid the keys to the car. He drove it to the movie theater and when he came out, the car was totaled. A semi-truck had run into it—a freak accident. Nobody was hurt, thankfully, but still."

"That sounds a little like a coincidence," I said hesitantly.

"I agree." He looked over at the toaster as the bread popped up. "But then it happened more and more. The family didn't let me go to prom. That year, the prom center had a sewage leak that ruined the entire event. They didn't let me play sports one afternoon, and a football came flying through the window the next day. They locked me in my room without supper, and the power went out and spoiled all the contents of their fridge. And that was just the beginning."

"How long did it take you to put two and two together?"

"A long, long time," he said. "I gave myself every reason to believe it was a coincidence, used every rationalization technique I could muster. It wasn't until my junior year of college that I started digging into my history."

I picked up the toast and set it on the plate, then turned to crack eggs over the pan. "That must have been a shock."

"You cannot imagine," he said. Then he hesitated and gave a shy smile. "Well, you probably can."

I laughed. "I've been here a few weeks, and I'm still not sure I believe it."

A friendly silence took over as I finished cooking breakfast and passed it to him.

"There you go. I'll stop asking questions and let you eat," I said. "It's nice to meet you."

"Same to you. Thank you for this incredible food."

"It's really nothing." I passed him the cup of coffee. "Simple."

"Island life. Nothing like it."

"Are you considering moving here?" I asked with curiosity. "If you enjoy it so much, what's holding you back?"

"Business," he said again, and I let it drop.

After a moment of slightly awkward silence, I busied myself washing my hands. The sound of the bell above the door tinkling merrily drew my attention as I wiped my hands on a towel. "Hello," I called to the new visitor. "May I help you?"

The new visitor didn't answer. Gliding across the floor, the figure moved like a storm cloud. Dressed in all black robes with a hood pulled over his head, I couldn't tell whether the figure was a woman or a man. He or she crossed to the far end of the bar and sat on a stool, bringing with him a layer of caution and a dose of foreboding.

I exchanged a "raised eyebrows" glance with Liam, then mouthed an "Excuse me," before shuffling down to the end of the bar. "Hi there, I'm Lily. Can I get you something to eat or drink?"

The figure's head was bowed so deeply I couldn't catch a glimpse of his or her face. Lining the rim of the hood was a silky black ribbon about one inch thick, glinting under the sun.

An arm snaked out from under the billowing black robes. He or she removed a napkin from the stack on the bar and put the tip of their fingertip to the paper, beginning to write in huge, sweeping movements. To my horror—and astonishment—black ink began to flow from the place where the nail met skin. When the figure removed his or her hand and passed me the napkin, I glanced at the message.

I blinked at the writing there: ELIXIR.

The Elixir was a drink that I'd only learned about, but never prepared. It was a potion meant for someone in desperate need. A potion meant only for a person on the edge of death. Once a person drank this potion, there was no going back: It was meant to preserve the spirit after death for a short time. Almost like a ghost. I'd only read about it in books, and I had no desire to see it work in real life.

"I'll... I'll be right back," I mumbled. "I don't have the ingredients here."

"Everything okay?" Liam asked. "The eggs are delicious."

"I'm so happy," I said distractedly. "I mean, I'm happy you like them. Sorry, I'll be right back. Can I get you more coffee?"

Liam waved for me to go on, which was a good thing since I already had one foot in the storeroom.

"Gus," I said to the old man hunched over the table. He didn't look up. "Gus!"

"I'm busy," he grumbled. "Doing your job, since you don't seem to fancy doing it yourself."

"Look at this." I slapped the piece of paper down on the table.

Though Gus tried to hide his interest, curiosity won out and he glanced at the writing on the napkin. He did a double take then looked up at me with a grave expression. "Who asked for this?"

"A guest," I said. "A visitor I've never seen before. He's wearing a cloak. What do you make of it?"

"The Elixir," he said slowly. "Is a touchy subject."

"I've read about it."

"You've read about it, but have you ever seen it in action?" he asked, a bitterness to his words. "Have you witnessed the effects of this potion?"

"No."

"It's a dangerous thing. Very dangerous," Gus said. "Only those mortally ill may request this potion. Even then, it speeds up the dying process. I haven't heard of a batch being made for at least ten years. There are strict regulations on those who may ask for it."

"Regulations?"

"There's a strict procedure you must follow by law."

"Is it difficult?"

Gus shrugged. "It's not time consuming, and it's not hard. Difficult... that depends on what you mean."

"Well, what do you mean?"

"The regulations state that you must give the requesting party a Truth Seeker potion first, followed up with a single question: *Do you understand the consequences of drinking The Elixir?*"

"Why?"

"Because of the nature of the potion, we require the user to fully understand the consequences before we may serve them."

"If the requesting party says yes, what happens next?"

Gus sighed. "If he or she fully understands the consequences, then they'll answer yes and you'll move along to the next phase. If they say no, they'll forget they ever asked the question, and their memory will be wiped of anything in conjunction with The Elixir."

"It's like an auto-detonate function," I said as Gus nodded. "Why so secretive?"

Gus bit his bottom lip. "The name of this potion is murmured only in dark and hopeless places. Those who seek it have a strong, desperate desire to use it. A desperate and hopeless man is a dangerous one."

I wanted to ask more, but I felt like I was using up all of my questions. Thankfully, Gus must have read my mind because he explained further.

"Imagine the things one may do if they obtain The Elixir," Gus said. "It gives someone life for hours, sometimes even days after they die."

"Like a ghost?"

Gus tilted his head sideways. "Of sorts. More like an apparition with certain... powers. If the person has dangerous intentions, imagine how much damage they could do with The Elixir. After all, they are already dead. There are virtually no consequences for them."

"They could... they could hurt people," I said. "And never be punished for it."

He nodded. "That exact situation happened only once before the regulations came into play; the repercussions were devastating."

"I don't feel comfortable with this," I said, turning around. "I'm just going to tell our guest that we don't serve the potion. I want no part of this."

Gus held up a hand. "I'm afraid you can't do that."

"Why not? I've never made the potion before, so I'll use that as an excuse. I'm inexperienced."

"If a person requests The Elixir from the rightful Mixologist, the Mixologist is required to accommodate them. That is also part of the regulations," Gus said with a shake of his head. "I'm sorry, Lily. You need to give your guest the Truth Seeker and go through due process. Those are the rules."

"Shouldn't I be allowed to choose if I want to brew a certain potion?" My heart beat quickly at the thought of mixing up something so potentially devastating. "I don't feel right about any of it—the whole concept—none of it. Wouldn't it be better to just avoid the whole thing?"

Gus stood up slowly. For the first time, he seemed to feel each one of his eighty-something years of age. A pained expression crossed his face as he gripped my shoulder with one hand. "The job of the Mixologist is not to 'play God,' for lack of a better saying. Your role is not to be the judge and jury; it is to offer help to those who need it."

"But you just explained how dangerous this potion can be if used wrong."

"How do you know he's intending to use it wrongly?"

I hesitated. "Maybe I'm being short-sighted, but I don't see any particularly great way to use it right. What could a person need to do so badly after they are dead that they're willing to die faster? The thought gives me a bad feeling."

Gus took a deep breath, releasing it slowly. "My grandmother took The Elixir."

My eyes widened. "She did?"

He nodded. "My mother was due to give birth to me just as my grandmother was being wheeled into the hospital. She was about to die from a terrible illness, just as I was about to be born. She'd been suffering for over three years, and the end of her life came as mine began. On the mainland, I believe humans call that disease Alzheimer's."

I raised my hand to Gus's, which was still on my shoulder, and squeezed it. "I'm so sorry."

"She knew the end was coming, it was just a matter of time." Gus removed his hand from my shoulder and crossed his arms. He rocked back on his heels and stared at the ground, looking nostalgic for the first time since we'd met. "They say people can sense when the end is near."

"I've heard that too," I whispered.

"She knew her life was finished that day, but she wasn't ready to let go." Gus exhaled a long breath. "At that time, the Mixologist was the predecessor to your grandfather. She summoned him and requested The Elixir. As per the rules, he gave her the Truth Serum first. With flying colors, she passed the test and asked again for the final potion. He made it, and he gave it to her."

Gus's eyes watered. I swallowed, unsure what words might ease his pain. For fear of saying the wrong thing, I remained silent.

"She passed away an hour before I was born, my mother tells me."

I gasped. "The Elixir preserved her…"

Gus bowed his head. "It kept her spirit alive long enough to meet her first grandson."

I waited a beat. "I'm sorry I jumped to conclusions. I'd never… I'd never thought of it like that before."

"That's why it's not your job to judge anyone," Gus said, his words surprisingly gentle. "It's impossible to know what they are going through when you have not walked in their shoes."

"I think we have a vial of Truth Seeker left," I said, striding to the cupboard where I kept a few pre-made, oft-used potions. I selected the correct container and returned to the doorway. I hesitated before stepping through. "Your grandmother sounds like quite a woman. I'm glad she got the chance to meet you."

"Lily, there's one more thing." Gus's eyes were hazy, as if he'd just woken from a dream. "It is not your job to be judge and jury, but always listen to your gut."

I squinted at him. "That sounds contradictory. I thought you just said I have to do this by law."

"You do. It is the rules, and the rules are in place for a good reason." Turning back to the table, Gus began delicately slicing a flower. "Someday, you'll understand. Sometimes, the rules are meant to be broken."

"How do I know when to follow them and when to break them?"

"Don't you have a customer waiting?" Gus growled in his normal gnarly tone. "Get to it."

"Sometimes I think you have multiple personalities."

Gus sighed and looked up. "You'll just know, Lily. There are some aspects of your job that I can't explain. You will have to decide for yourself when the time comes."

"What if I make the wrong decision?"

Gus raised his eyebrows. "That's a hazard you'll have to accept when the time is right."

Somehow, Gus left me more confused after his explanation than before. Holding the vial of the Truth Seeker in my palm, I glanced down at it, steeling myself for the task ahead.

CHAPTER 3

WHEN I RETURNED TO THE bar, the first thing I noticed was the absence of Liam. His plate sat empty on the counter, his coffee cup drained. In place of the food, he'd left a napkin with a note scrawled on it. Despite the hooded stranger waiting at the far end of the bar, I quickly scanned the note under the guise of putting the dirty dishes in the sink.

"I'll be right with you," I mumbled, stalling for time as I picked up the paper.

Lily,

It was a pleasure getting to know you. I had to run, but I'd love to come by sometime. Maybe when you're less busy? I have a few days on the island and if you're up to it, I'd love to buy you lunch. Or get a tour of The Isle from a local. I'll be staying at the B&B.

Liam

I sucked in a breath, playing the note over again in my mind as I counted the money he'd left on the counter. US dollars meant nothing to the wizards and witches on The Isle. Gold coins and trading were the most common currency, and Liam had left me at least three times the amount needed for his meal. I pocketed it, fully intending to give all of it back the next time I saw him.

As for the lunch date... well, I didn't want it to be a date. But the conversation had been fun, and he was a nice person. It might be enjoyable to have a chat with someone who understood the mainland. All the islanders pretended to understand my human customs and traditions, but it just wasn't the same. Reminiscing about McDonalds and movies and books from back home sounded like a nice distraction from the day's stress.

A small twitch of guilt tugged at my stomach. I fought it back, knowing the root cause of my discomfort was the man who went by the pseudonym Ranger X.

We'd kissed once; it had sizzled like a flash in the pan, and then his soul-searching eyes had taken me to a place I couldn't seem to forget.

However, we had a problem. A big problem.

Rangers were not allowed to marry or have children, and even serious relationships were frowned upon. Loved ones were viewed as a liability. Rangers worked hard jobs, long hours, and dangerous assignments. Their lifespan was half that of a normal witch or wizard, if they were lucky, and it was unfair to the ones they left behind when their time on earth was done. Therefore, they tried not to leave anyone behind. At least, not anyone who'd miss them.

Maybe making lunch plans with Liam wasn't a bad idea. It could help get my mind off of Ranger X. Jangling the coins in my pocket, I decided to swing by later and offer Liam a tour around The Isle.

The tap of a fingernail against wood drew me from the depths of my thoughts, startling me. I looked to the hooded figure hunched over the counter. "I'm so sorry, I was lost in thought."

I opened my fist, which had inadvertently closed tight around the vial, and strode to the end of the bar. I tried to get a peek under the hood, but it hung too deeply over the figure's face and shielded everything down to the person's chin. Judging by the very light stubble there, the figure was a man.

Clearing my throat, I held the vial out in front of me. "Do you understand the process?"

He gave no indication that he'd heard me, so I went on to explain.

"According to the regulations, I need to issue you the Truth Serum first. Then I will ask you a question, and you will have to answer it under the influence of the serum. Do you understand the procedure?"

I was just about to give up when finally, the man gave the slightest of nods. He extended a hand, and I slowly dropped the vial into his outstretched palm.

"You'll need to swallow all of it," I said. "The side effects of the potion itself will fade shortly. However, if the answer you provide to the question isn't sufficient, you may experience permanent memory loss."

"I understand." The voice was gravelly, as if formed from years of smoking. Or quite possibly, the raspiness could be a sign of illness. "May I?"

My pulse increased. "Yes."

He held the vial under the sunlight streaming across the countertop. Inside the glass, black and white liquid swirled together, never mixing. The two were repelled from one another, symbolizing the delicate balance of truth and lies. No matter how hard a person shook the bottle, whether they boiled it or froze it, burned it or dumped it, the dichotomy would never bond.

Suddenly, the stranger uncapped the bottle and drew it under his hood, swallowing the Serum in one motion. He set the empty vial back on the counter before I had time to blink.

"Do you understand the consequences of The Elixir?" I asked in a rattling voice. Then I took Gus's advice and listened to my gut instinct, adding a question of my own. "And do you intend to use it for good?"

Without a second's pause, the gravelly voice answered in a slightly sing-songish tone typically present when the truth serum was active. "I both understand the consequences of requesting The Elixir, and I have only the purest of intentions for its use."

"I need to prepare it," I said, after waiting to see if the man's memory aborted. When it didn't, I cleared my throat. "It might take some time."

"I'll wait," he said. "I'll wait as long as it takes."

⌖

"That should just about do it," Gus said as I sprinkled the most finely ground Baby's Breath into a miniature cauldron perched in the center of the table. It sat over a green flame, a special flame that we'd had to build from the twigs of the oldest weeping willow on The Isle. "Stir this while I grab the last ingredient."

I stirred the potion, more grateful than ever to have Gus by my side. Without *The Magic of Mixology* spellbook, I would never have figured out the concoction on my own. Mixology ran in my blood, but it didn't all come naturally. There was an element of experience and knowledge that I hadn't yet built up in my short time on The Isle. Gus had memorized the book front to back, however, and remembered even the smallest nuances of the intricate potion.

I wiped sweat from my brow as Gus returned with a tiny eyedropper filled with red liquid.

"What is that?" I asked warily. "I don't think I want to know."

"Then why'd ya ask?"

"Do I want to know?"

"No," Gus said firmly. "Take this and release exactly three drops into the cauldron. We wait one minute after that. If you've done everything correctly, the smoke will turn black."

My hand shook as I took the dropper from Gus's hand. My concentration was disappearing rapidly after having focused hard for the past hour, but I took everything I had left and squeezed exactly three drops of the solution into the pot. The seconds ticked by, turning into the longest minute of my life.

Even Gus tapped his foot against the wooden floor in impatience. He wasn't a particularly patient man, but he rarely let his nerves show.

"It worked!" I gasped. "The smoke—it's black!"

Gus reached forward and doused the green flame with a special white powder. The fire vanished, smoke coughing black puffs toward the ceiling.

"Quickly, pour this into a goblet," Gus said. "It doesn't last."

"This potion is time sensitive?"

"It expires one hour from creation."

"Is that another regulation?" I asked as I grabbed a large goblet from the shelf. It was gold and encrusted with gemstones. Such a pivotal moment in a person's life felt as if it deserved our finest glassware.

"Intentions can change in a second," Gus said. "The expiration date is for the protection of everyone. Should the person asking for The Elixir change their mind in a day, we'd need to re-test them with the Truth Serum."

My back straightened. "What if he changed his mind in an hour?"

Gus licked his lips as he shook his head. "That's a risk that we can't possibly prevent."

My chest tightened as I took the goblet. "He drinks this... all of it. Then what?"

"Then he'll likely carry on with his business until..." Gus cleared his throat. "It's best if you close up shop for the night and spend some time with your cousins."

"But the shop doesn't close for another two hours," I said, glancing at the clock. "You've always taught me that we never close early."

"Sometimes rules are meant to be broken," Gus said. "I have the feeling that you won't be doing much good here tonight after you've served The Elixir. You've concentrated hard, and frankly, I don't trust you to make a cup of coffee, let alone a potion. Magic & Mixology will close tonight."

He was right. Already I couldn't concentrate on anything except the bubbling potion in my hand. It felt weighty. Like the decision itself, the potion was a heavy one. "I'll spend some time with Poppy and Zin, then."

"You've done good," Gus called as I took a few steps toward the bar. "The Elixir is a taxing potion on both the consumer and the Mixologist. It's natural if you don't get much sleep tonight."

I savored Gus's compliment for a moment; they came few and far between. However, his words also gave me pause. "Why would I not sleep tonight?"

Gus gave me a crooked smile, the slightest hint of pity in his gaze. "Maybe you won't have trouble sleeping. Who knows."

As I proceeded back outside to give the hooded figure his potion, the sinking feeling in my stomach grew stronger, and Gus's warning returned. I suddenly understood.

How could I sleep after administering a potion that meant certain death to the recipient?

CHAPTER 4

"**Y**OU'RE COMPLETELY AWARE WHAT DRINKING this entails?" I asked again, clutching the potion near to my chest. "There is no going back once you drink this."

"I understood the risks long before I came here," he said, a raspy lilt to his words. "It's time."

The minutes were indeed ticking down. Another fifty minutes and the potion would cease to function. "There's no way to come back after you drink this—"

"I told you, I knew the risks coming in here."

Taking the final few steps toward the man in the hood, I wished I could convince him not to drink The Elixir. For both his sake and mine. "This is the first time I've made it; I can't guarantee its quality."

"I know who you are. The smoke is black, and the old man in the back helped you. Doesn't matter if it's the first or the last time you make it as long as it works. That's all I care about."

"I've never seen anyone drink it before. I don't know what's supposed to happen."

"Well, like your old man said, you aren't the judge nor are you the jury. Whatever happens after I drink this is my business."

"Mine too," I said in a hushed tone. "I have to live with whatever happens to you."

"I am doing this as much for you as I am for myself."

"What?" My mouth fell open. "I don't know you, and I don't want you to drink this! Why would you think that?"

"Give me the glass."

I hesitated.

"Give it to him." Gus stood in the doorway, his face creased in a contemplative stare. "You've given him your advice and provided him counsel. If he doesn't want to listen to it, that's his choice."

"But—"

"Listen to him," growled the stranger. "You must give me the potion. Those are the rules."

My gaze flipped between Gus and the stranger, my heart gaining momentum with each beat. Extending a shaky hand, I set the potion on the bar, just far enough away so the hooded man had to lean forward.

From underneath his flowing robes, he snatched the goblet and brought it to his lips. There, he hesitated for one brief second. He looked into the mixture, the black smoke swirling up and distorting his features. Suddenly, he tipped his head back and poured the liquid straight down his throat. As he did so, I caught the briefest glimpse into his eyes. A murky gray.

He set the glass down, his eyes burning holes in my skin from under his hood. As quickly as the hood slid back, he pulled it forward once more.

"Are you okay?" I asked, expecting more of a reaction. Some gagging maybe, or a vile expression. Instead, the whole thing was relatively anti-climactic until the man's lips curled into a smile brimming with disdain. I raised my shoulders. "Can I get you water or something?"

"Good night, Lily Locke." He stood and withdrew gold coins from within the depths of his robes. Throwing all of them on the table, he turned and strode toward the door.

"Wait!" I called after him. "This is too much! Ten times the amount due!"

The figure paused at the doorway, his chest rising and falling beneath his robes. "Where I'm going, gold is useless."

I wanted to call after him that I could help, that maybe there was some antidote. I wanted to shout advice, take back the entire potion, and throw it away for good. But I found myself unable to do any of it. Instead, I stood frozen in place and watched as he left. Gus's eyes never left my face, his stare pinning me to the wall with its intensity.

"Let it go, Lily," Gus said quietly. "Let him go, and close up shop for today. Your work here is done."

CHAPTER 5

I CLOSED UP SHOP JUST AS Gus had ordered, taking my time as I wiped down the glassware and washed leftover dishes. Though the sun was high in the sky and the day was only half gone, my shoulders slumped in exhaustion, my mind as fried as if I'd been memorizing herbs for ten hours straight.

The light jangling sound of coins reminded me of the two visitors from today. Both had overpaid their bills significantly, and as I scrubbed the top of the wooden bar clean, guilt tugged at my insides.

Exhaling a sigh, I finished cleaning the bar, locked up, and disappeared back into the storeroom.

"What now?" I asked Gus. He sat at the table with a pair of glasses perched on his nose, studying what looked like a tiny twig on the table. "I've never had a day off before."

"You talk as if I'm a slave driver," he said without looking up.

I made an "if the shoe fits" sort of shrug, but luckily, he was too busy slicing the twig in half with a very sharp knife to notice.

"I saw that," he said. "I can tell if you roll your eyes at me from a mile away."

"I didn't roll my eyes!"

"Did you make a face?" Gus looked up, his eyes magnified at least ten times behind his glasses. "You made a face."

"Well, it's true. I don't usually have days off. Can I please help with whatever you're working on? It'll make me feel better."

"No."

I crossed the room and sat down on the bench opposite him. "Please?"

"It's not my job to make you feel better," he said. He remained tense for a moment, hiding his thoughts until finally his hands relaxed and he spoke softly. "Don't you want to rest?"

"Don't *you* want to relax?" I shot back. "The shop is closed. Why don't you go enjoy the day?"

"I like spending my time here." Gus didn't look up, but he paused ever so slightly as he said the words. "I don't have a life outside of this place."

"I like it here too," I said softly. "I'd be happy to help you."

Gus let out a slow breath. At first it looked like he wanted to argue. Then he pushed the glasses up on his head and gave me a curious stare. "You want to help?"

"I need the distraction."

"Five minutes," Gus said. "That's all I have left here. Believe it or not, I do have plans tonight."

"Are you going on a date with Mimsey?" I asked in a sing-song voice. "Dinner plans?"

"You talk like that and I'll switch up Dragon's Breath with Foxtail when you're not looking. Then we'll see who's laughing when you have hives across your forehead."

"I'm just asking," I said, taking the twig from Gus. "What do I do with this?"

"Slice it very thinly."

"Is it toxic?"

Gus raised an eyebrow. "No."

"What's it called?"

"It's a damn vanilla bean," Gus said. "Nothing except flavoring."

My cheeks colored. "Oh, okay. Never seen one like this before."

Gus's sigh sounded frustrated. "Well, then learn."

We lapsed into silence. The task took much longer than five minutes. Before I knew it, an hour had passed. The time had been pleasant, and Gus had been surprisingly cordial as he explained in great detail the process of scooping out the seeds.

"Thanks," I said once we were all done. "That helped take my mind off things."

"You're gonna need someone else to distract you now," Gus said. "I ain't yer babysitter."

I stifled a smile as Gus's gruffness returned. "Maybe I'll see what my cousins are up to."

"Maybe that's a good idea."

I put the ingredients away and filed each jar in its rightful place before starting up the stairs to the attic. "Thanks for everything, Gus. I couldn't have done it without you."

"That's a lie. You did it all on yer own, I just supervised."

"Have a nice night, Gus."

"Lily," he called, almost as an afterthought. "You did good. That's a hard thing for even an experienced Mixologist to do."

"Which part?"

"All of it," Gus said. "Creating The Elixir is just the start. It gets more difficult from here on out."

"Did I do the right thing?" I asked, taking a few steps back down the stairs. "Because it doesn't feel like it."

"You did what you had to do, and that is the nature of your job."

"I just wish the last Mixologist was still alive. I have so many questions about everything."

Gus thunked his cane across the room and came to a stop in front of me. "You don't need to hear opinions from the outside when it comes to your instincts. You don't need me, or your aunts, or your cousins, telling you what is right or wrong."

"I don't like making those decisions."

"The Mixologist is chosen based on many criteria," Gus said. "Part of the criteria is the notion of good and evil. By nature, you are a good person. We have never had an evil Mixologist, and I doubt it's possible."

"I thought it was all based on blood lines."

"Blood lines play a role in it. Zin, Poppy, all of Trinket's other rascals—they all could've become the Mixologist based on blood alone, yet you were the one chosen. Trust that you inherited this place for a reason," Gus said, gesturing to the storeroom. "The knowledge and instincts run through your veins. Instead of turning outside to find the answer, you must turn inside and listen. When you learn how to listen to your heart, you'll find the difference between right and wrong."

"What if I can't hear it?"

"You can, and you will. It takes time, like all things." Gus returned to the table, a sign the conversation was rapidly coming to an end. "Next time you're faced with a tough decision, use it as practice. Take a moment to be silent... and just listen."

CHAPTER 6

THIRTY MINUTES LATER, I'D SHOWERED, splashed on a bit of makeup, and slipped into a light, summery dress. My mind whirred at an incredible rate, but Gus's words had helped calm my pounding heart. Standing in front of the mirror in my bedroom, I did a quick twirl and watched as the dress floated around my knees.

It felt good to get cleaned up and put on a nice outfit. I rarely had a night away from the shop, and when I did, it was usually reserved for dinner with the family. In recent weeks, Mimsey had forced Gus to let me out early once per week, and she was a strict enforcer of family meals. It was nice to have someone watching out for me, since most of my life, I'd fended for myself.

The sun was setting outside, casting beautiful glows of red and orange and pinks across my room. The attic had been converted into a quaint bedroom with fluffy white pillows and a snowy, lush comforter. I was sorely tempted to crawl under the soft covers and just sleep.

"No you don't, Lily Locke," I said, muttering to myself in the mirror. "You have one night off, and you will not spend it sleeping."

Throwing a thick shawl over my shoulders, I made my way downstairs. Gus was gone already, so I did one final sweep of the storeroom, careful not to step on any of the yarn or wires still out from our theorizing the night before. Both the interior and the outside bar were deserted, so I turned the key in the lock and bounced down the front steps.

I trudged through the sand, the warm, dazzling crystals cascading over my toes as I walked. I'd lived in flip-flops ever since I'd arrived because really, anything else was impractical. I strolled toward The Twist, the garden labyrinth outside of Hettie's house that kept visitors—welcome or not—at bay.

My plans for tonight were simple. First, I would stop by The Twist to see if my cousins were available for a stroll. I wanted to return the extra coins Liam had left on the counter, and I figured the walk across The Isle would be a lot more fun with company. After that, maybe the three of us would grab a bite to eat at the restaurant near the B&B. Knowing the girls, all I had to do was offer to pay for food and they'd leap at the opportunity to join.

However, my plans went off track before I made it to The Twist.

Spotting one of my cousins on the way, I stepped from the sandy beach onto a green expanse of grass, raising a hand to shield the setting sun. Ten feet away, Zin sat as still as a stone statue, her eyes shut and her hands on her head. Close to me stood my grandmother, Hettie, dressed in a tiara that dazzled from the glow of the lake and a hoodie that read "Dance Mom" in blinging letters.

I walked up to Hettie and nodded at the hoodie. "Do any of your kids dance?"

"Not yet," Hettie said. "But it's never too late."

I sized up the rest of her outfit, and then quickly wished I hadn't. She wore purple leggings over her starting-to-sag legs, the fabric tight as latex. Over the leggings she'd pulled up leg warmers so woolly she may as well have attached two cats to her calves. The thick gold chain hanging around her neck wouldn't look out of place on Mr. T.

"You like my outfit?" Hettie asked. "I see you peeking at all the hot stuff I've got to offer. I can get you a matching one if ya like."

"Oh, no thanks," I said. "I don't think I could quite pull it off like you do."

"You're darn tootin' you can't. I didn't work eighty years on this body for nothin." She gave her booty a slap with her hand then cackled. "Give yourself another few years and you'll have the confidence to wear this."

"If I'm ever that confident, then shoot me," I mumbled. "Put me out of my misery."

"What's that?"

"Nothing. What is Zin doing?"

"I'm training her."

"Training her to do what... fall asleep?"

Hettie turned and winked. Then she gestured for me to take a few steps away from the clearing. "She wants to become a Ranger, so I offered to train her."

"Training includes napping? Maybe I want to be a Ranger, too."

"Nah, I'm teaching her how to not be an idiot."

I blinked. "What?"

"I told Zin to sit down and put her hands on top of her head and close her eyes. She's been sittin' there not moving for an hour now. She didn't even ask why."

"And you're just watching her?"

"It's hilarious!" Hettie threw her head back and laughed so hard she choked a little on her own spit. Then she wiped the tears from her eyes and put on a very serious expression. "No, that's not funny at all. I'm instructing her. See, she needs to learn to question authority. No good Ranger ever became famous because they followed all the rules."

"So you're just trying to get her to ask questions."

"Ask questions, fight back, rebel against The Man—you name it."

I shook my head. "You have a funny way of instructing people."

"I learned from the best."

"What do you mean?" I glanced at this tiara-wearin', booty-slappin' grandmother with a wary eye. "Who did you learn from, and what were you learning?"

"Come to Ranger HQ with us, and I'll show you."

"You've been to Ranger Headquarters?" I couldn't keep the astonishment out of my voice. "I don't even know where that is."

"I worked for the Rangers," she said. "In fact, how do you think Poppy got her job? I helped her out. But do I get a kick back from her salary? No…"

I was stunned into silence. "Wow, I had no idea."

"Never judge a grannie by her leg warmers," she said with another cackle. "That's a second lesson for you today. I'm even teaching you for free. How do you like that?"

Finally, Zin peeked one of her eyes open. "What are you two talking about? Hi, Lily."

"Just watching the training," I said with a shrug. "Very interesting stuff."

"Hettie, will you tell me if I'm doing this right?" Zin asked in annoyance. "I've been sitting here forever, and I'm starting to get hungry."

"You're doing it right," Hettie said. "Just keep going."

Zin snapped her eyes shut and let out a long sigh. "This is stupid!"

"You've got to stop this," I mumbled to Hettie. "You're making her look like a fool."

"I'd rather I make her look like a fool than someone else," Hettie said, twirling to face me, a sharp cut to her words. "The Ranger career path is not an easy one. She's got to learn."

"But—"

"You think I want her to be a Ranger?" Hettie grabbed me by the arm and pulled me a few steps away. "Do you?"

I was a bit taken aback by her forcefulness. "Uh, Zin wants the job, so I suppose she'll try for it regardless."

"Of course she wants the job. She can do it, too," Hettie scoffed. "I didn't raise any imbeciles, and neither did my daughters. Zin can be anything she wants to be. But a Ranger? That's a hard life. It's a tough path, and the likelihood of her makin' it another ten years in that business is slim."

My palms began to sweat, and I wondered if maybe I should encourage Zin to pursue a career with a lower mortality rate. "I didn't realize you felt so strongly."

"I know the truth because I worked there," Hettie said. "And if my granddaughter is going to take that job, you'd better believe I'll be proud of her. I'll wave her flag from every rooftop these old knees can climb, but what I will not do is send her in unprepared. If she's going to succeed at the Ranger lifestyle, she needs to learn."

I swallowed, feeling a bit out of my league with some of this island business. A couple of weeks was not long enough to understand its nuances and culture. Plus, Hettie had a point. I'd rather Zin be rejected from the Ranger program until she was ready to face what was waiting for her on the other side.

Zin peered through one eyelid again. "I'm really starting to need to use the restroom. Any chance I can take a break?"

"No," Hettie said shortly. "Keep going."

I made a disgruntled noise in my throat, but my grandmother silenced me with one look. We stood in silence for another minute, watching Zin sit there in pseudo-meditation.

"Why are you here anyway?" Zin asked with another peek at me. "Who knows how long I'll be here. This training business isn't for wimps."

"No, it's not," I said, hiding a small smile. "However, I was wondering if you and Poppy were available for dinner tonight?"

"You're not inviting your old Gran?" The gray-haired, sparkle-covered head whipped toward me. "Bummer, dude."

I cleared my throat and revised. "You too, Hettie. You can come if you'd like."

Hettie waved a hand and laughed. "I'm just messin' with y'all. You both need to stop taking everything I say so seriously. I have plans, anyway. Spend some time with your cousins."

"Are we going to be done training by then?" Zin asked. "How much longer will this take?"

"How much longer do you want it to take?" Hettie looked nonchalantly down at her nails. "I never told you how long to sit there."

"What?" Zin's screech could likely be heard back at the bar. "You were making me sit here for no good reason?"

"Oh, there was a good reason," Hettie said. "I always have my reasons."

"Are you going to share what that reason was?" Zin let her hands fall to her sides and opened her eyes. A cloudy expression covered her face as she pieced the puzzle together. "Were you just messing with me?"

"Sorta." Hettie grinned. "I'm teaching you to make your own rules. I was just telling Lily that well-behaved women rarely make history."

"That's not what you were telling me," I mumbled. "You were saying—"

Hettie waved a hand to shut me up. "Same thing. I am teaching you to think critically. I told you to sit there, and you did it for an hour. You didn't even ask why!"

Zin flew to her feet. "That's it. I knew you were going crazy, old lady!"

"Calm down! It's a proper lesson," Hettie said, shaking her finger at Zin. "When you become a Ranger, you will be given assignments. Sometimes those assignments will be hard, and sometimes they won't make sense. Are you going to be one of those Rangers who just blindly follows orders like a big, clumsy giant? Or are you going to think for yourself?"

Zin fell silent. "You said when. You really think... *When* I become a Ranger?"

Zin was hung up on the first part of that question, while the last part had resonated with me. Maybe Hettie's musings were directed at more than one person. Based upon the glittering look in her eye as she swiveled her gaze toward me, I was all but convinced she knew what I was thinking.

"Of course *when*," Hettie said. "All of my granddaughters can become whatever they'd like in their lifetimes. It's a matter of deciding what you want, how badly you want it, and what you're willing to do to get there."

"How is she supposed to know when to break the rules and when to follow them?" I blurted out. "You know, when she's a Ranger."

Hettie sized me up with her calculating eyes. "That's the second step. The harder step. Unfortunately, that is something I can't teach, and neither can anyone else. Not even the best of Rangers."

"That's reassuring," Zin grumbled. "Doesn't leave me a lot of hope."

"On the contrary." Hettie peered at both of us closely before responding. "That should give you the greatest hope of all."

"How?"

"It should reassure you because at the end of the day, the truth comes from inside you," Hettie said. "No amount of teaching or rules or regulations can tell you what is right or wrong. In order to decide that, one must look within and listen to what their heart is saying."

"That's not very clear," I said, slightly annoyed by all of this *'look inside yourself'* junk. I thought I'd left Tony Robbins behind when I'd left the mainland. At the moment, I was trying my best to look inside, but the only thing I found was a bit of fear and a lot of confusion. "How about more of a *'paint by numbers'* style of learning?"

Hettie tsked. "You'll learn in time. You're thinking about this in all the wrong ways. You already have the answers."

"But it doesn't feel like it," I said, my voice growing louder. "I don't feel like I know much of anything at the moment."

"I didn't say it was going to be easy," Hettie said. "But it's true.

You already have the answers. It's like a gold coin that's been buried under a mound of dirt for centuries."

Zin squinted. "Now we're talking money?"

Hettie shook her head. "At first, you don't even know that coin is there. Maybe it's buried on your lawn, and you don't even know to look for it. Then one day, someone tells you that you have all of the money you need, you just need to start digging."

She paused a minute, looking between us and leaving a moment of silence for us to catch up. "You start digging, but it takes some time. See, there's no road map to this coin, you just know it's there. Somewhere inside of your yard. So you dig, and you dig, and you dig. You make mistakes and dig in the backyard when it's buried in the front. Maybe you don't dig deep enough, or wide enough, or fast enough."

Zin moved a few steps closer, and we stood shoulder to shoulder as Hettie faced us both.

"Then one day, you find that gold coin. It's buried in your yard alright, it just took some time to find it."

"That's it?" Zin asked. "Then it's over?"

"No, then the hard part is just getting started," Hettie said. "See, now that you've found the coin, it's likely crusted over with mud, maybe a bit tarnished and dirty. Slowly, carefully you need to polish it. Dust it off. Let it sit for a bit and clean it a little every day. Then one day out of the blue, you'll look over and that dirty gold coin you never knew existed will shine like the sun itself."

I stood still, listening to every word.

"Throughout all of this, you can't forget one thing." Hettie's eyes slid between the two of us. "At one time, you never knew that coin existed. Patience, girls. You must work a little at it every day and have patience. Then one day, you will see exactly what I'm talking about."

CHAPTER 7

HETTIE WRAPPED UP HER LECTURE and, a few minutes later, called an end to training for the day.

"What's next?" Zin asked. "I thought you were working tonight, Lily."

"I was looking for you and Poppy," I said. "We closed up shop early, so I wanted to see if you two wanted to go out to dinner. On me."

"Go," Hettie said, directing her words to Zin. "And put some nice clothes on. You're not a Ranger yet, and I'm still holding out hope you'll find a man who'll change your mind and marry you."

"I'm an independent woman," Zin said. "Maybe there's more to life than swooning at big muscles."

"Girl, of course there is," Hettie said. "You start swooning, and I'm gonna have to have a talk with you. Look at me, I'm an independent woman. I worked with the Rangers and I had kids. They're not exclusive."

Zin raised a finger, resting it thoughtfully on her lip. "Hang on a second, how do I know you're not lying about working for the Rangers? Is this another test?"

"I can prove it to you." Hettie crossed her spindly arms. "My Ranger-ness, that is."

"I don't believe you."

"Let's go," Hettie said. "Lily was looking for Poppy anyway. Let's go pay her a visit."

"Where is she?" I frowned. "I was headed to The Twist."

"She's at Ranger Headquarters, of course," Hettie said. "It's her day to work dispatch."

"I've never been there," I said. "Never even seen the place. Am I allowed inside?"

"Stay behind if you want," Hettie said. "But I've got some Ranger-ness to prove to my other granddaughter. C'mon, Zin."

I took a few jogging steps to catch up to my grandmother. "Where is it? What does this place look like? So we're just allowed to waltz in and visit?"

"You're exhausting with all your questions," Hettie said. "Isn't your mouth tired? How does Gus do it? Just wait and see. We'll be there in a few minutes."

"Will I be able to talk to a Ranger?"

"Any Ranger?" Zin winked. "Or Mr. X?"

My cheeks burned at her suggestive gaze. "Any Ranger. I just want to get an update on the missing spellbook. See if they have any information or leads."

"Oh, sure, you can talk to 'em," Hettie said. "They have a customer service department. But first things first, I have a very important call to make."

Zin rolled her eyes. "Don't do it, Hettie. It's not funny."

"What's not funny?" I asked. "What's she going to do?"

"Poppy works dispatch," Zin said. "Hettie likes to prank her."

"I think I'll order a pizza today," Hettie cackled. "Let's make a bet. Who thinks I can keep her on the phone longer than three seconds?"

Zin took the "under" bet, so I was stuck with the "over three seconds" bet.

Hettie pulled out a small device that looked similar to a phone, but functioned more like a walkie-talkie. The contraption didn't have any numbers on it, just buttons and dials in a variety of colors. I hadn't seen anything like it on The Isle. Hettie pressed the largest, reddest button. "Yes, hello, I'd like extra cheese on my pizza—"

The line went dead almost immediately.

"I win." Zin grinned. "I'll let you buy me dinner, Lily."

"Drat that was fast," Hettie said. "She's learning."

Hettie pressed another combination of dials. "Buzz us in, will you Poppy?"

"This is the emergency line." Poppy hissed. "I told you not to use it."

"This is an emergency," Hettie said. "Zin needs to use the restroom."

Zin raised her hands in annoyance. "I can wait."

"And Lily needs to talk to her man," Hettie added. "Be a darling and let us in."

Poppy sighed. "Don't make a scene in here, okay? They're still mad at me for buzzing you in the last time."

I looked at Hettie as Poppy disconnected. "What'd you do last time?"

She shrugged. "Nothing."

"She drew mustaches on the wall of photos," Zin said. "The wall with pictures of all the head Rangers for the past fifty years."

"It was a joke," Hettie mumbled. "People need to relax."

"A joke that didn't wipe off," Zin said. "You drew a handlebar moustache on the greatest Ranger of all time. And another one had a goatee."

"Are we here?" I looked around, but I didn't see anything out of the ordinary.

We had passed The Twist. As the sun sank lower in the horizon, the wild jungle in front of us turned a shade of dark that sent shivers rattling through my body and increased my pulse with every step. "I thought we weren't supposed to go into The Forest. What about that big, black building on the other side of The Isle? I thought that was where HQ would be located?"

"That's where they want you to think it's located," Hettie said. "But that's just corporate. The only people working there are the finance folks. Rangers hold some meetings there for show, but anything top secret is taken care of here."

"Where is here?" We stood just on the outskirts of The Forest. "I really don't think we should go in there. It's getting dark."

"Poppy should be buzzing us in anytime now," Hettie said. "Keep an eye out."

"An eye out for what?"

"There," Zin said, pointing. "Did you see that?"

If Zin hadn't alerted me, I would've missed it. Between two of the largest trees on the edge of the woods, a miniscule bolt of lightning shot between them. "What is that?"

"The portal to the entrance," Zin said. "Sort of like human elevators from what I hear. You walk through, and it takes you to a new level."

"That's not at all like an elevator," I mumbled. "I don't see any door, and I don't see any other 'floors' located around here. Can't we just wait for Poppy to come get us?"

"Don't be silly." Hettie grabbed my hand. "We only have a few seconds before it closes."

"Is the entrance always here?" I asked as my grandmother pulled me toward the space where a thin stream of lightning had danced just seconds ago. "How do you get in without Poppy's help?"

"You don't," Hettie said. "The entrance can be between any two trees. It's completely random, and is rarely the same two trees. The gateway is impossible to find without an invitation."

"What if someone wants a meeting with a Ranger?" I asked. "How do they find one?"

"People don't set up meetings with Rangers," Zin said. "Rangers come to them."

Hettie nodded. "She's right."

"But what if someone needs help?"

"It's the Rangers' job to know about it before the situation gets to that point," Hettie said. "Now, will you stop talking a moment so I can concentrate?"

I shut up quickly, letting Hettie grab my elbow in her bony fingers. Zin stood close by her other side, and the three of us strode toward the trees.

A tugging sensation began deep behind my navel, and I was taken back to the moment when I'd first arrived on The Isle— transported from the mainland by a boat the size of a dingy that had carried us into massive wave. Some sort of portal like this one, except now, I knew what to expect.

However, knowing what to expect did not prepare me for the process. My rib cage constricted and my breath vanished as I hurtled headfirst through blackness. When I came to, my feet hit firm ground, and I collapsed in a heap on the cold, tile floor.

"Sorry about that," Hettie was saying when I managed to open my eyes and blink away the stars. "First timer, here."

I blinked furiously, trying to clear away the stars as Hettie and Zin each hooked an arm through mine and hauled me to my feet.

"C'mon now, use your legs," Hettie said. "You look drunk. People are gonna assume we're bringing you here to detox."

"What happened?" I asked, a bit dazed. "You have to warn me next time we go hurtling through a black hole."

"Black hole," Hettie scoffed. "That was a tiny portal. You'll get used to it. Until then, at least try to land on your feet. People are staring."

"Welcome to Ranger Headquarters!" A familiar, peppy voice sounded, and I turned my attention to Poppy, who was waving us in. "How ya doin', Lily? Sorry about that. The entrance can be rather abrupt."

I climbed to my feet and gave her a begrudging hug. "You don't say."

"I've been meaning to show you around the place, but Gus keeps you so dang busy counting herbs, or whatever you do locked up in your bungalow, that I haven't gotten a chance to steal you away."

Zin and Hettie also greeted Poppy, and I took the opportunity to glance around the space. "Wow," I breathed. "This is... something else."

"It's comfortable." Poppy shrugged, clearly unimpressed by the space. "You want a tour?"

"I'd love one!"

"Follow me, you'll need a badge."

I followed Poppy to a counter that looked like the reception desk for the Ritz. Stepping through the portal between the trees had landed us in a hallway with ceilings so high I could barely see the top.

The walls were black and shiny, the furniture a combination of dazzling metals and spotless white. Black leather couches and coffee tables formed a square in the middle of the space, giving off the feel of a modern, uber-sleek lounge. Soft music played in the background as one or two men dressed in sharp suits crisscrossed through the room, disappearing into a dark hallway.

A woman stood behind the front desk. When she smiled, the motion was so striking I did a double take. She laughed and extended a hand. "Hello, you're a friend of Poppy's?"

I nodded, trying not to stare at her features. I quickly shook her hand which felt as delicate as paper-mache.

With hair as white as a star and eyes as blue as sea glass, I doubted she was human. The creature wore a tight black dress that fell midway to her thigh, covered by a gauzy shawl over thin arms. At least three inches taller than me, she had the height of a supermodel and the fashion wardrobe of a CEO. Stunning was not a strong enough word to describe her beauty. Ethereal, maybe.

"No problem," she said with a wink, her laugh sounding light and airy. "Let me print up a pass for you."

"Do you need my name? Information?" I tried to peek over

the counter, but there were no computers anywhere in sight. No machinery, gadgets, or technology of any sorts. "I'm—"

"I know who you are," she said. "You're the new Mixologist."

"You're famous." Poppy elbowed me. "This is Elle. She's the secretary here, but don't let the job title fool you. She runs this place."

Elle shook her head. "I've just been here a long time. Knowledge seeps in over the years, you know."

"Surely you haven't been here more than five or ten years," I said. "You're not old enough."

Both Elle and Poppy broke out in a laugh. "Try five hundred years," Poppy said. "Elle is Fae. Here on The Isle, Fae live long lives. She never forgets anything, either, which can be a real bummer for people who try to cross her. Someone stole her lunch three hundred years ago, and the poor witch still doesn't have a parking spot for her broomstick."

"It's a blessing and a curse," Elle said with a grin. "Here you are, Lily. Just put your wrist out."

I extended my wrist, shooting a curious glance at Poppy.

"It doesn't hurt," Poppy explained. "Relax."

Elle took my wrist in her long, delicate fingers and held it so that my palm faced up. She pressed her thumb onto my forearm for a long second.

"You have a beautiful manicure," I said, trying to ease the awkwardness as Elle continued to press down on my arm with a cool touch. "I like that color."

Elle gave a half smile and glanced at her glittering silver nails. "Thanks, I'll give you the name of the witch who does it. Really skilled."

"Wonderful," I said. Running out of things to talk about, I gazed around the room some more until Elle's fingers heated against my skin. "What's happening?"

"We don't use those human badges," Poppy said. "Not needed.

My mom told me about those plastic cards. We use a much simpler and foolproof method here. A Fae's touch leaves a dusting of magic on your skin. It'll allow you access to all of the places you need to go, no more and no less. It wears off in about an hour, so we should get moving."

"It was great to meet you, Lily," the beautiful creature said. "I've been meaning to stop by Magic & Mixology, but I haven't gotten around to it."

"I imagine they keep you busy down here." I couldn't help but return her smile. Somehow, even her intense beauty couldn't offset her genuinely pleasant personality. That a person so gorgeous could also be so kind, however, made me wonder if there was hope for the rest of us on this island.

"That they do, but I enjoy it." Elle grinned. "Never a dull moment here."

Poppy took my arm, whistled for our cousin and Hettie to follow. They didn't seem to hear.

"What are they doing?" she muttered. "I can't take them anywhere."

A few more stern whistles got their attention, and soon Hettie and Zin had marks on their arms courtesy of Elle. We set off down one of the long, dark hallways, the only light to guide us stemming from tiny, star-like dots along the wall. It took a moment for my eyes to adjust.

"It feels like we're on the Milky Way," I whispered. For some reason, the eerie quiet seemed sacred.

Poppy's laugh echoed off the walls. "We're so far from space that you're more likely to see the center of the earth than the moon. We're underground. Deep underground."

"How long have you worked here?"

"On and off since I turned eighteen," Poppy said. "I still split my time working dispatch and the supply store. We have a few other girls on dispatch rotation, so it's a pretty flexible schedule. Good benefits, and all of those 'adult' things, you know."

"I'd have never guessed," I said, my eyes still drawn to the dark, mysterious walls. "Benefits. That's funny for some reason."

Poppy raised an eyebrow. "Vamp Vites aren't cheap, ya know. How are those coming along, anyway?"

"I'm missing one ingredient," I said with a sigh.

When I first arrived on the island and learned about Poppy's blood-intolerance issue, she'd explained that our grandfather, who was the Mixologist at the time she was born, had concocted a beverage that provided all the nutrients a normal vampire might need.

"I can't figure out where he ordered Dust of the Devil. There are no stores on The Isle that carry it. I've checked them all. I even asked Harpin."

"How is that possible? Where else could he get it from?" Poppy led the way out of the tunnel, showing us into a hallway that was all reflective gray. Metallic walls below, above, and to our sides. "He was getting it from somewhere."

"I know," I said. "But Gus has no clue, which in itself is quite strange. Normally Gus does all of the ingredient orders. He catalogues them and puts them away, but he told me he's never been asked to restock Dust of the Devil. Our grandfather and Neil were the only Mixologists to make this potion, right? Did they ever say anything to you—a hint or a clue or *something*?"

Poppy shook her head. "If they did, I wasn't listening. Mostly, I just wanted the potion to work. It's not fun if it starts to wear off. The cravings get pretty bad, pretty quick."

"It's not fun for any of us," Hettie said, waving a hand in front of her face to signal a noxious smell. "We're forced to feed her raw meats, and that doesn't sit well with her stomach if you catch my... drift."

Zin snorted. "Clever."

"Funny! You guys are really funny," Poppy said sarcastically. "You try to live without half of the nutrients you need and tell me how that sits with your stomach."

"It's more like you ate a vat of broccoli, topped it off with a bit of asparagus, and then devoured a bathtub full of beans," Hettie said. "I mean really, it's impressive. That could be your Uniqueness if you wanted to be a Ranger."

Poppy's face reddened, and she opened her mouth to speak, but I interrupted first.

"I'll find it, don't worry," I told Poppy. "I've talked to Gus in depth about it, and we're on the lookout. He's asking all of his suppliers for advice."

Poppy sighed. "I appreciate it."

We reached the end of the hallway made of metal, which was a good thing because I was getting so dizzy I couldn't tell which way was left or right, up or down, but I could say for a fact that the contents of my stomach were about to come up.

"This is the lab," Poppy said, pointing off to one side. "Lily, I thought you'd like this in particular."

The metal had melded into a series of hallways made from clear glass. Sort of like a carnival fun house. Without Poppy, I would've knocked myself unconscious by waltzing straight into a solid, see-through panel. Thanks to her slow, guiding steps, however, we made it to the lab in one piece.

A glass wall surrounded the lab, and I stood as close as possible without smudging it. Inside, men dressed in sharp suits covered by white coats moved with purpose from one station to the next.

Small flames licked the top of one table, while another table held a container the size of a small whale filled with teensy glowing fish. Above the fire sat a series of eight vials, each of them different sizes and shapes. Some were tall, some were short, some were green, and some were gold. All of them sparkled as liquid bubbled and brewed inside.

"What are they making?" I glanced out of the corner of my eye at Poppy.

"I have no clue," Poppy said. "It's way over my head. I can try to get you a pass sometime though, if you'd like. It's not unheard of to bring guests into the lab, and I bet they'd be happy to have you."

I made a face. "I bet not. I'd just get in their way."

"Wrong." Poppy's grin brightened her face. "Lily, don't forget. You are the Mixologist. You can ask people to do things for you. A lot of folks would bend over backwards for the chance to share their work with you. This island has been waiting for the next true Mixologist for a while. We're really happy you're here."

I sighed. "I don't know about that. Lately, I've been feeling like I have no clue what I'm doing. There's so much to learn, so little time to learn it, and so many things to accomplish. The list is so long, and I haven't even gotten started yet."

"You're not alone. Gus is around to help, and so are we," Poppy said. "You are practically royalty here."

"Royalty..." I said with heavy sarcasm. "Definitely not royalty."

Poppy waved a hand in dismissal. "You're a big deal. People listen when you talk. Even if some don't realize it yet, they will soon enough. Even Elle knew who you were before you introduced yourself."

"I think that's her job."

"Yeah, well..." Poppy bobbed her shoulders up and down. "She didn't know my name when I was first hired, and I've lived here all my life. Just ask Hettie and Zin. Speaking of... Hettie? Where'd they go? Zin?"

My head swiveled in all directions as well, but the two ladies were nowhere in sight. Though it was hard to imagine where they could've disappeared to, seeing how all of the walls were made of glass.

"They do this every time," Poppy said in annoyance. "Did you know they banned Hettie from this building for seven years? She kept disappearing and causing trouble. I told her to watch it or they'll kick her out again."

"What sort of trouble?" I had to pick up my pace to stay with Poppy. "Poking into business that wasn't hers?"

"That, among other things. For a while, Hettie used to sneak into the bathrooms and take the little bottles of hand soap."

I burst out laughing. "Why would she do that?"

"She likes the scent!"

I laughed, struggling not to run into any of the clear walls. "Do you know where they went?"

"I have a feeling," Poppy said. Then she whirled around and stomped toward the edge of the maze. "Before we find them, I have to ask you one thing."

"What?"

"You don't have to whisper. Nobody can hear us."

It was eerie being here, surrounded by enough glass to build a castle. Everyone could see one another, but nobody could hear whispered secrets. It was a bit of a thrill. "Is everything okay?"

She stepped so close that her nose was an inch away from mine. Then she ignored her own advice and dropped her voice to a nervous whisper. "I'm running low."

"Low on what?"

"The Vamp Vites. I only have a week's supply left."

"A week?" My jaw flew open. "Poppy, you should have said something!"

"You told me you were looking for the missing ingredient!"

"I was! I still am. But you should have given me more advance notice that you were almost out. Some of our suppliers take two weeks to ship the goods. Even if we find it, the stuff might not get here in time. Not to mention, I don't have the potions book right now. With *The Magic of Mixology* stolen, I don't have any of my recipes."

"How have you been operating in the meantime?" Poppy frowned. "Gus has to remember, right?"

"Probably," I said. "But I haven't asked him about the details because I haven't had all of the necessary supplies."

"You can do it. I know you can, Lily."

"Do what?" My voice turned into a bit of a screech. "Find a book stolen by a professional thief? Find an ingredient that Gus and I have never once seen? All in one week?"

"Yes." Poppy's voice was firm as she nodded. "I have faith in you."

"How? I haven't done anything yet."

"You've done plenty," Poppy said. "You don't think Gus brags about you when you're not looking? I've heard the stories. Plus, I know all about why you had to close up shop today. Creating and serving The Elixir is serious business."

"How do you know about The Elixir? That just happened this morning."

"I work dispatch with all of the Rangers, and when things out of the ordinary are happening, it's their job to know about it. If you think they'd miss something like a request for The Elixir..." Poppy blew out a breath. "Let's put it this way. They knew the second that man walked into your bungalow."

"But how?"

"There's a lot you don't know about Rangers, and it's going to have to stay that way. They don't share their secrets and techniques for a reason, and I really shouldn't be talking about it. Especially here." Poppy's gaze shifted around the room as if she thought we were being watched. "Let's go find Hettie."

"Poppy..." I reached for her hand. She stopped abruptly at my touch, and I gave her fingers a squeeze, offering her an olive branch of a smile. "I'm going to find the missing ingredient. Between Gus and me, we've got the situation under control. Don't worry."

Poppy gave a serene smile. "I'm not worried."

CHAPTER 8

AFTER WEAVING OUR WAY THROUGH a few more glass hallways, the scenery changed from clean and modern into old and regal in an instant. We passed through tall, stone arches with columns rising high on either side of a path covered by plush red carpet. Purple tapestries dangled from the doorways, hushing the hallway. Statues in all forms of undress posed around us, and for a moment, I might've believed I was standing on Mount Olympus itself.

"This place is beautiful," I said with a note of reverence. "What is it called?"

"The Hall of Fame." She, too, spoke in a hushed voice. "It's where we honor the greatest of supernatural beings."

"And this is where we'll find Hettie?"

Poppy gave me a sideways glance. "You'll understand in a minute."

"Let me guess, Hettie considers herself one of the Greats?"

"She calls herself a goddess," Poppy trilled as she attempted to stifle a laugh. "It's not nearly as funny as when she was caught trying to steal a set of fake grapes from an Aphrodite statue. She said they'd look better on her dining room table than in this dusty old hall!"

I covered my mouth to contain my own laughter as we toured deeper and deeper into the regal space.

"That woman, I tell you…" Poppy and I turned a corner, stopping short at the sight before us. "Just like I said."

Hettie and Zin stood before a wall of trophies. The room was full of them, floor to ceiling. Silver and gold statues, plaques, and other memorabilia.

"I'm just pointing out the statue of myself," Hettie said without turning around. "Zin doesn't believe I worked with the Rangers. She was trying to tell me I was in no position to train her. Well, I give you... this. Am I a goddess or what?"

Joining Hettie on her other side, I looked to where she was pointing. The tiniest of all the statues sat at the end of her fingertip. The figurine reminded me of a little army man with a parachute attached to his back, the kind found in the bottom of cereal boxes. Except this statue was of a woman wearing a tiara with a smirk that distinctly matched my grandmother's. Below the figurine was a tiny plaque that read: Most Valuable... .

"What does that say?" I squinted. "The last word is all smudged out."

"I can't read it either," Zin said. "It sort of looks like pinhead?"

"It does not say pinhead!" Hettie flounced a hand on her hip. "How rude."

"What does it say?" Poppy asked. "I've never heard of anyone who knows what the original award was for."

"No matter," Hettie said as a pink flush decorated her cheeks. "Isn't she beautiful?"

"Lovely," I said.

"Really impressive," Zin agreed. "And this should explain why you're allowed to train me... how?"

"Because!" Hettie crossed her arms and puffed out her chest. "Not just anyone gets a statue here."

"True," Poppy agreed. "I don't even have one yet, and I fancy myself an integral part of the workforce."

"I'll have one," Zin vowed, her gaze leveling at the statue. "Just you wait."

"Come on, let's get out of here before someone starts asking questions," Poppy said. "Pretty soon they're going to stop letting me show people around because all of my guests cause trouble!"

"Maybe if I could just touch this one last thing..." Hettie reached forward to run her hands along the abs of Hercules. Just as she did so, loud, angry voices erupted behind her.

"I will not accept that as an answer," a male voice said. "We need to let her find out on her own."

"We don't have an option," a second, quieter male voice said. "We need to hurry. They're already here."

"You don't think she'll notice all the robes? They're flocking across The Isle."

Hettie's eyes widened, and Poppy's matched hers.

"We've gotta hide," Poppy said. "That's the director's voice."

"We're not allowed to be in here?" I blinked at her. "Why'd you take us in here then?"

"I didn't! Hettie did."

We both turned on Hettie, who crossed her arms and made a disgruntled noise in her throat. "I refuse to be intimidated by the two of you. I have a statue in here with my name on it. I can be in here if I want."

"You're supposed to have special clearance," Poppy muttered. "Quick, just duck! Duck behind there and we'll let them pass."

The four of us scurried behind a partial wall that held a display of marble statues posed like sprinters in the Olympic races.

"This is fun," Zin said with a dark, mischievous smile. "Really, really fun."

"It is not fun," Poppy whimpered. "You guys are going to make me lose my job."

"Relax," Hettie said. "I was basically the first female Ranger."

"No, you have a statue the size of my thumbprint on the wall. That doesn't make you a Ranger," Poppy said crossly. "You had a moment of glory, and it does not allow you to wander free around Headquarters three decades after you earned it."

"Sure it does," Hettie sniffed and pointed her nose upwards. "Plus, I'm an old, senile woman. I can wander wherever I want and blame it on my age."

"Nobody thinks you're senile," Poppy said. "Crazy, maybe. But that has nothing to do with you being old."

The two glared at each other until I gestured for them to keep things down. The voices in the hallway were still loud and still angry, and they were getting much closer to us. It didn't take long for their voices to wash throughout the room as they paused a few paces away.

"Let's not talk about this here," the second voice said calmly. "I'm sure there's a logical explanation for everything. Would you like to come up to my office?"

"We'll talk about it in here," the director said. "And we'll talk now. What is going on?"

We all pushed closer against the wall as the voices lapsed into silence. When the conversation resumed, they were whispering.

"Answer me," the director said. "Why are they here so soon? I thought we had more time."

"We can't be sure, sir."

"What do you mean? Are you not in charge of Foreign Affairs?"

"This is hardly a Foreign Affair. They're part of the community just like the rest of us."

"Anyone who is not from The Isle is foreign for my purposes," the director said sternly. "This is most certainly foreign."

"Their presence here is not forbidden."

"Do we need to make it forbidden?"

"No sir, that would be a drastic measure." The head of Foreign Affairs sighed. "We believe they're here to recruit new witches and wizards."

"Now is not the time to be focusing on recruitment," he said. "I thought we agreed that until the business with The Faction is done, schooling takes secondary priority."

"Yes, but there are no laws against it."

The director paused. "So be it. But what I won't have is my Mixologist threatened."

"The Mixologist was threatened?"

"One of the cloaks requested The Elixir. That's something no Mixologist should have to serve, let alone a beginner."

I froze at their conversation. Poppy, Zin, and Hettie's eyes all landed on me, but I looked at the ground. Were people watching my every move?

"The Elixir?" The head of Foreign Affairs asked. "No. That doesn't make any sense."

"The potion was served successfully this afternoon."

"I'll... I'll get in contact with the Headmaster," the head of Foreign Affairs said after clearing his throat. "I apologize. Is the Mixologist handling things all right?"

"As best she can, from what I hear."

"I'll take care of it."

"Pass along this message to the Headmaster, will you? Tell him kindly about the high number of cloaks we've seen lately. Let him know... we're watching."

"Yes, sir."

"And Ranger M, one more thing."

"Sir?"

"If we must ban all recruiting from The Isle, we will. I'll ban all cloaks if I have to. If they want to be here, I need to know what they are up to, and why. Understood?"

"Yes, sir."

I imagined the head of Foreign Affairs bowing, or nodding, or whatever it was that Rangers did to acknowledge one another. Did they salute? Footsteps shuffled away shortly after, but only one set of them. The four of us remained crunched behind the wall, waiting to see which of the men had gone and which had stayed.

After a few seconds' wait, another set of footsteps approached in the hallway. A different voice spoke. A familiar voice. "Director?"

Hettie exhaled an almost audible sigh of relief as the director took a few steps away from the wall.

"What is it, X?"

"There's a guest for you in the main lobby, sir," Ranger X said. "Do you have a moment?"

The director hesitated before responding, and for a long second I worried he'd spotted us. "Of course. Will you be joining me?"

"No. It's a private matter for you, sir. I'm just the messenger."

"Thank you, X. Any word on the other issue I asked you to keep an eye on?"

"Still working on it, sir."

"Keep me posted."

"Of course."

The now-familiar jaunt of the director's footsteps sounded as he strode quickly down the hall. Behind the wall, a barely audible sigh sounded as Poppy's shoulders sank at least three inches in relief.

"Why, hello ladies," Ranger X said, stepping around the corner. Somehow, he'd made his way across the room soundlessly. "What brings you into hiding today?"

"Oh, you know..." Poppy said, coughing as she straightened up. "Business."

"Really." Ranger X raised an eyebrow. "So you have clearance to be in here, then?"

Poppy grinned like a lunatic while Zin wore a scowl on her face that'd have a lesser man shaking in his boots. Hettie licked her lips as she stared up at Ranger X's tall form. Meanwhile, I watched it all like a dork.

Ranger X wore a suit made of the finest materials money could buy. The fabric begged my hands to touch the sleeves, to run my fingers over its soft contours. The man inside the suit was just as impressive.

With eyes like black diamonds and hair curling into a wavy, matching shade of darkness, the only thing cheerful about him was the twinkle in his eye, and the soft curve of his lips. When he crossed his arms, the jacket moved with him like a suit of armor.

"You look fancy," Hettie said, breaking the silence. "Did someone die?"

Ranger X looked stunned for a moment, and then gave a low, throaty chuckle. "No, not that I'm aware."

"You never wear a suit," Hettie pointed out. She hauled herself to her feet and took a few steps closer to the man, sizing him up as if she were a seamstress about to tailor his clothes. "What's the big deal?"

Ranger X cocked his head to the side and studied my pint-sized grandmother. "I'm in the office. We dress nicely here."

"You normally wear those jeans that give your rear end a really nice shape. At least, when you're out and about that is." She circled Ranger X, stopping directly behind him and staring at said butt. "You know, I suppose this isn't all that bad either. Can I touch it?"

"No!" the three of us girls chorused. "Hettie, stop it. This is a professional workplace."

"What's the point of working hard if you can't have a little fun?" Hettie eyed Ranger X's backside again like it was a particularly juicy apple. Then with a sigh full of rattling frustration, she shook her head. "Fine. Lily, give it a poke and let me know how it feels."

"No!" My face burned. "I'm not... we're not... Hettie," I chided. "Stop being inappropriate."

"I'm old and senile. I can say whatever I want."

Ranger X cleared his throat. "Then tell me what brings you ladies here today."

"Well, uh, I wanted to visit Poppy," I said. "I had the day off from the bungalow, and I'd never been here before."

A flash of recognition blitzed through his eyes as I mentioned the shop closing early. "And that led to you hiding from the director... how?"

"You know Zin is training for the Ranger trials," Hettie said. "I want to be her instructor."

Ranger X waited patiently.

"You know how grandkids can get," Hettie said, twirling her hand in the air in front of her body. "Difficult."

"I actually know nothing about that," Ranger X deadpanned. "Since we're not allowed families."

"Well, they're difficult, I tell ya. They think they're on top of the world."

"Is that right?"

"Darn tootin'," Hettie said. She thumbed in Zin's direction. "This one thought I didn't know boo about being a Ranger, so I came in here to show her my statue."

Ranger X glanced over his shoulder, his gaze falling briefly on the army-sized figurine behind him. "I see."

"Then the director waltzed his way in here, not even minding his own business. So we hid."

"Why didn't you just walk out?"

"What's the fun in that?" Hettie raised her arms above her head. "I'm old. I'm gonna die soon. Are you really gonna deny me fun in my final years? What if this was the last fun thing I got to do here on earth? I'm bonding with my grandbabies, you know. They're gonna look back on this moment fondly."

"As am I," Ranger X muttered. Then he mumbled words that sounded like crazy and nutcase, or something along those lines. I didn't blame him much. "Do you plan to creep around the building for the rest of the day, or would you like me to show you out?"

"Nah, I've had my fill of creeping for today," Hettie said. "I'm hungry. Girls, are you ready to go?"

Cautiously Poppy stood, followed closely by Zin. I joined them, hooking my arm through my grandmother's so she wouldn't get lost. Again.

Then Hettie surprised me by twirling out of my grasp. She

danced over to Ranger X, her little fists circling in front of her face like a boxer. "Come on, Ranger X. Let's duel. I can tell Zin's not convinced about my strength from that statue."

"I'm not dueling you," he said. He gave me a 'please, help' sort of stare.

"Hettie, it's time to go," I said, reaching for her. "He's not going to duel you."

Hettie muttered something under her breath about *I'll show him.* Then she held up her hand and shot a tiny lightning bolt straight from her palm toward Ranger X's chest. But he was faster. Ranger X blocked the bolt and had Hettie draped over his shoulder like a sack of potatoes before I could blink.

"I'll walk you ladies out," Ranger X said, turning on his heel with my grandmother bobbing over his shoulder on the way out the door. "I'm sure you don't mind."

Poppy raised her eyebrows. "Do what he says!"

The three of us followed close behind Ranger X.

"Hettie, are you okay?" I asked cautiously. Her body resembled a limp noodle hanging over his shoulder. Her arms flopped down to his waist, waving to and fro like a lazy sprinkler system.

I almost reached out to stop Ranger X so I could take my grandmother's pulse, but at the very last second, she turned her head up and winked. That woman winked at us, and then she went right back to dangling over his shoulder.

"She loves it," Zin whispered. "Can you believe her?"

Poppy shook her head. "Maybe you should let her train you for the Ranger program. I don't know anyone like her."

"Did she just pinch him?" Zin whispered as Ranger X's back shot ramrod straight. "The guts on that woman!"

"Maybe we all need to be trained by her," Poppy said a bit wistfully. "She's older than us by decades and she still gets more action than all of us put together."

I couldn't draw my eyes away from where Hettie was pretending to squeeze Ranger X's buns like a pair of ripe cantaloupes at the supermarket. It was like a train wreck. I didn't want to see it happening, but I couldn't look away.

Ranger X turned around as we stopped whispering, and Hettie went limp.

Ranger X's eyes scanned the three of us for a long time. When his eyes landed on me, it heated my stomach, and goose bumps prickled my arms. His eyes didn't pull away from mine for a long while.

"Stop staring," Zin said. "This is getting weird."

I yanked my eyes away and looked down. Unfortunately, Hettie's head was "down," and she waved enthusiastically back up at me.

"Put the grandma down," Poppy said. "It's time for them to get going anyway. I have to get back to work."

Ranger X didn't listen. Instead, he marched all the way through Ranger HQ with my grandmother hanging over his shoulder. One or two folks directed funny looks in his direction, but it wasn't until we reached Elle at the front desk that anyone addressed the issue.

"I see you've met our guests?" Elle asked, her blue eyes falling on Ranger X. "Aren't they lovely?"

Something in her innocent voice and beautiful face sparked a small curl of jealousy in my stomach. I fought it back. Ranger X and I had nothing going between us, except for a polite business relationship. I had absolutely no reason to dislike Elle. In fact, I liked her a lot. I just didn't like her too close to Ranger X.

"It's not our first meeting," Ranger X said, glancing around at us, his gaze landing on me. "But lovely is one word to describe them." He carefully placed Hettie's feet down on the floor.

"Describe me, maybe." Hettie pointed at herself. She leaned an elbow on the desk and twisted her head to face Elle. "Did you know I have a statue in the Hall of Fame?"

"I did." Elle nodded politely. "You've shown it to me before... many times."

"So many times," Poppy echoed. "Too many."

"It ain't just anyone who can get a trophy erect in there," Hettie said. "But I did."

Poppy, Zin, and I all flinched at Hettie's choice of words.

"Erected, Hettie," Poppy clarified. "You know what? Just cut that word out of your vocabulary entirely."

Elle covered her mouth with those long, dainty fingers, stifling a giggle. Even as that wisp of jealousy hovered inside my stomach, I couldn't help but join in the laughter. She was just so pleasant to be around.

"Lily, may I have a word?" Ranger X shifted his weight from one foot to the other. "In private."

I pointed at myself. "Me?"

"No, the other Lily," Hettie said sarcastically. "If you'd like to whisk me away, Ranger, feel free. I'm up for grabs."

"Hettie!" both Zin and Poppy said at once.

I followed him across the lobby, the soft background music creating a false sense of relaxation as our footsteps padded across the thick carpeting.

"In here." Ranger X rested his hand on my lower back, causing a jolt of electricity to sizzle across my skin.

I tried not to shiver at his touch, but it was like trying to stop a sneeze. Our close proximity amplified his motions; every breath, every footstep felt intensely personal. I stepped away from his hand as he pushed open the door to a dark room. I wanted to tell him to leave the light off for a moment so we could be here together. Quietly. Just the two of us.

But he flicked the light on, and I blinked twice as my eyes adjusted.

"Hi," he said, more softly now. "Thanks for coming."

I didn't bother to correct him. Really, I'd just stopped by to see Poppy, but I wasn't going to burst his bubble.

"I know you came to see Poppy," he said quickly. "But it worked out well because I needed to talk to you anyway. Please tell me everything you remember about the man who ordered The Elixir."

"I can't do that."

"Why not?"

"First of all, I pride myself on keeping my clients' business confidential. If I started blabbing what everyone ordered, I'd lose half my clientele. Nobody wants the entire island to know they've ordered a Balding Beverage or a Height Helper. That sort of stuff is private."

"Not when it's a matter of security."

"How is this a matter of security?" I sat down at the conference table, two seats away from Ranger X. The distance helped me think. "Gus was there the entire time. I hadn't known about The Elixir before my guest requested it, so I was as clueless as the next person. It was Gus who guided me through everything."

"And you trust Gus?"

I looked at him curiously. He was the second person to ask in one day. "Of course I trust him."

Ranger X glanced down at the table where he'd folded his hands.

"How do you even know about The Elixir?" I broke the silence. "It was just this afternoon the visitor came in. It took over an hour to brew, and I only served it to him thirty minutes ago or so."

"There's strong magic in that spell." Ranger X leaned back in his chair and rested his hands behind his head. "Ranger HQ is responsible for the safety of The Isle. We have triggers in place to alert us of potentially harmful magic."

I scrunched my nose up. "How can you tell?"

"Magic has an equal and opposite reaction; it leaves a trace. The spell doesn't just disappear. It takes energy to create a spell, and during a very intense spell, a void emerges. We have our own hexes to sense these voids."

"That's why it's harder to perform bad magic." I gave a slow nod. "Someone—was it you?—explained to me when I first arrived that The Faction has a harder battle ahead of them than we do because they're using their powers to harm instead of help."

He nodded. "Exactly. We can detect bad magic. That doesn't mean we can always prevent it, but we usually send someone to check it out."

"You sent someone to Magic & Mixology?"

"We were about to, but then you showed up here." Ranger X eyed me. "You read my mind."

"That was all Hettie," I said with a laugh. "I was trying to find someone else."

"Someone else?"

For a brief moment, I wondered if that glint in Ranger X's dark irises didn't also walk the line of jealousy. Then I pushed the thought away. The glint disappeared much faster than it'd arrived. "Okay, my turn. Tell me where you are at with the investigation for *The Magic of Mixology*."

He exhaled a sigh. "We're no further than when I updated you yesterday."

"But you hadn't made any progress when you updated me yesterday."

"If I could change that, I would," Ranger X said grimly. "I've never seen anything like it. There are no traces of magic. None of our sensors detected foul play, there is not a hint of a fingerprint in the room, and nobody saw anything."

"I need it back!"

"I'm well aware." Ranger X's jawline tensed. "I'm working on it, as are many of my best men. They're scouring The Isle now asking for help from less than... traditional members of The Isle."

I didn't bother to ask. Whether he was referring to werewolves or gnomes or giants, I really wasn't sure I needed to know the nitty-gritty details. "Do you think that'll actually help anything, or is it a long shot?"

"At this point, it's all a long shot. Investigations normally don't take this long."

"I mean, I used to watch television, and sometimes investigations took months."

"You're talking about humans. I'm talking about the supernatural."

I fell silent. "So where does that leave us? I can't become a Mixologist without that book. It contains everything."

"You're doing just fine now."

"Just fine is not good enough. I'm struggling as it is, and I lean on Gus for everything."

"You're allowed to use other people for help, Lily. The job might be a solo one, but it doesn't have to be a lonely one."

"I wouldn't have known where to start with The Elixir if it hadn't been for Gus. He explained the rules, he remembered the ingredients, the recipe... everything. Without him, I'd be lost."

"Then keep Gus close."

All at once, a silence descended on the room, heavy and full of trepidation. "Gus went out tonight," I said slowly. "Gus never goes out."

"Did he say where he was going?"

"Not in so many words. I assumed he had dinner plans with Mimsey."

"Are they dating?"

"Not really..." I hesitated. "But I think they want to."

"How do you know that?" he asked with too much curiosity. "Gus doesn't strike me as the type to open up about his personal life."

"People don't need to say when they like someone, either as a friend or as a romantic interest. You can just feel it."

"And you think the nature of this evening's visit was romantic?"

I wrinkled my nose. "I don't like to think in those terms when talking about Gus. Or Mimsey."

To my surprise, Ranger X laughed. "He's a man, just like any of us."

"What's that supposed to mean?"

He cleared his throat, and this time it was Ranger X's face turning the color of ripe tomatoes. "Nothing."

"In all seriousness, do you think Gus is in trouble?"

He paused a moment. "He really likes Mimsey, huh?"

"He enjoys her company," I hedged. "I haven't seen them together long enough to know if it's love, but there is something between them."

"Do you think he was lying when he said he was going out tonight?"

I shook my head. "He was too awkward about it. If Gus wanted to do something in secret, he just wouldn't have told me, and I'd never have known."

"It doesn't hurt to check in with him," X said. "I'll make up an excuse and say it's Ranger HQ business. Does he have a way we can reach him?"

"I've never needed to try," I said thoughtfully. "He doesn't carry a Comm device. Usually we're right next to each other, so I shout across the room. If Gus needs something, he finds me."

For some reason, all of our modern technology from the mainland did not work quite right here on The Isle. Maybe my cell phone would've worked if it hadn't been washed away by the giant wave, but it was unlikely. The amount of magic zipping through the air rendered most devices useless, and I hadn't seen a computer either. Even receipts and bookkeeping were done by hand, bringing me back to Little House on the Prairie days.

"Let me call in Glinda, she's our Emergency Contact Specialist," Ranger X said. "She consults for Ranger HQ."

"So what does Poppy do as a dispatcher, if she can't call people?"

"She dispatches internally. As you might know, each Ranger has a specific talent or skill set. If we get word that someone needs healing, she'll direct the request to the medics. If someone's lost, she'll contact Ranger F, who's known for his ability to return things to their rightful owner. The list continues."

"So about this Ranger F, can I get him working on my case? Maybe he'll have some luck finding the spellbook."

Ranger X narrowed his eyes at me. "He's already on it. He's the reason I'm saying the future is bleak for that book. His track record is impeccable. He's solved almost everything in just under three days. Yours… it's been going on weeks. Short of a wild breakthrough, I don't see this case closing anytime soon."

"But I need it—"

"We're not abandoning it," Ranger X interrupted. "If anything, we'll be setting an example. When we find out whoever did this, we'll come down, and come down hard on them. The longer this goes the more interest it generates. The more interest it generates, the more of an example we need to make with it. Now, let me call Glinda in here so we can talk to Gus."

CHAPTER 9

FIVE MINUTES AND A LOT of pink glitter later, a witch who looked nothing like the beautiful Glinda from the Wizard of Oz had set up shop in the middle of the conference room.

This witch looked like she'd gone out and had a good time at Mardi Gras last night. Smudges of mascara lined her eyes, while her weathered face gave off the impression of a long, hard-earned life. She wore a dress that looked sort of like Peter Pan had fought a tutu. Pink tatters of cloth flapped around her waist in a bedraggled skirt and fluttered about as she pulled out a crystal ball. The woman herself stood no taller than four feet high, and her body was made of rolls and curves and sassiness.

"So, who're we talkin' to?" She chomped some gum, and strangely reminded me of an attraction from the New Jersey boardwalk. She looked to Ranger X and stuck a hand on her hip, but he nodded toward me. She whirled in my direction. "You gonna speak, chickie? I don't got all day."

She did some snapping with her fingers, and I jumped to attention.

"Uh… his name's Gus?" I spoke extra loud, competing with the jangling bells dangling from her fingers.

"You sure about that?" she snapped.

"Yes?"

"Then why you askin' me a question, sweetheart?" Glinda put something that looked like a crystal sphere on the table and waved one hand over it like she might a magic eight ball. "Gus who?"

"Gus... of the bungalow?"

"Sound a little confident. I know you're new here and all, but ain't you supposed to be the Mixologist?" Glinda closed her eyes. When I didn't respond right away, she peeked underneath one eyelid. "Cat got your tongue?"

Startled, I shook my head. "Sorry, I thought you were concentrating. I *am* the Mixologist."

"I can multi-task," Glinda said. "Now tell me about this Gus."

I looked to Ranger X, but he looked mildly amused more than anything else. "Uh, he's medium-old, really crabby most of the time, and spends the majority of his time in the storeroom over at the bungalow."

"Good," Glinda said. "Except I sense you're lying about something."

My heart raced. "I'm sorry, I wasn't trying to lie. I don't even know what I was lying about?"

"Let me tell you. If it's the Gus I know, then he's super-duper-ancient, old as dust, really. He's crabby on a good day and vicious on a bad day, and he spends so much time in that storeroom I think he might've smoked too much of the fun weeds, if you know what I'm saying."

I covered my mouth, but couldn't help snorting at her description. When I pulled myself together, I caught the slight glimmer of satisfaction in her eye. "If you knew who Gus was already, why'd you ask me?"

"Just curious what you thought of him. Everyone knows Gus. He helped make a Pimple Popper that changed my life."

I laughed again, surprised at how much I enjoyed the company of the strange, old witch. "You're funny."

"Not funny, I just speak the truth, sweetheart." Glinda laid her fingers on top of the crystal ball and closed her eyes again, this time for a longer moment. The silliness disappeared, and her forehead crinkled and twitched in concentration. "Okay, I need a few minutes now. I sent the signal out."

"How does that work?" I asked, taking a hesitant step forward.

"You're from the mainland I hear, yeah?" She looked at me, waiting for an answer. When I nodded, she mimicked the gesture. "That's what I thought. Another reason why I wanted to meet ya. I'm from there too. New York."

"New York? Wow! I've never been."

She shrugged. "Fine, I'm from Jersey. But it sounds better to say New York, and most of these munchkins don't know the difference anyway. You're the first person in years who's called my bluff."

I slid a sideways glance over at Ranger X to see how he liked being called a munchkin.

"He's my munchkin, aren't ya?" Glinda reached over to pinch Ranger X's cheek, but the man was faster. He was on his feet with Glinda's wrist in his hand before anyone could say Hocus Pocus. The threatening gesture didn't scare Glinda. She leaned forward, winked, and cooed at him. "There's my little munchkin."

"I'll turn you into toad droppings," Ranger X said. "I've told you that before, and I'll say it again."

"He's sensitive." Glinda winked over her shoulder at me, even while she was still captive in Ranger X's grasp. Their bodies were close. Too close. I worried X might snap her right in half. "It's okay though. I think he's just being extra manly because he's got a crush on you and he wants to show off them muscles."

At the same time I blushed, Ranger X lifted the tiny witch's hand so high that her entire body came off the ground. He dangled her before him and looked her in the eye. Even now, she didn't seem to mind.

In fact, she did a little shimmy and winked back at him. She winked so often I wondered if it was a nervous tick. "This is kinky."

Ranger X let go of her wrist without warning. Glinda dropped to the floor, grabbing the table for balance as she looked around the room and brushed down her ragged tutu.

"Are you okay?" I rushed forward, giving Ranger X the evil eye. "Are you hurt?"

"Not even my pride," Glinda said cheerily. "I swallowed that a long time ago, which is great because now I can say anything I want and not worry about lookin' stupid!"

"That's not a bad idea," I said. "I kind of like it."

"I do not," Ranger X said. "A bit of a filter is never a bad thing, especially in a professional work environment."

Glinda rolled her eyes at me. "They keep trying to run me out of the workforce. They say I don't dress appropriately, can you believe it?" She reached down and played with the end of a few strings flapping around her waist. "They want me to dress in all black and wear pretty makeup and pin my hair back. Sorry, but that's not me."

"I like your style," I said, searching for the right word. "It's eccentric."

"Exactly! They want my magic, they're gonna have to deal with eccentricities." Glinda twirled around. "Okay, that spell should be almost cooked. Are we ready to find Gus?"

I huddled over the ball with her while Ranger X watched from the back.

"You never did say how this works," I said. "Is it a secret?"

"Not at all. Have you met a Forest Fairy?"

"No, not yet."

"Good. You don't want to meet one in the wild." She looked up at me. "See, this magic ball is mostly glorified nonsense. But it's the unique talent that got me a cushy job at Ranger HQ—"

"Are you a Ranger?" I asked. "Sorry to interrupt."

She shook her head. "I'm a certified Emergency Contact Specialist. I got no desire to be a Ranger. I couldn't wear my outfit!"

"I see. About the Forest Fairies?"

"They are teensy tiny creatures, about this big." She held up two fingers hardly an inch apart. "Annoying little creatures. Tricky as can be, and mischievous. If you're not lookin', they'll give you a wedgie, steal your lunch money, and whisper your deepest, darkest secrets to those you care most about."

"They sound terrible."

"They are," she said. "In the wild. Until I came along, folks looked at them as pesky insects. At worst, they'd be squashed. At best, caged. They're not fun when they're running around loose, but that's where I come in. The little buggers understand me."

"You're... you're their leader or something?"

"I'm not one of 'em, never mix that up," she said. "It's impossible to fit in with another species entirely."

"I'm sorry, I don't understand."

"Lily, sometimes it's not about fitting in. Sometimes it's about leading without abandon. I train these Forest Fairies, and they listen to me."

"Are they human?" I hesitated. "Well, not human, but... are they like us? As people?"

"You're worried I'm being cruel?"

I bobbed my shoulders up and down. "I guess you could say that."

"It's not cruel at all. In fact, we have a pleasant arrangement. If the fairies work for me, they are allowed to use The Isle and move about freely. They mostly stay within the cover of the trees, but not always. Because of my work with the fairies, I've enacted a law to protect them. Currently, there's a ban against catching fairies. It's illegal to hold them captive, cage them, or otherwise detain one. That law never existed until I came around. They were treated in a bad way. So for most of them, our partnership was a relief."

"Don't they deserve their freedom regardless?"

"You weren't here before," Glinda said. "You have to understand that they wreaked absolute havoc on our society when they roamed free. Most of them were locked away in prison when I came around, and I worked out a deal to free them. In exchange, they run a few errands a week for me. It's not a bad trade."

"So they listen to only you?"

"She's the only one sassy enough to talk back to them," Ranger X grumbled. "They're terrors. Horrible creatures."

"And I love 'em." Glinda gave a wide, cheesy smile. "In this crystal ball, I have a spell that I created with the help of fairy magic. It gives me the ability to speak to any specific fairy on my roster. They may be annoying creatures, but they can cover the circumference of the island in under a minute, and usually it takes less than ten seconds for my little army to locate a person."

"Wow," I said. "That's impressive."

"That's why they pay me the big bucks," Glinda chortled. "Right, X? Isn't it about time for a raise?"

"Just find Gus," Ranger X said. "Now."

Glinda squeezed her eyes shut and turned back to the ball. Underneath her fingers, a picture started to appear as if a movie screen had popped up in the middle of the ball and begun to play. "That's called fairy magic."

I leaned in closer and watched the picture unfold. Gus, dressed in a nice suit, walked toward The Twist. As the image sharpened, it became clear that I was seeing him from the view of a fairy. Almost as if I were watching a home video recorded from a camera attached to the fairy's head like a Go-Pro.

"Message," a robotic voice said, filtering through the crystal ball. "Message from Glinda."

Gus's head jerked up onscreen, surprise scrawled across his face. He narrowed his eyes at the fairy. "Is that you, Glinda? What do you want? I'm busy!"

Glinda laughed and leaned into the ball. "Hi there, Gussie. Out on a date?"

Gus reached out and swatted the space in front of him. He was probably swatting at the fairy, but it looked like he'd aimed at us. "Leave me alone, Glinda. I'm busy tonight."

"I'm with Lily."

"Lily?" Gus's eyes swiveled back toward the fairy, and I had the eerie sensation he was staring directly into my eyes. "Is she okay?"

Glinda nodded at me. "Go ahead, dear."

"Gus, it's me," I said, still getting used to the setup. "You've got to be careful tonight. Where are you going?"

"I told you where I'm going," he growled. "And I'm always careful."

"You didn't tell me where you were going," I said. "I assumed you were meeting Mimsey, but you never confirmed it."

"Well, you figured right."

"It's nothing to be so secretive about!"

"Did you call to ask about my dating life?"

"No, I'm at Ranger HQ—"

"How'd you get inside?"

"Visiting Poppy," I said. "Anyway, Ranger X and I were talking."

"Is that all you were doin'?" Gus asked. "I don't interrupt you during your private time."

I made a disgruntled noise in my throat.

"You bother me about my dating life, I'll bother you about yours," Gus said. "Not that I care about it or anything. But if you start slacking in your work because you're a lovestruck were-pup, I'll start caring a whole lot more."

"You're the only person who knows the contents of *The Magic of Mixology*," I said, ignoring the whole bit about my dating life. X was not part of my dating life. He never had been, and he never could be. Plus, I really didn't want to get into things in front of Glinda. "Ranger X was telling me the case will likely stay open a long time, so I'll continue to need your help."

"It's already been open a long time."

"Well, it might be a lot longer time," I said. "Without you, I'd be lost. The Isle would be in trouble."

"Then don't get rid of me," Gus said. "What's the problem?"

"We need you to be safe," I said. "We can't risk anything happening to you."

Ranger X waved a hand. "May I?"

I nodded and stepped back, giving him control.

"Gus, it's X. I want to be clear. You can handle yourself, we don't doubt it. Let me give you a Companion for a few days."

"A Companion?" I asked, at the same time Gus said, "No!"

"A Companion is a shape-shifter," Glinda whispered to me. "They don't use any other forms of magic, so they're virtually undetectable. A dog, a grasshopper, you name it. We have a small fleet of Companions that serve as security detail to high-risk targets."

"I refuse," Gus said. "I can refuse a Companion at any time. It's my right. This conversation is over."

With that, the video went blank.

"Can we get him back?" I asked. "Maybe I can try to talk some sense into him."

"This Forest Fairy is tired. It takes a lot of work to transmit a signal, plus Gus swatted at the poor thing," Glinda said. "If you want another, I can send one. But if you want my advice, I'd say let Gus have his date tonight, and in the morning you can talk to him when he's fresh and happy."

"Gus is never happy," I said. "Or fresh."

"Well... less crabby," she said. "Who knows? Maybe if his night goes well enough with Mimsey, he'll actually be happy."

I closed my eyes. "Ew. I prefer not to have the imagery."

Glinda laughed. "I'm off, unless you two need anything else?"

X shook his head. "Gus is almost to The Twist. Once he's there, he'll be fine."

The Twist, an enchanted labyrinth, was the master plan and life's work of my grandmother. Nobody was allowed in, and nobody was allowed out. The only way through the maze was with a person who had West Isle Witch blood. If Mimsey led Gus through The Twist, nobody else would be able to follow without getting so irreparably lost, they'd be stuck there until they were set free by one of my aunts.

"The Twist. That Hettie is a genius," Glinda said. "I always did like her. Us weirdos gotta stick together. You, me, and your Gran. Well, I'm off. It's been fun. Toodles."

With a flap of her skirt, she disappeared from the room. I turned to Ranger X. "I'm not that weird, am I?"

He didn't answer.

I poked him in the shoulder. "You consider me to be in the same league of weird as my grandmother and Glinda?"

His stony expression spoke volumes.

I fought a smile. "Do you need anything else from me? Speaking of my grandmother, I should really find my family and herd them home."

"Do you have plans tonight?" Ranger X blurted. "For dinner. Just dinner, I mean."

My hands twisted in front of my body. "X..."

"Never mind." He waved a hand. "I shouldn't have asked."

"It's not that. It's just... I am busy. I have plans tonight."

His eyebrows knitted together. "With your cousins?"

"Sort of."

"Sort of plans?"

"I'm meeting with someone later."

"Is it a date?"

"No." I answered quickly, but Ranger X's suspicious gaze had me doubting that he believed me. "It's not a date. I just have to return something. Maybe a different night?"

"Of course." He cleared his throat. "Well, I think that's everything, then."

I debated telling him about Liam. Explaining that I was

returning his money, end of story. I turned around, finding X watching me as I rested a hand on the doorknob, and began to explain. He beat me to it.

"I shouldn't have pried into your business," he said, the words soft. "I hope you'll understand that I was just finishing up here for the day, and I was going to grab a bite to eat at Sea Salt." He shrugged. "I like your company is all. I wasn't trying to dredge up old... things."

There had never really been a "thing" between us. Attraction, sure. In spades, even. But that was the end of it. He could never get married or start a family, and I was not only the Mixologist, but a brand new witch. I had enough to focus on without worrying about men and dating and all of the other things people did for fun.

"It's fine," I said. "You didn't dredge anything up. There's hardly anything to dredge up."

My light laugh sounded a bit hollow even to my own ears, and Ranger X only cracked a sad sort of half smile. "I suppose."

A long beat passed, the tension thick enough to eat with a spoon.

"Have a nice evening," X said, reaching out and resting a hand on my shoulder. He gave it a reassuring squeeze. "We'll find your spellbook, okay? And Gus will be fine."

I met his gaze, those dark eyes of his lacking the spark I'd gotten so used to seeing. It'd been replaced by a gritty determination. An expression that told me he wouldn't stop until he'd solved every piece of this puzzle. "I have one more question."

His eyebrows shot up as if he'd forgotten we were still talking. Withdrawing his hand from my shoulder, he crossed his arms. "What's up?"

"Talk to me about Zin. What are her chances?"

"For?"

"I heard about the trials. Both you and I know that she wants to become a Ranger more than anything. What are her chances?"

"I can't possibly say."

"What do you mean?" I blinked. "You're the leader. The top dog. The head honcho. Surely you have a say?"

"We have regulations in place that prevent favoritism."

"Can't you still tell me her chances?"

"Honestly? They're not good." Ranger X shot me an apologetic gaze. "You asked for honesty, and I gave it to you. Rangers are usually not women because some of the tasks are physically too difficult. There are biological differences between us. This is not a judgment on either side, it is merely a fact."

He continued, watching my reaction. "Lily, you have to understand that if I have two people equal in all things— intelligence, professionalism, and every other mental front—then I will take into account how fast the person can run. How much weight they can lift. How quickly they can make the decision to save a life or end one."

As he paused, my breath came in short bursts. The intensity with which he spoke rubbed off on me. For a moment, I forgot it was Zin who wanted the position, not me. "And you'll pick the person who can run faster any day," I said. "I've heard this argument before. If you're trapped in a burning building, you want to make sure the person on the outside can save you."

X shook his head. "No."

"No?"

"No, I don't think about myself in that way." He stepped closer to me, his spicy, winterfresh breath tickling my neck as he brushed a stray piece of hair off my collar bone. "I think about you."

My breath hitched, the patch of skin burning where he'd touched me, tendrils of heat radiating to all limbs of my body.

"When I decide to make someone a Ranger, I do it because I trust them with the lives of those most precious to me." The weight of his words fell heavy in the room. "I would never accept a Ranger into the program who I couldn't trust one hundred percent to save you, should you need saving."

I licked my dry lips, my gaze falling to the floor. "But—"

"No. That is final, and it is my absolute decision that can never be changed," Ranger X said sternly. Then he pulled me closer to him, his hands circling my lower back. He pressed a light kiss to the top of my head. "You can never change my belief on that."

I rested my head on his chest. "But it'll break Zin's spirit if she can't get in."

"I didn't say it's impossible, I just said that I choose the best person for the job." Ranger X stroked my hair. Somehow all of the awkwardness had faded between us, and everything felt natural again. As I leaned into his chest, his breath tickled my skin and his hands soothed my worries away. "My advice to Zin is simple. Be the best."

"Easier said than done."

"Yes, of course," he said. "I never said it would be easy."

"How can I help her train?"

X gave a half sort of smile. "Convince her to listen to your grandmother."

I pointed to myself. "My grandmother? Hettie? The Hettie who was just hiding in the trophy room?"

"The one and only."

I gave him a skeptical look. "You're pulling my leg."

"I'm dead serious." Ranger X let out a low laugh. "In fact, I'm more scared of her than anyone else on this island."

CHAPTER 10

"WHAT ARE YOU GUYS DOING for dinner tonight?" I asked. After waving goodbye to blue-eyed Elle, Poppy led me, Zin, and Hettie out of the building. "Anyone want to grab a bite to eat? I'm never off work at this time. The only date I've had in the last few weeks is Gus, and he's not particularly chatty."

"We're your second choice?" Hettie turned to me. "I'm not being your sloppy seconds. You should choose your family over Gus."

"It's a work date! I was kidding. Usually we just eat dinner as I read and memorize more herbs."

Hettie wrinkled her nose. "You need to get out more, child. Else you'll never find a man."

"Good thing I'm not looking for one," I grumbled. "What about you two? Any plans?"

Zin wrinkled her nose. "My mom is running some committee or another tonight, so I have to watch the rascals."

"I would normally love to go," Poppy said. "But my mom's on a date with your mentor, and she asked me to feed her guinea pig."

"Her guinea pig is fat enough," Zin said. "His name is Chunk for crying out loud."

"You're just mad because you transformed into a hamster last week and I made you race Chunk," Poppy said. "And you lost."

"He had like, three pounds on me!" Zin crossed her arms, her eyes blazing. "You know I can't help my size."

Poppy winked at me. "I know, and I can't help teasing you about it."

"I'm going home," Zin said. "I have to feed the twins dinner."

Hettie followed her with a brief wave. "I'd love to go, but I can't either. VanderVamp Rules is on the projector tonight. Can't miss my show."

I raised my eyebrows at Poppy. "What do you say to a quick bite?"

"I'm really sorry, but my mom will kill me if I don't feed Chunk," Poppy said. "You can come with me if you want, though."

"You hate that guinea pig."

Poppy blushed. "Yeah, but you know Mimsey. She loves that thing."

"You're lying."

"Fine!" Poppy threw her hands up in the air. "I worked a double shift. I helped out Mimsey and Trinket at the supply store this morning, and then went straight to fill in for another six hours at Ranger HQ. I kind of want to watch VanderVamp Rules with Hettie and have her cook me some pasta. I'm tired, that's all. My feet hurt, I'm all talked out, and Hettie makes me age ten years every time she sets foot in HQ. I have to watch her like a hawk and it's exhausting."

"That's all you had to say," I said with a grin. "Look, I get it. I have errands to run tonight anyway, so it's probably best if I just get on with it. I was mostly procrastinating."

"Are you sure? You can absolutely come by and hang tonight if you want. I'll even share my bottle of wine. I just don't want to put clothes on and head over to Sea Salt."

"Really, don't worry. I'll see you later, okay? If I'm done in time, I'll stop over on the way back."

"Okay, great. Be safe! You don't need anything, do you? What about your Hex on the Beach potion to keep the guys away?"

I dug into my pocket and pulled out a small vial of the potion, waggling it in front of Poppy's face. "Got it. Plus, I have a good old tube of Pepper Spray around my keychain. Have a good night, Poppy."

She pulled me in and kissed both cheeks European style. We parted ways, Poppy hurrying to catch up with Hettie while I strolled in the opposite direction. The coins jangled in my pocket as I set my sights on the path that would take me across town to the B&B where I'd hopefully find my target.

The Isle was relatively small. It was similar in size to that of a condensed city, not unlike the square space of downtown Minneapolis. It was entirely walkable, though a jaunt from one side to the other could take up to thirty minutes.

My feet carried me across a white sandy path in lazy twists. The path started at the beach in front of my bungalow, wound its way past the dock and the supply store, curled over the open ground, and finally across the Lower Bridge. A canal cut The Isle in two, leaving us with a West and an East side.

Hettie, Mimsey, Trinket, and their children—along with myself—were the only witches who dared inhabit the West side of The Isle. Most people chose to stay on the opposite side of the bridges for safety reasons. Hundreds of creatures lived in The Forest, and those creatures were much more likely to wander down to the bungalow than across the bridge and into the highly populated East side.

I crossed the Lower Bridge, since the Upper Bridge was reserved mostly for Rangers. The latter led deep into The Forest, and most of the islanders would suffer a ten-minute detour just to use the safer route.

Giant goldfish swam in the canal beneath the bridge, and I paused as one particularly orange fish swam circles around his silvery friend, their movements smooth as a dance. It was so mesmerizing I lost track of time standing there, until a crack startled me from my flip-flops.

The crack came from the bushes to my left, jolting me out of my trance. I pressed deeper into the East Isle territory, the air full of spells, protective hexes, and many other safety precautions.

The sizzle of magic surrounded the entrance from the West to the East side, but it didn't do much to calm my nerves. With one last glance toward the bushes, I picked up my pace and didn't slow down until I'd reached Main Street.

Main Street was a small section of the East side neighborhood. The narrow, cobblestone paved street wound its way between a few local shops and food stands. Decorative white lights dangled from the palm trees lining the sidewalks, and despite the late hour, many folks milled about the street. Families waltzed between the stores, some of the children carrying candies and balloons that roared and squeaked, just like the animals after which they'd been molded. The younger adults held lemonades or iced slushies in their hands, while the older witches and wizards carried much larger beverages in the vein of Pina Coladas and Strawberry Daiquiris.

My breathing eased, my chest finally loosening as I realized how uptight I'd been on the walk over. Between the men in cloaks, the theft of the spellbook, and my mentor's odd behavior, strange things were happening, and it had me on edge.

Strolling down Main Street, however, allowed me to relax. Shop owners sold their wares and conversed with the townsfolk while parents whistled, chatted, and skipped through the streets with their kids. The sense of normalcy was refreshing.

By the time I reached the end of Main Street, I was smiling again. I'd returned the pepper spray to my keychain and the vial of defensive potion to my pocket. Turning off of the cobblestone road, I entered a smaller walkway—not much more than a garden path—that led to the sole B&B on The Isle. I followed the flat stones to the front steps of a quaint, cottage-like building.

I raised a hand and knocked on the front door. Yellow walls made for a bright, cutesy building with pink shutters and a sky-blue door. The theme was very Cozy Country Escape, despite the tropical setting.

The door opened a second later, though I couldn't see who was behind it.

"Can I help you?" squeaked a voice somewhere around my knees. "I'm Midge, I run this place."

"Oh, hello." For a moment, I debated getting on my knees, or at least crouching down so that we could see eye to eye. As it was, she was staring at the scar just above my knee while I was looking down at the top of her head. "I'm here to visit a friend."

"A friend, you say? I wasn't told to expect any guests." Midge turned around and bounced her petite frame over to the front desk. "What's this friend's name?"

Her gray hair was knotted in a bun on top of her head, and her face was wrinkled from years and years of living. But her wrinkles weren't the tired, sun-worn battle scars of a hard life. No, her wrinkles were pleasant, as if they'd been formed from smiling instead of frowning, from looking at the world with kindness instead of judgment. I immediately liked her.

"His name is Liam," I said, still standing in the doorway. "He said he was staying at the B&B, and I only know of one. I assume it's here?"

"We're the only B&B on The Isle." Her face crinkled in an amused expression. "You're new here, aren't you?"

I nodded.

"Well, what are you doing standing over there? You look harmless, come on in." Midge waved a hand for me to enter the room. I took a step forward as Midge took six steps upward and stood on a platform behind the desk. Now, we were eye to eye. "Liam, you say?"

I nodded again, sneaking a glance at the step stool she'd used. It looked like stacks of old, hardcover books in a language I didn't recognize. "Liam, that's right."

"He's here, but he didn't say he was expecting company."

"Well, he didn't know I was planning to come," I said. "But he did invite me to come by... sort of."

Midge's pleasant gaze froze. "May I ask the nature of your business before I call up to him?"

My face must have turned into a beet. "Um, I'm just returning something of his."

"Let me call him."

"If it's too much trouble, I can just leave it here and he can pick it up later." I jangled the coins in my pocket for emphasis. "He overpaid me earlier, so I just wanted to return the extra. I didn't realize how late it's getting..."

She shook her head, distracted by some sort of Comm device pressed against her ear. A moment later, she shook her head again. "He's not in his room, but he might be grabbing a bite to eat in the dining area. Follow me."

Midge hopped down her stack of books and gestured for me to follow her through a doorway on the far side of the lobby. "Even if he's not eating, you should really consider giving our chowder a try. It really is to die for."

I laughed. "I bet. It smells heavenly."

"No," she said, peering up at me. "Literally, someone once died for it."

I winced. "I ate already, thank you."

"I'm kidding," she said, turning around and winking at me. "Nobody has died for it."

"Oh." I forced a false laugh. I'd had enough talk about dying and potions lately, and it was getting hard to tell what was real and what was fake. "You're funny."

"Nobody's died... recently," she corrected. "Oh, look, there he is."

I didn't get a chance to ask if she was kidding a second time because just then she pointed across a small, romantically lit dining room to a table for two. However, one of the place settings was empty. Behind the other sat an impeccably dressed man.

"Shall I set you a place?" Midge asked curiously. "Or mention that you're here?"

Stepping back from the doorway just as Liam glanced over in our direction, I shook my head. "I'll go over myself. But first, may I ask you a question?"

"Sure."

Lowering my voice, I took a few steps back into the lobby, out of Liam's sight. "What do you think of him? He's new here too, right?"

She squinted at me. "Hold on a second—you're the new Mixologist."

I blinked. "Yes, I am. How did you know?"

"I'm ancient. I know these things. Plus, small town. Word—"

"—gets around," I finished for her. "So I've heard. Do you know anything about Liam's story?"

"May I ask why?" Midge leaned in, keeping her voice on the quiet end of the spectrum. "I don't mean to be rude, but the reason I've been in business for centuries is because I keep my guests' information private. Their names, their room numbers, and most importantly, their business. I thought you just wanted to deliver coins."

I decided to play the card that Liam himself had handed me. "There's a little more to the story."

Midge raised an eyebrow. "Do tell. Tit-for-tat, you know."

I tried for what I hoped was a semi-embarrassed, flirtatious sort of wink. Mostly, it just felt like an eye twitch, and I lost my train of thought.

"Are you okay?" Midge asked. "I can recommend a good doctor if you're feeling ill."

"No, no, I'm fine." I slapped a hand over my twitchy right eye. So much for my powers of seduction. "I'm just wondering what you think of him. Liam. He asked if I wanted to get coffee. He's new, I'm new... I hope you understand."

"Oh!" Midge let out a high-pitched giggle. "I see how it is now. Liam is a perfectly nice gentleman. There's only one problem."

"What's that?"

"Well, the reason I didn't put two and two together sooner is because everyone knows that Liam isn't interested in your type. No offense darling, it's not just you. It's all of us."

"All of us meaning... witches? Magical people? Islanders?"

Midge laughed. "No, you're not understanding. Women. Liam is not interested in women."

My spine went ramrod straight. "Wow, I missed all alarm bells going off with that one."

"He's a very manly man, you know," she said. "And he's been coming here on and off for the last ten years on business. I can tell you one fact—he's never once laid a finger on a woman in any sort of way, especially not a romantic way. He's never been on a date as far as I know, and I know everything. He's just not interested. I'm sorry, but maybe your alarm bells are broken."

"Guess so," I said, doing a mental head scratch. "I could be wrong, I suppose."

"I suppose you're right." Midge patted my shoulder. "Don't worry, you're certainly not the first, and you won't be the last. However, he's a lovely conversationalist, and he's not bad to look at, either. If you're wondering whether or not it's a good idea to get a coffee with him, I say why on earth not? Go for it! You'll probably have to work with him on business at some point, anyway. Most of the islanders do."

"Business? What does he do?"

"Why don't you ask him yourself?" Midge put both of her hands on my shoulders and manually spun me around. She marched me straight over to the table in the corner where Liam looked up, an amused smirk on his face as Midge grinned broadly. "Liam, I believe you've already met Lily. Lily, this is Liam."

"How do you know my name?" I asked in a hushed voice while awkwardly smiling at Liam. "I never told you."

"Dear, I know everything," she whispered. "Now, sit down. I'll have coffee and a snack brought out. It seems like you two have a lot to discuss."

CHAPTER 11

"THANK YOU," I MURMURED A few minutes later as Midge herself dropped by our table with two cappuccinos and a small plate of biscotti. "This looks delicious."

Liam leaned forward from his seat across the table and winked. "Why do you think I've stayed here during every business trip all these years?" He cast a teasing glance over at Midge. "Not for the company, surely."

She gave him a good-natured swat on the shoulder. "Keep that up, and I'll start putting a pinch of Forget-Me-Not into your potion. You'll be swooning over me every time you walk into this lobby."

Liam laughed. "Thank you, Midge. You're a dear."

She gave a quick bow of her head, and then studied both of us once more before vanishing from the dining room back toward the lobby.

"She seems like the perfect person to own a B&B," I said once she'd gone. "Friendly, but strict. Private."

"Not to mention the cappuccinos." Liam raised his glass. "A toast before we jump straight into business?"

I raised my mug, and we clinked glasses. I took a sip of the frothy beverage, the creamy warmth just what I needed after a long day at the bungalow. Closing my eyes, I sighed with happiness. "This is good."

"Wait till you dip the biscotti into it." Liam reached for the plate and picked up a long, thin cookie with a light frosting made to look like a magical wand. He dunked it into his own cappuccino, and then held out the end. "Try this."

I hesitated. As positive as Midge was that Liam wasn't interested in "my type," I couldn't help but think this was feeling an awful lot like a date. I didn't want to be on a date. However, I did want that cookie. Leaning forward, I took a quick bite, smiling despite every intention to be one hundred percent business. "That is tasty."

"I told you! Now, hold on, you've got a little something..." He trailed off, reaching across the table, his finger gently brushing something off of my top lip.

I blushed. "Well, that was embarrassing."

"It was just a bit of foam." He winked. "I thought it was cute."

For lack of a follow-up, I reached for another cookie.

"What brings you by?" Liam asked. "Did you get my note?"

"Yes!" Grateful for the change of subject, I reached into my pocket and dug around until I extracted all of the money he had paid me. "I also got the coins you left for your meal, and it is far too much. I can't accept it. So, here you go."

Liam's eyes followed my movements as I extended my closed fist across the table, turning it over and exposing the coins on the palm of my hand. It felt odd to dump them on the table, so I waited patiently.

"That's everything." Liam hardly glanced at the coins. "You didn't keep any payment for yourself."

"The meal was on the house. You're a visitor. Plus, it was just a few eggs."

"Keep it all. I left it as a tip. It wasn't an accident."

"Don't be ridiculous. You ordered eggs, but paid for an entire chicken coop."

Liam laughed as he reached forward and closed my fingers around the coins. "Keep it. I want you to have it. Really, you're making a big deal out of nothing."

"It's too much!"

"It's my money. I earn it, so I get to spend it how I like, and I would like for you to have it. I wasn't tipping for the eggs. I was tipping for the service. It's been a while since I've been to The Isle, and it was pleasant to receive a warm reception. Don't read deeper into it."

I frowned. "You normally don't receive a warm reception?"

Liam grinned. "You like to ask questions."

My cheeks likely reddened, and I gave an embarrassed shake of my head. "You don't have to answer that. I'm nosy by nature. Don't worry, it's not just you, I pester everyone with questions."

"Unfortunate. I rather liked the idea of it being just me." Liam winked. Then he nodded at the coins in my hands. "It's yours."

"Thank you," I said, pulling my hand back. "Then I insist you come back for breakfast before you leave The Isle. On me."

"Of course. How does tomorrow sound?"

"Great!" I tried for cheery, but my distraction won over. "Listen, I need to ask you one thing."

"Go ahead." Liam's gaze was clear and pleasant. "I'm an open book."

"Well, it's less asking and more telling."

"Then I'm listening."

"I just wanted to put it out there that I'm a little confused why you're being so nice to me," I said. "And I feel obligated to tell you that I'm not looking for anything right now—in terms of romance, at least. This is super awkward to say since I don't know if you're even interested in me at all, or if maybe I'm reading this whole situation wrong. You seem like a nice man, and I'd love to have you over for breakfast. I'm babbling, so if you want to jump in and spare me more embarrassment, that'd be lovely—"

"Breakfast is just breakfast, and cookies are just cookies." Liam gestured toward the tray. "Don't worry. I appreciate your honesty, but I'm not looking for anything, either. Well, nothing more than some good food and decent conversation if it's available."

I exhaled a big sigh of relief. "Whew, okay good."

"Now that you feel sufficiently awkward, put those coins back in your pocket and have another biscotti. The ones with the fruit tart in the middle will make you melt in happiness."

Five minutes later, the two of us had a pleasant conversation going, and I wondered if I'd been wrong all along about this feeling like a date. Already, it felt like a catch-up between old friends. Laughing, chatting, telling stories. Liam didn't reach for my hand or pry into my personal business, and I didn't say anything too stupid. Plus, the cookies with the jam in the middle were some of the most wonderful pieces of dessert I'd ever eaten.

"I need to get that recipe," I groaned, leaning back in my chair. "I shouldn't have eaten so many sweets. I hardly had dinner."

"I can order you some food," Liam said, already glancing around for the server. "I recommend the Magic and Cheese. The type of cheese Midge uses is to die for—"

He stopped talking, which caused my gaze to wander across the room. Two men in cloaks drifted into the dining room, their robes skimming the floor. At least, I assumed they were both men due to their tall, broad-shouldered stature. Similar to the visitor earlier in the day, both had hoods draped low, their facial features hidden entirely.

Liam watched my gaze as it followed the two of them across the room. "You're staring," he said finally. "Do you know them?"

I blinked and shook myself back to reality. "Sorry, that was rude. I'm just surprised. I've never seen anyone on The Isle wearing cloaks before, and now I've seen three in the same day. Does it mean something?"

"You're referencing the other guest at your bar today," Liam said slowly. "He arrived after me."

I jerked my chin subtly toward the opposite side of the room. "Do you think he might be one of them?"

"I know for a fact neither of them is him."

"How? You can't see their faces."

Liam slid a sideways gaze at them, his voice low. "Look at the line of fabric around their hoods. The man from the bungalow today wore a black ribbon. These two are orange and red ribbons."

Despite my best efforts not to stare, I found myself leaning a bit toward the two cloaked strangers. The cloaks draped over the figures' bodies were long, black, and swooshy.

Their hoods were no different. When pulled over their heads, the fabric almost grazed the tips of their noses. At the very end of their hoods, however, was a thin strip of satin-looking ribbon around an inch thick. One of them had an orange stripe and the other a red one, just as Liam had said.

"I didn't notice the color before," I said. "Earlier today, I mean. The black ribbon likely would've blended right into the cloak itself. What does it mean?"

"You've never seen a Cretan before?"

"A Cretan?" I blinked. "Never even heard of it. Or them."

"Cretan Darham Hall is a school located in upstate New York. Very cold, wildly secluded. It's known to be one of the finest schools for witches and wizards in the nation."

"Why am I sensing there's a catch?"

"Because there is," Liam said. "There is one very big caveat."

"Which is?"

"Let me back up for a second. Cretan is a very prestigious school. The alumni community is an incredibly proud group, and former students can be seen wearing their cloaks to represent their history. It's a brotherhood of sorts, and the members are extremely loyal to their own kind."

"So I can't buy one of those cloaks at the thrift store?" I asked, the joke falling flat. "They're not accepting applications?"

Liam gave me a small smile. "No, and let me just say this. When I say they are a brotherhood of sorts, I mean that quite literally..."

He shifted uncomfortably in his seat, and it took a moment for the meaning to sink in.

"Oh," I said finally. "They're not friendly toward women."

Liam nodded, a slightly sad expression on his face. "It's not just women, it's anyone who doesn't fit in with their belief system."

"That sounds cult-ish to me."

Liam didn't bother to disagree. "Still, nobody can deny that Cretan churns out great, great magic users. Mostly wizards, with one or two other paranormal creatures who have exceptional abilities. They've gone on to invent many of the spells that allow our culture to exist the way it does today."

"There's still that catch," I said. "What aren't you telling me?"

"I'm telling you everything, but I need to clarify. The school creates great and powerful wizards. However, great and powerful is not synonymous with good."

"It's evil?"

Liam shook his head and spoke sharply. "The school itself is not inherently good or evil. I don't believe things or places have the power to be good or evil, but the people who inhabit them do."

"And the people who inhabit Cretan…"

"Have a complicated track record."

I raised an eyebrow. "I won't share any details."

Liam glanced to his left. The two cloaked figures had only ordered water. They sat deep in conversation, their heads leaned close together, seemingly oblivious to everything else going on around them. "It's rumored that half the barrel of apples is good, and half is bad when they leave that school."

"That is a lot of bad."

"It's also a lot of good," Liam said. "As one might imagine, it is a very touchy subject."

"Understandably."

"There has been talk on more than one occasion about completely shutting the school down."

"In order to prevent the bad?"

Liam nodded. "But it's never gotten past the discussion stages. Without the good coming from that school, we'd be ages behind The Faction in terms of technology. You've heard of The Faction?"

I nodded.

"The argument is that it'd be easier to maintain balance in our universe if the school was shut down completely. The less-than-honorable wizards would have to find other ways to receive an education—"

"—but they'd do it anyway," I said. "Where there's a will, there's a way."

"That's exactly what the Board agreed upon." Liam smiled. "You might be new, but you catch on quickly. The Board members agreed that in the end, it's better to keep an eye on the students than have them running wild, completely off of our radar."

"Do the less-than-honorable wizards leaving the school join up with The Faction?"

"Some of them, but not all. The Faction certainly tries to recruit hard there, but Cretan is a bit different that way. It's... the Ivy League. You know the Ivy League?"

"Harvard, you mean? Yale, all of those schools?"

"Yes. Cretan is more along those lines. It takes money to get in. A lot of money. Our coins that is, not human dollars. Many of the wizards who graduate from the school—both good and bad—consider themselves to be 'above' the rest of us. They waltz around in their cloaks, their heads freshly full of knowledge. They have big plans. Big dreams. Bigger than The Faction— at least to them."

"Bigger than The Faction? I thought The Faction was the biggest dream of all. The largest threat."

"Oh, they are the largest threat, but you must remember that fighting for The Faction means fighting for a cause. Those Faction wizards believe in something, even if it's an evil something. Most

Cretan wizards aren't interested in causes. The overwhelming majority are, hmm. How do I put this?"

"Selfish?"

"That's a good word to describe it." Liam gave a tight smile. "Let's just say most of the wizards would rather be famous for coming up with a new potion or a cure. They want the fame and the glory. Fighting for a cause is not always about fame and glory, now, is it?"

"I suppose not."

"To fight for a cause—good or evil—is still to fight for something. It is not, by nature, a selfish act."

I considered all of this for a moment. "How do you tell a good wizard from a bad one?"

"How do you tell a good person from a bad one?" Liam shrugged. "Difficult, isn't it?"

I sighed.

"Now you see our dilemma."

I glanced over at the two figures still deep in discussion, wondering if they were good or bad, or any number of places in between. "What do the colorful ribbons mean?"

"They signify the highest level of study achieved by a wizard at school."

I turned my attention back to Liam. "Sort of like a bachelor's degree versus a PhD?"

"In a sense. But this goes much further, much deeper than that. It's not only a class they took or the level of achievement; it's their mastery of skills."

"Is red or orange more prestigious?"

Liam raised an eyebrow at me. "That is the wrong question, my dear."

"Then what is the right one?"

"The answer you are looking for is Black," he said with a low, almost reverent tone. "The guest you had at the bungalow today had obtained the highest level of mastery that a witch or wizard could ever hope to achieve."

"Really?"

"Only five wizards in the past thousand years have achieved a Black Ribbon."

"I had one of the five in my bar, and I didn't even know?"

He shook his head. "You spoke with two of the five today."

"Two?" I gaped, my mouth falling open. "Do you have a Black Ribbon?"

He shook his head. "Not me."

"But—"

"Someone very close to you." Liam leaned in, his gaze scanning the room. "Someone skilled, intelligent, and accomplished. It just might be the person you know best on this island."

I blinked. "My cousins aren't witches and wizards. I pretty sure it's not Hettie…"

"Think. Who is the person closest to you?"

I looked up. "No."

Liam flashed a tight smile. "Yes."

"Gus?"

"I'm not surprised he didn't tell you," Liam said. "He likes to keep it a secret."

I stood up, my head spinning. "I… I have to get going. Thanks for everything."

I left the coins on the table, bid Liam a distracted goodbye, and turned for the door. My mind whirred with thoughts of Gus, the person I trusted most outside of my family. I hadn't expected him to tell me everything about his history, but something this huge seemed important enough to share.

My blood ran cold even as Liam called after me to wait up. I couldn't help but think that, even after all this time, I really didn't know Gus at all.

CHAPTER 12

IDGE WAVED AS I WALKED out the door, my mind in
another dimension. I think I told her goodbye, but
I might've thought it instead. As I stumbled down the
curvy path from the B&B, I let my thoughts float in the clouds and
my feelings go numb.

Gus hadn't lied to me. I'd never asked where he'd gone to school
or how he'd learned every herb and potion in such detail. I'd always
assumed that he'd learned it training with previous Mixologists as
an apprentice, and he'd let me continue to believe that.

My feet carried me away from Main Street. The families
mingling about were beginning to thin out at this hour, but I didn't
feel like being around anyone at all. I didn't want to go home either.
That left me with nowhere to go. My cousins were busy, and even
my aunts had plans. Hettie had a date too, even if it was only with
her weekly program. I was alone.

Kicking sand up from the ground, I debated joining Hettie and
Poppy. It'd be better than sitting at home alone, letting my mind
dwell on all of the events of the day. The Elixir, the news about
Gus, the cloaked strangers... Gus had been right. I wouldn't be
getting much sleep tonight.

I took a detour instead of heading straight to The Twist. I
walked along the sandy beach up the northeastern side of The Isle,
my gaze alternating between the glittering white sand sprinkled
beneath my toes and the last, lingering fingers of sunlight on the

horizon. Waves lapped at the shore, and a light spray misted against my ankles.

Slipping off my flip-flops, I carried my shoes in my hand and let the coolness of the ground soothe my aching feet. Working all day in the storeroom had gotten me in better shape than ever. I wouldn't be running marathons anytime soon, but it was more movement than I'd gotten sitting in a cubicle and heating up Hot Pockets for lunch.

At the bungalow, I had an endless supply of fruits, eggs, toast, and all sorts of tasty, fresh food. Plus, I had the luxury of going to Hettie's house at least once a week for a home-cooked meal. In the few weeks I'd been living on The Isle, my body was already adjusting. My skin darkened, my hair lightened, and my body slimmed down, while still building muscle. Island life was growing on me.

By the time I looked up, I had almost reached the northernmost point on the East side of The Isle. Just in front of me sat an all-glass building that jutted out over the lake. A sign sticking a bit crooked out of the ground read Sea Salt.

I stood still for a moment, trying to remember if I'd come here on purpose, or if it'd been my subconscious guiding the way. Even as I failed to convince myself that it'd all been one big accident, my gaze landed on the one man I desperately wanted to see.

High above the water sat Ranger X. He was perched in the loft-style restaurant at a table in the corner closest to me. From the looks of it, he was alone. I made my way over to the base of the building, never once taking my eyes off him. All four walls were clear glass while the floor was made of a frosted panel so that wandering eyes couldn't peek under a lady's skirt. I watched as Ranger X placed his order with a cute blond waitress.

His eyes didn't follow the waitress as she bobbed away. Instead, his gaze turned toward the lake. Resting against the back of his chair, he simply sat still and watched as the waves jumped and leaped in the distance, both calming and excited all at once. I was used to people playing with their phones, sending texts, and scrolling Facebook during wait times, but not X. He just sat and watched as if waiting for something to appear on the horizon.

"Hold on a second, I'll be right with you." The same blonde who'd taken Ranger X's order passed by me, turning to look over her shoulder as she waltzed down the path. She shouted to someone else I couldn't see. "Benny, get back in here. Your break's over, and we've got customers waiting."

I stood off to the side as she turned around and waltzed back.

"Sorry," she said with another smile. "It's not a busy night, but Ben likes to 'vanish' and take a few sips of the Kool-Aid from our extra supplies if you know what I mean. Can I help you?"

I laughed. "Oh, no thanks—I'm okay. I was just out for an evening stroll."

"You hungry? We have extra seats." She thumbed upstairs. "Tacos are on special tonight. Really tasty and pretty inexpensive."

I hesitated. It wasn't like I was hankering to go home and cook a meal for one. Ranger X and I were allowed to eat at the same restaurant, even if he didn't want my company. "Sure. I'd love to try the tacos."

"Great! Follow me." She grabbed a menu and flounced up the stairs. I hurried to keep up as she twirled into the main room. "Where would you like to sit?"

I planned to tell her I'd take a seat at the bar. Somehow, it felt rude to intrude on X's dinner, even if he had invited me. What did I know? Maybe he'd handed my invitation off to someone else. That'd be awkward. However, as I glanced past the server and began to request the bar, my gaze landed once more on Ranger X. The expression on his face, peaceful, but maybe a bit lonely, did the trick. "Actually, I see one of my friends. May I go say hi first?"

The server's face fell a bit, and this time her smile wasn't as friendly. "Oh, the table in the corner? Sure. I just took his order. Have a seat and I'll be right over."

I suspected her fallen expression had something to do with the fact that Ranger X was not only the most handsome man in the bar by tenfold, but he was also the only man under retirement age.

Hesitantly, I made my way across the restaurant as if the floor might crack and shatter at any given moment. It wasn't until I was a few steps away that Ranger X noticed my presence. He did a double take as I neared his table, and I gave a shy wave which he returned with a lopsided smile.

"Fancy running into you here," I said. "How's it going?"

"You mean, since I last saw you an hour ago?"

"Only an hour? Time flies."

He smiled, but didn't offer for me to sit down. "What brings you around here?"

I coughed, a sound that rang false to my own ears, and tried to ignore the prickling sense of embarrassment creeping down my neck. "Just out for a stroll."

"Nice night for a stroll."

"Yeah, it is." I paused. "Well, have a good dinner, X. It was nice to see you. Thanks again for the tour today."

Feeling overwhelmed with stupidity, I wished that I could sink into the glass floor and dissolve until I was transparent underfoot. What had I been thinking? He'd probably already made a date with someone else. Likely he'd only asked me earlier since I'd been the convenient option.

"Do you want to sit down?" he called after I'd taken a few steps away. "There's an open seat here."

"For me?"

He grinned. "Come eat. The menu is great here."

I walked back to the table and slid into the seat, lowering my voice. "Are you sure you're not expecting someone else?"

"The only reason I didn't ask you to sit right away is because I thought that *you* were here with your friend."

I did a mental facepalm. "Even after I told you I didn't have a date, you thought I had a date?"

"You said you had plans with someone else." He shrugged. "How did I know? I'm sure you have men around The Isle clambering to take you out. This is the best restaurant in town, so it's not an unlikely scenario."

"Me? What about you?"

"We're not talking about me. Even if we were, I'm not exactly into men."

I laughed. "Women. The rumors say there's a line halfway around The Isle for a date with you."

"You can jump straight to the front every time. I'll allow it."

We carried on easy small talk. By the time the server came back to take my order, I was hardly bothered by her frown and snippy tone.

"The shrimp, please," I said, pointing to an entree I couldn't pronounce.

"How about two glasses of wine?" X raised an eyebrow at me. "Sound good?"

"Sounds great. I'll have the Cab."

"Make it two."

"I'll bring them right over," the server said before leaving us alone once more.

"This is nice," I said as we both looked out over the water. "It's my first time here."

Ranger X murmured in agreement before we lapsed into silence. The only sound to break the quiet was the distinct clink of glass as the waitress placed our wine on the table.

"Cheers," he said, raising a glass. "To finally being able to steal you away from work for a night, even if it was an accident."

I raised my glass and clinked his, taking a sip of the rich, velvety liquid before setting it down. "If you had asked me, I might have snuck away before this," I said. "It doesn't take a serving of The Elixir for me to get the night off."

"I don't know. Gus runs a pretty tight ship."

"Speaking of Gus, I have to talk to you about something."

"I was hoping we wouldn't talk about work," he said with a sigh. "But I suppose it can't be avoided."

"Do you know the school Cretan Darham Hall?"

"It's infamous."

"Did you know Gus is a graduate?" I asked. "Not only a graduate, but he's a Black Ribbon?"

Ranger X sat back and took another drink of wine, and then two more as he mulled over the information before replying. "I'm not surprised. I didn't know for sure though."

"What do you make of it?"

He raised one shoulder. "I don't make anything of it. It's just a fact. A fact I'll file away for the future, should it ever be of use."

"I just learned that fifty percent of wizards who graduate from that school are bad."

"According to your math, that means fifty percent would also be good."

"True," I agreed.

"Where'd you get your information?"

I inhaled a breath. "Do you know a man who goes by the name of Liam?"

"Brown hair, little bit older than me, polite guy?"

"That's him."

"I've seen him around, but we're not close," X said. "Did you talk to him?"

I quickly explained the sequence of events that had landed me at Sea Salt for dinner. From Liam's morning visit to the bungalow, to his overpayment of the bill, to my returning the money at

Midge's B&B. "After all of that, I'm still not sure what Liam does for a living, or why he's here."

"He buys and sells goods."

"What sort of goods?"

Ranger X raised an eyebrow. "We'll call them... hard to find goods and services."

I sucked in a breath. "Illegal stuff? Does he steal things?"

"He's a don't ask, don't tell sort of guy."

"Hold on a second." I raised a hand and put it on the table. "You're basically the police here on The Isle. If you know he's doing something wrong, then why haven't you gone after him? Put him in jail?"

"I never said that he's involved in anything illegal."

I waited a beat. "Help me out then. What does he do?"

"There are gray areas and fine lines in any industry," X said. "And every now and again, a good person needs materials for a good cause, yet sometimes those materials are difficult to obtain."

I squinted at him. "So he walks a fine line between right and wrong, is that what you're saying?"

"More or less. His business is legal, and I trust him. He's helped Ranger HQ on several different occasions."

"Has he helped you?"

"One of my men." Ranger X shifted in his chair. "A Ranger had been badly injured. A bite from a troll that'd become infected after a trip into The Forest. All of the medicine we had on hand combined wouldn't have saved his life, and none of the healers would touch him. They said he was too far gone."

The slight note of pain in his voice surprised me. I'd pictured the leader of the Rangers to be able to speak about situations like this with a note of detachment. "You called Liam for help?"

"I did. He was able to deliver a new potion not yet on the market. It's highly dangerous with the potential for extremely terrible side effects. It wasn't approved by the MPA—"

"MPA?"

"Magical Potions Association. They test newly developed potions and verify their safety before allowing them to go to market for public use. This is why Liam's job tiptoes in a gray area. It's not illegal to use the potion, merely... unconventional."

"And difficult to obtain, I'd imagine."

"Very much so," Ranger X said. "Liam's specialty is less in the potions side of things, and more on the relationships. He knows more people than you'd ever care to meet, and he knows their strengths and weaknesses, their desires and fears. Liam isn't dangerous in the traditional sense, but if you need something from someone, he's the man to get it for you."

A thought crossed my mind, something from earlier today. "Have previous Mixologists used his services?"

Ranger X's forehead creased in interest. "Do you have a need for them?"

"I'm not sure," I said slowly. "I'm missing one ingredient for Poppy's Vamp Vites. She's running low on her supply, and she's starting to experience side effects."

"Can I help?"

I smiled. "That's kind of you to ask. But unless you know where I can find Dust of the Devil by the end of the week, I'm afraid I don't think so."

"Liam would know." X gave a firm nod. "Ask him tomorrow. I'm sure he'll be able to work out something for you."

"I can't figure out where the last Mixologist secured it from, and Gus doesn't know either. It's quite strange."

"Maybe not as strange as you think. Liam is known for his utmost discretion. Most people don't know what he does for a living. They assume he's living off old money and traveling around living the high life, but that is as far from the truth as one can get. Liam built up everything himself, and that's why his relationships are rock solid. He has never once betrayed my trust, or anyone else's that I know of, and that's why he's successful. It's also why we do not want him in prison, but on our side."

"So it's possible that the previous Mixologist went through Liam, and Gus wouldn't have known about it?"

"It's not only possible, I'd be surprised if it's never happened. Liam makes a habit of knowing anyone important in the magical world, and you, my dear, are the most important thing since the invention of sliced Pepper Wheel."

"I have no clue what Pepper Wheel means."

"Let's just say that word about your arrival on The Isle is spreading. Here on the island people found out quickly about you, but it takes longer for word to cross over to the mainland. I'm sure that the arrival of Liam is the tip of the iceberg. Before long, a flood of strangers, businessmen, and bystanders will arrive, all hoping to catch a glimpse of this long-awaited Mixologist."

"That sounds terrible. I don't like people coming by the bungalow just to stare."

He laughed. "They'll have to order something. It'll be good for business!"

"I don't care about the business, I need to study!" I said with a smile. "I don't feel very important."

"Hire some help if it gets too overwhelming," Ranger X said. "That's my only advice because sweetheart, you are important and there is absolutely no getting around that fact."

The server arrived with our food, and the conversation slowed to a minimum. We murmured thank yous as she offered pepper and grated cheese. When she asked if either of us wanted a refill on wine, X leapt to answer before I could say no thanks.

"Sure," he said with a wink in my direction. "I'm up for it, if the lady is."

"This lady?" I pointed to myself, sensing a challenge. I gave him a wicked grin before nodding to the waitress. "Top off our glasses, please."

After our wine glasses had been refilled and the server disappeared back behind the bar, I looked over at Ranger X.

"You know, this is starting to feel like a date," I said quietly. "I just meant to say hi when I stopped in here, not start anything between us."

"Do you want it to be a date?" His breath stalled in his chest as he waited for an answer. "Never mind, stupid question. We've already talked about this."

To fight the warmth heating my cheeks, I raised my glass. "To complicated relationships."

His eyes sparkled with the same mixture of happiness and sadness, and we clinked glasses.

"Eat, before it gets cold." He pointed to my plate. "What do you think of it?"

"Delicious." I took a few bites and then set down my fork. "Except I can't shake one thing."

"What's that?"

"Have you ever been betrayed by someone close to you?"

X laid his fork down. "Are you asking because you want to know, or because you feel betrayed and want advice?"

I shrugged. "Both?"

"If this is about Gus, then I don't have much advice for you. That's your relationship, and only you can decide when to trust, when to question, and when to believe on blind faith."

My gut twisted. "That's what I was afraid of. No offense, but that doesn't help me any."

Ranger X gave a low chuckle that didn't stem from a place of happiness. "I know, but that's the fact of the matter. Relationships are hard, and often there are no right answers. I could tell you what to do, but that's not the right answer, either. You need to learn to trust yourself."

"I don't trust my instincts. They've been wrong before."

"Then don't trust your instincts, trust what's in here." Ranger slid his plate to the side of the table, then reached across and wrapped his hand over my shoulder. His thumb rubbed just over the place where my heart beat like crazy. "You know it already, somewhere deep down, the ultimate truth. You just have to find it."

"What if I can't?"

"You can and you will, eventually. It might take time, and it might take a series of mistakes and failures before you unearth the truth, but that's okay. That's what life's all about." X surveyed me with a soft expression. "I've made mistakes—grave mistakes. In my line of work, trusting myself can mean the difference between life and death."

"Like when you called Liam for the troll bite."

"Exactly." X cleared his throat. "Unfortunately, the man never recovered."

I blinked. "What? But I thought the point of your story was that Liam saved him!"

"He lived another two years. Long enough to say goodbye to everyone. Long enough to set his affairs in order. Without the medicine, he would've been dead within hours."

"You gave him borrowed time."

He nodded. "The answer isn't always good or bad. In fact, it's usually not. Sometimes, it is a mixture between the two, and you have to take the good with the bad."

The food on my plate smelled delicious, and it looked like a piece of art, but I couldn't bring myself to eat. "I don't know how to bring this up with Gus."

"If you can truly trust a person," X said carefully. "That shouldn't be an issue."

"I trust him, but that doesn't make it any less uncomfortable."

"Difficult conversations are always uncomfortable. But with the right person, you can have those conversations." Ranger X hesitated for a second. "I told you I can't give you specific advice, and I meant it. However, if you want my two cents on the matter, it's this: Give Gus a chance. You've already developed a relationship with him, a good one by the sounds of it. You'd be doing him a disservice to assume certain truths about him. Before you judge, give him a chance to explain. He might have reasons for keeping secrets from you."

"You're right." I exhaled a long sigh that released a huge wave of tension off my chest. "I must've just let the stress of the moment get to me. I wasn't thinking clearly."

"It's easy to do." X smiled. "Speaking of not thinking clearly, this second glass of wine has gone straight to my head. I don't indulge much, but this felt like a special occasion."

I could only manage a shy glance up through my lashes, but when my gaze landed on his it caught hold. His black eyes sparkled in a mesmerizing dance, and a slight pinkish tinge made his naturally tan skin glow in a vibrant array of colors. When his lips quirked up in a wide grin, I realized he might have a little buzz going. When he continued grinning, I knew he had a buzz.

Laughing, I shook my head. "You're a little tipsy!"

"It doesn't happen often, so take a picture." He winked, leaning forward and dropping his voice to a whisper. "And don't you dare tell anyone because if they saw me like this, I'd never hear the end of it."

I zipped my lips. "I'll never tell a soul."

"You look beautiful tonight," he said, his voice a bit raspy. "You look… I wish…" He sat back in his chair, letting out a pained groan.

I gave a reluctant shake of my head. "Don't say anything you'll regret. You're two glasses of wine in, and I will remember everything tomorrow."

"I wish this had started out as a date tonight," he said firmly. "A real date. Where I picked you up, took you someplace nice, and held your hand. This feels too much like an accident."

"I told you not to say anything," I warned. "You know this can't be a date."

"You told me not to say anything I'd regret," he clarified. "I might be a bit more candid than usual, but I'm not drunk. I'm not going to forget tomorrow what I've told you tonight. I'm just telling the truth. I don't—and I won't—ever regret telling you how I feel."

Suddenly, the food on my plate became very interesting. I poked at the shrimp and fiddled with some noodles as my brain worked at warp speed to come up with a response.

The server came and asked if things were going okay. I made a noise of agreement in my throat while Ranger X pushed his empty plate toward the edge of the table. She looked to me. "More wine?"

I shook my head no, and I couldn't help but think that she'd noticed the awkward silence over the table. She gave a knowing smile and a curt nod and took the empty dishware to the kitchen. Even after she'd gone, the lingering memory of her grin irked me, as if she was just waiting for me to make a mistake so she could swoop into my seat.

"What are you thinking?" X's voice startled me out of my reverie.

I swallowed hard, deciding to go all in. "I'm thinking this doesn't have to be a date. Why don't we just enjoy our night and see where it leads?"

Reaching across the table, he pulled my hands into his. "The date part is not the problem. The problem begins when I let myself care for you more than I already do..."

"You already care for me?"

"Of course I do," he said, blinking in surprise. "But don't ask me why."

I blushed, about to respond with a joke, when he continued.

"That's what makes things difficult. The rules Ranger HQ have against dating and marrying isn't... it's not the actual dating that's the problem. It's the decision-making. When a Ranger makes decisions with his heart instead of his head, everything becomes more dangerous. For all people involved, not just myself, not just you. It puts all of the other Rangers at risk, and we are brothers. We can't put each other at risk. I've lost enough men over the years without accidents, and I refuse to let that number grow higher."

"If you already care for me, isn't it already too late?"

X's gaze dropped to the plate of food in front of me.

I pushed it forward. "Want some?"

"No, I'm fine," he said. "We shouldn't be here tonight."

I caught the server watching us closely from behind the bar, and something about her nosiness into private matters got on my nerves. At the same time, it gave me a bit of courage that I didn't have before, tempting me to throw caution to the wind. "You're a Ranger, yes? You've been at it most of your adult life?"

"All my adult life."

"Listen, I understand it's your duty to protect and serve The Isle, and all of those wonderful things you do. But what about yourself? What's that thing telling you?" I reached over and tapped on his chest. "You're not on the clock right now. A little distraction might help to relax you. We don't even have to put labels on it. Let's just have a fun night. No strings attached. A non-date."

"A non-date." He turned the words over in his mouth.

"Yes," I said emphatically, squeezing his hand. "We've both been super busy. Let's finish our dinner, grab some dessert, and then I'll let you walk me home. Nothing date-like. No holding hands, no kissing, no pressure. Just some company and conversation."

One of his eyebrows rose. His eyes wanted to say yes, but his lips couldn't seem to form the word.

"Fine. Change of plans, we're done with dinner." I winked. "I'm ready for dessert, and you're coming with. Have you tried the cotton candy from that vendor near the B&B? It looked like a cloud, and I need some of it now."

He laughed. "I don't think I have a choice."

"That's right, you don't. I am forcing you to have fun." Reaching over, I grabbed his hand and pulled him up. "Oh, shoot. Money."

Fishing around in my pockets, I realized I'd dumped all of my coins onto the table back with Liam.

"Stop it." X leaned over and rested his hand on my arm. "It's on me. You were my guest."

"I'm just trying to keep things from being date-like."

"It's a non-date starting…" He paused, pulled out more than enough coins from somewhere inside of his suit, and dropped them on the table. "Starting now."

Chapter 13

STROLLING AROUND THE ISLE WITH a handsome man dressed in a suit, his dark hair wind-blown, and the fresh, sharp scent of him wafting in the breeze, was more than enjoyable. I hooked my arm through his, and he didn't push it away. Hand holding was off the table apparently, but elbow-hooking was fair game.

"It's polite," Ranger X argued, gesturing toward our intertwined arms. "It's not date-like, it's just manners."

"Exactly. And we all know you have great manners."

He stopped walking right then and hooked that arm even further through mine until it slid all the way around my lower back. He bent me backward, dipping me so low that my hair dusted the sand on the ground, while his arms held me tight and his breath tickled my exposed neck. He held me like that for several moments, the distance between our lips taunting a kiss, the sugary scent of cotton candy lingering in the air.

"I have wonderful manners," he said eventually. "You haven't even seen the start of it."

My breath came out faster than normal, and there was nothing I could do to stop it. However, I was tipped so far upside down that the blood rushed to my head and I suddenly felt dizzy. His words, his closeness, all of it was too much. I tapped his shoulder and said in a squeaky voice, "Excuse me? Head rush."

With a reluctant gaze, he righted me and once more, we continued on our stroll around the outskirts of The Isle. The way things were going, this non-date was beginning to feel very much like a real date.

Walking arm in arm with a man who drew the gazes of everyone we passed, sharing the sticky sweetness of pink and blue cotton candy on a stick, trying my best not to swipe away the tiny, flyaway cloud of sugar that'd landed low on his cheek—all of it was wonderful. Together we spent the night wandering about, as if time was of no essence and morning was a distant worry of a distant day.

"I had a really nice time tonight," X said as we reached the end of Main Street near the B&B. The families had all but disappeared. The shop owners had packed up their wares and closed their doors. One or two of them made eye contact with us as they swept off the stoops of their stores, their soft, knowing gazes telling me that they all thought this was real, too.

"You're welcome for forcing you to have fun," I teased. "You should try it more often sometime!"

"What about tomorrow?"

I stopped walking as he turned to face me.

"Is that too forward?"

"I work tomorrow," I said. "You work. We have so much going on. *The Magic of Mixology* is still missing, there are men in cloaks seeping into this town left and right, and I don't know what to make out of any of it. Plus, I now have this whole thing with Gus to figure out. And Poppy's vitamins. Not to mention the fact that I can't stop thinking about the man to whom I served The Elixir today. Where is he? What's happening to him?"

By the time I finished speaking, my voice came in flurried waves, my chest rising and falling like the water lapping at The Isle's shores. Suddenly my heart felt like it would beat right out of my chest, and the whole thing—everything—it was too much. Crouching down, I put my head in my hands and collapsed into the smallest ball possible right in the middle of the street.

Only a split second passed before X was right down there with me, pulling my hands away from my face.

"Hey, stop," he said gently. "Everything you just listed is something we need to think about. Together. I'm on the case, as are ten other Rangers who are highly qualified and very skilled. Gus—I know you have concerns about him—but up until now, he's been nothing but helpful to you from what I can see."

"Minus his grouchiness," I said, the smallest of smiles peeking through my lips. "That's not always helpful."

Ranger X gave a low laugh. "Of course, but that's the nature of the beast. You take what you can get from Gus and let those snarky spells pass. My observations probably don't mean much. I haven't spent nearly as much time with him as you have, but he's seemed happier lately."

"Maybe because he finally has a date?"

"Or maybe… because you finally arrived."

"Me?"

"He's been waiting for you most of his adult life. Think of it from his point of view: He's aging, and he has a lot of knowledge in that brain. Though he'll never be a Mixologist, he can help you become a great one. Not only great, but the best. He sees something in you, and for a teacher, there is no greater joy than finding a student with the willingness to learn, the capacity to do great things, and the natural ability to succeed. Those three things are a rare combination, and Lily, you exude them in spades."

I hid behind my hands again. Taking compliments wasn't really my thing. "I don't know what to say," I mumbled from behind my hands. "It's too much pressure."

"Then share some of that pressure." Ranger X clasped his hands over my wrists and gently led me to a standing position. I let him peel my hands away from my face, and what I found looking back at me was a gaze filled with hope, tenderness, and confidence. "You are not alone on The Isle. Remember that. Even if you don't want my help," he said, pausing for a wink. "You have plenty of people on your side."

"Thank you." I stepped forward. Even though we were only inches apart, it still felt too far. "Thank you for everything. Come on, let's go home. We have a busy day tomorrow, and we should both get some rest."

"I'm sorry to see this night end."

"Me too, but—"

"I know, you're right." Reaching over, he smoothed my flyaways from my face. He leaned forward and pressed a kiss so gentle against my forehead that even as he pulled away, I wondered if it'd actually happened. "Are you ready?"

This time, we dropped all pretenses of our non-date and held hands.

CHAPTER 14

UNFORTUNATELY, THE WALK HOME WAS not without incident. As Gus had predicted, I couldn't stop thinking about the man who'd requested The Elixir. Why had he done it? Where was he now? What was he planning to do? The later the hour of night, the more I worried.

Then, there were the thoughts of Gus's secret past that insisted on bubbling to the surface. How many other things didn't I know about him? The niggling warning from Poppy and Zin—to examine those closest to me—was more relevant now than ever. The more I fought the notion that Gus was involved with something, the more skeptical I became.

Ranger X and I made it halfway across The Isle, and we were just about to cross the Lower Bridge when a familiar voice drew my attention, taking me away from the thoughts swirling through my head.

"Quick!" I yanked Ranger X's hand and pulled him to the side of the path leading up to the bridge. A small ice cream hut surrounded by bushes blooming with all shades of pink and purple flowers perched crookedly in the grass, giving us just enough protection to hide.

X began to ask a question, but I clamped a hand over his mouth before he could finish the first words. If my hand wasn't enough to quiet him, then my blazing glare must've done the trick. Without further argument, he followed me behind the ice cream hut and crouched down.

"I don't think you've taken me here for romantic reasons," he said in a barely audible whisper. The two of us were cramped. We sat crouched on the ground with sticks and brush poking every exposed part of our bodies. The only pleasant aspect of the foliage was the scent. Flower upon flower bloomed across every branch, and the floral scent was almost intoxicating. "So who are we hiding from?"

I held a finger to my lips. The voice came closer and closer, along with a few sets of footsteps, and before I could inhale another breath, the visitors were upon us.

"...too many of you here. If you're not careful, you'll get everyone else suspicious."

My spine stiffened. It was Gus speaking, and he spoke in a guarded tone. He didn't want to be overheard, that much was obvious. I slowly turned my head to Ranger X and raised my eyebrows. He gave a nod of understanding, and together we sat silent as a tomb.

"Let them be suspicious. There's no proof of anything," a second voice said. "We have every right to be here."

"Then be careful!" Gus said sharply. "If she sees me with you, she's going to start asking questions. She's smart. Too smart to be fooled by you."

"Some might say you have a soft spot for her." A third voice spoke, this one calm and cool and calculating. It, too, was familiar. Too familiar. It belonged to Harpin. "I thought we'd discussed this."

Harpin owned a tea shop on the East side of The Isle, and during my first days here, he'd almost killed me. He'd said it was an accident, that he was just toying with me, but still. When he took away my breath and left me to choke without oxygen, it was hard to forgive easily. Not to mention that he had been angling for the job of Mixologist for years and was not happy to see me come to The Isle and accept it.

"You have nothing to say about her as far as I'm concerned, Harpin," Gus spat. "What would you know about a close relationship?"

"Now boys," the only unfamiliar voice said. "We're all working together here, so calm down. We mustn't fight among ourselves. We have enough of that going on outside of our control."

Gus grumbled something, and despite the severity of the moment, I almost smiled. I'd thought he'd only needed to have the last word when it came to me, but apparently his habit extended to everyone else on The Isle, too.

"I'm just saying," Harpin said coolly. "If Gus is unable to act objectively, we may have a problem."

"Gus has not given us any reason to believe he cannot act objectively," the second voice said. "Until he does, we'll no longer discuss the matter."

"I think that's the reason he doesn't want her to see us together," Harpin continued. "Gus doesn't trust himself to lie to her."

"Gus will lie if he needs to lie," the mediator said. "Won't you, Gus?"

"How about you don't blow my cover?" Gus growled. "Then I won't need a reason to lie. All it takes is a bit of careful planning. Is that so much to ask?"

"I'm not exposing us," Harpin said. "I'm just expressing my concerns."

"I'll express my concerns up your arse—" Gus wasn't done with his insults, but the smooth-talking peacekeeper broke up the fight anyway.

"Stop it, gentlemen, or we will forget this whole thing if you can't get along. I thought your differences would have been forgotten by now, but I can see that past transgressions have long memories..."

"We're fine," Gus said. "I'm fine, at least."

"I can be professional," Harpin said. "As long as he doesn't let his feelings for the girl get in the way."

"I don't have any sort of feelings for her," Gus said. "She's my trainee, and that's all. The way you're talkin' it sounds like you think I'm about to ask her out on a date."

"I didn't mean those sort of feelings, I meant..." Harpin trailed off. "As if she's your daughter. Or better yet, your granddaughter, old man."

"I'm her hired help, and that's the end of it," Gus said. "Thomas, can we finish our conversation before I shove my finger so far up this man's nose it comes out his ear?"

Next to me, Ranger X's shoulders shook quietly in the night.

"Are you laughing?" I whispered. "This isn't funny."

X swiped a hand underneath one of his eyes. "Gus is a firecracker."

I started to respond, but something was wrong.

Listening closely, I shut my mouth and waited. The conversation on the path in front of the ice cream hut had halted and the footsteps stopped. I shot Ranger X a wild-eyed expression, but he just leaned back against the wall and looked up to the sky, his breathing silent and his body stilled. I copied him as best I could, but my heart sounded like a jackhammer against my ribs, and if the three men in front of the shack didn't start walking soon, I was afraid my palms would sweat enough to flood the entire island.

Thankfully, the man named Thomas spoke up again. "We'll need to bring her in at some point."

"Then we do it on my terms," Gus said. "When I say, where I say, and how I say."

"That's not how this works," Harpin said. "We don't do what's best for Gus, we do what's best for all of us."

"All of us?" I mouthed to Ranger X. "Who?"

He gave a brief shake of his head, but I couldn't tell if he had no idea, or if he wanted me to be quiet.

"Do you want my help or not?" Gus asked. "I'm in this all the way, but if you still doubt me after everything... if you need more proof, then maybe I should just get out while the gettin's good."

"That's not what Harpin was saying," Thomas said, once again ironing things over. "What he's trying to say is that we'll have to bring her in eventually, and that there'll be a narrow window of time to do it."

"Fine," Gus said. "I can work with that. But you have to give me warning, and you have to give me a chance to talk to her first. I'm going to be the one to tell her everything and that is final. If that deal can't be made, then consider me done."

"Not a problem," Thomas said. "You'll receive at minimum twenty-four hours warning. Will that suffice?"

After a beat, Gus replied grudgingly. "Fine."

"Does she suspect anything?" Thomas asked. "You said she's smart."

"She is damn smart, but I don't think she suspects anything yet. We haven't given her a reason to, but I can't be seen with you any more in public. It's only a matter of time."

"Good. Let's keep it that way for as long as possible," Thomas said. "We need her oblivious for now."

"What about the rest of the Cretans?" Gus asked. "How long are they staying?"

"It's their right to be here as long as they want," Harpin said. "What's it matter to you?"

"It matters to me because Lily's gonna start asking questions. Curious and smart can be a dangerous combination around someone who has a secret," Gus said. "And I've got plenty of secrets."

"Then lie." Harpin hissed. "You said you could do it."

"Enough, we have to keep moving," Thomas said. "You have the information we need, Gus?"

Another long beat. "Yes."

"If you're lying, I can talk to her," Harpin said. "It's been a while since we've spoken."

"Because she despises you," Gus said. "Which is fortunate, since she'll never expect us to be partnering on something of this magnitude. She knows I dislike you just as much as she does."

The silence that followed was laden with tension. I couldn't move, couldn't speak. I couldn't even bring myself to look at Ranger X.

"We're done," Thomas said. "You have one day, Gus. Tomorrow night, we'll meet."

"I need longer than a day."

"You don't have longer than a day, so get it done," Thomas said. "Goodbye."

Ranger X and I sat still for a long while. The first two pairs of footsteps to fade into the distance belonged to Thomas and Harpin, their robed figures vanishing into the night as they headed east. I strained my eyes to see the color of their ribbons, but I could only make out that they were a bright color, which contrasted against the black of the hood. Meanwhile, the third set of footsteps never disappeared.

"Is he gone?" I breathed to Ranger X.

He shook his head.

It was a good thing we waited because the footsteps belonging to Gus didn't sound again for at least ten minutes. Though we couldn't see him from behind the ice cream hut, I suspected he might have been sitting. Sitting and staring up at the stars because when he finally walked away, his face was pointed toward the sky as he moved at a slow, deliberate pace.

However, I didn't expect him to be wearing a robe. An all-black robe with an all-black ribbon around the hood.

My eyes met Ranger X's gaze, and together we watched as one of the most powerful wizards to graduate from Cretan disappeared into the night.

CHAPTER 15

"HE WAS SUPPOSED TO BE on a date with Mimsey," I said as we made our way over the bridge to the West side of The Isle. "What does all this mean? What did he need to prove to these men?"

We'd waited behind the ice cream hut for at least thirty minutes, maybe longer, before setting out on foot.

"Maybe the date ended early."

I sighed. "Does that explain why he'd go and put on his graduate robes and meet some old buddies? I don't know what to think."

"I don't either."

"What am I supposed to do?"

"About what?"

"Everything!" I threw my hands into the air. This time, I didn't notice the fish swimming below the bridge or the lovely scent of lilacs lingering on the night breeze. "What was that all about? Gus working with Harpin? What on earth could be so important that two arch-enemies agree to work together? They hate each other's guts. Anyone could've seen that from the two seconds they stood next to each other."

"There are things important enough for people to overcome their differences," Ranger X said. "The only question left is what is so important."

"That could be anything!"

"No, I don't think so. I'd argue it's quite limiting." Ranger X slipped his hand to my lower back, guiding me over a rough patch of cobblestone. "Consider it this way. You dislike Harpin, yes?"

I could barely hide the curl of my lips into a frown. "You could say that."

"So what would it take for you to work with him?"

"A lot."

"Exactly," he said. "You wouldn't go over there to ask him for a hand if you needed furniture moved, no matter how much you wanted that furniture moved. You wouldn't ask him for money, you wouldn't do anything that might require a favor of you in return unless..."

"Unless something, or someone, I loved was at stake," I said quietly. "But what does Gus care so much about?"

"That's for you to think about," X said. "But remember what I said earlier. Before you judge him, ask. It sounded like he doesn't want to lie to you back there. Maybe all you need to do is ask and he'll explain things to you."

I hesitated. "I don't want to put him at risk. That Thomas guy sounded like he meant business. As for Harpin, he's his own force to be reckoned with."

"Don't you think he owes you some explanation if you're going to be involved?"

"When you put it like that..."

"I'm not swaying your opinions either way. You heard what you heard, and you saw what you saw. You have a missing spellbook that was stolen by an impossibly adept thief, and you witnessed a meeting of strangers where one of those men, a man you care about, was supposed to be somewhere else. I'll leave it up to you how to proceed."

"What could they be working on?" The answer felt just out of reach, hovering around the edges of my consciousness and begging for me to name it. "I feel like I should know this, but it's just not coming to me."

"Then forget about it for tonight. Gus is gone for now, the rest of The Isle will soon be asleep, and you need your rest. You'll have another day tomorrow at the bungalow and plenty of time to think about it then. Best to do it with a clear head."

"I suppose you're right," I said slowly.

"More importantly, I don't want to end this non-date on a sour note. Can we enjoy the last five minutes of our stroll?"

I smiled. "I'd like that."

True to form, the next five minutes passed too quickly and too easily. They were such happy minutes I didn't want them to end. Ranger X had pointed out the various sea shells on the shore, describing their names, their patterns, and how they were formed. When we reached the beach in front of the bungalow, we stopped.

"Here," he said, holding out his hand. "I found this at the very start, but I wanted to save it for last."

"Best for last?"

He nodded, and then opened his palm. I leaned in, gasping at the sight of a beautiful pebble.

"That is the most incredible color I have ever seen. May I touch it?"

"It's yours."

I reached for the stone as reverently as if it'd fallen from the sky itself. Blue on the outside, swirls of silver danced through the middle, illuminating the rock from the inside out. A fuzzy, golden halo circled the outer rim, reflecting off a blue so pure it looked like bits of another world had been gathered and packaged in a bundle full of air. "What is it called?"

"Angel's Breath," Ranger X said. "These pebbles are known for their luck. Carry it in your pocket for when you need it the most."

"Does it work?"

"They say each time a soul enters the afterlife they are given one pebble to leave behind on earth. Whenever a person wishes on the stone, it's that soul's duty to determine if their intentions are pure. If the answer is yes, your wish will be granted, the stone will lose its glow, and their spirit is able to move on."

"That is an incredible story," I said, turning the rock from one palm to the next, the smooth outside feeling like a mixture of satin and glass. "But you didn't answer my question. Does it work?"

"You'll have to find out."

I slipped it into my pocket. "Shall I test it now?"

"Save it for when you need it most," Ranger X said. "Right now, you don't need luck. But I would like one thing."

"What's that?"

"A non-kiss."

"But—"

"This is a non-date, and a non-kiss. It's only fair," Ranger X said. "I have manners, and I won't bring it up again, I promise."

My head told me to say no, but my heart, my body, and my soul all said yes. Three against one were tough odds, and this time, my head lost the battle. "Make it good."

Curling me into his arms, Ranger X's lips met mine in a furious tangle of heat. The heady taste of wine mixed with the fresh sea salt. As his tongue slipped between my lips, all thoughts disappeared. No worries lingered and no fears surfaced. It was just the two of us, his strong hands twisted between my locks, pulling the hair tight against my scalp as he trailed his lips down to my neck. I shivered, my own arms snaking around his neck and just holding on, absorbing the moment until he pulled back, his dark eyes swirling with desire.

"That was some non-kiss," I said. "Wow."

"I would like to non-kiss you again," he said. "A lot."

"We might as well get it out of our systems, right?" The irony was not lost on me—he'd said that exact phrase just weeks before. Apparently, we weren't out of each other's systems yet. "What do you say?"

"One more can't hurt."

This time, he lifted me into his arms and walked a few steps into the water. The spray from the waves lapping at his ankles misted around us, wrapping us in a cloud of fog. My skin was chilled and his lips were warm, while a furnace burned in my stomach. He held me in his arms and kissed me until the goose bumps overtook my skin and my lips were raw.

Finally, we walked toward the bungalow together, hand in hand. All pretenses of our non-date gone.

"Thank you for the amazing night," I said. "And for all of your advice."

He raised a hand and ran his fingers along my exposed collar bone. "I hope we can have another non-date sometime."

We stood still, neither of us able to break apart first.

"I should be going," he said eventually, without moving.

"Yes, I should get some sleep." Instead of turning toward the porch steps, I threw my arms around his neck and hugged him tightly. No kissing, no touching, just an embrace that made me feel safe. My eyes closed, and I nearly drifted off to sleep. His hands gently unlocked mine from around his neck, and I forced my eyes to open.

But instead of locking on his gaze, something in the distance caught my eye. I took a step back, stumbling, gasping, spluttering at the sight in the distance.

"Lily, are you okay? What is it?" Ranger X held me close. "What's wrong?"

"Look!"

Together we turned, and thankfully, he had a good grip on my waist because my body sagged against his side. There, floating in the lake, was a pile of robes. As each wave crashed to shore, the bulk grew nearer and nearer and nearer until the truth was unmistakable.

Inside that bundle of robes lay a body.

CHAPTER 16

I MUST HAVE FALLEN ASLEEP AT some point during the night, but I couldn't remember when my nightmares became real and my thoughts dissolved into dreams. After discovering the body washed ashore, Ranger X had leapt into action. He turned on a dime, transforming from non-date mode to Ranger mode in a second.

After sending for help, we huddled together until backup arrived. Then the minutes turned into hours, and everything became a blur. Into the wee hours of the night we were answering questions, surveying the area, and trying to figure out how a body had ended up on the beach outside of my bungalow.

The body had not been formally identified, but I could venture a guess as to who it might be: black robes, black ribbon across the hood, male facial features—it didn't leave a lot of options. I explained about the hooded stranger asking for The Elixir to the Rangers, and they'd nodded and muttered to one another, never bothering to clue me in on their theories.

Hours later, the Rangers finally left. In their wake, the cool calmness of the night turned into a black void—a scary, lonely place that had me jumping at every cricket chirp and stick crackle. The body had been removed and the spotlights turned off, but even then, sleep didn't come, just as Gus had predicted.

The only Ranger who didn't leave was X. He insisted on staying at the bungalow and keeping watch, despite my best attempts at protesting. Eventually I gave in and pulled him into the kitchen where we shared a cup of coffee and some somber silence. I was too wired, too tired to talk, too exhausted to feel any emotions.

I didn't remember walking up to bed or undressing, but I must have done it because the next thing I knew, light was streaming through my windows and I was tucked safe in my bed.

I couldn't remember the last time I'd slept uninterrupted. I secretly thought that Gus loved to wake me abruptly from my dreams by shouting as loud as physically possible from the bottom of the staircase. Speaking of, where was Gus?

A sudden memory of offering Ranger X the couch downstairs hit me then, and I realized that Gus had probably shown up this morning ready to shout up the staircase as usual, but Ranger X had likely demanded I be left alone. I sighed. As much as I had insisted that Ranger X didn't have to stay over, I had to admit, it felt nice to know someone had my back.

"How on earth did you not tell us?" a familiar voice chided. Poppy poked her head up from the side of my bed, and I leapt up so hard I nearly smacked my head on the ceiling. "You kept it a secret from us, how dare you!"

I clutched my hands to my chest. "What are you doing here? You just about gave me a heart attack. And how did you get in?"

"Well, we had to climb in the window, seeing how you had a surprise guest staying over downstairs."

"We?"

"Hi," Zin said with a wave, popping up from the other side of the bed. "I'm here too."

"What are you guys doing here?"

"We came by to check on you. Poppy didn't see you setting up shop on her way to work at the supply store this morning, so we poked our heads in to see if you were around."

"We were quite surprised to see X sitting in your kitchen drinking a cup of coffee—"

"—with a definitely 'slept in' couch and blanket set up over in the corner."

Poppy waggled her eyebrows. "Why'd you send him down to the couch without you? Doesn't he know he's supposed to cuddle you in the morning? At least on a first date."

"We didn't do anything!" I said. "It wasn't a date."

Poppy and Zin shared a look, rolling their eyes at one another.

"What are the kids calling it these days?" Poppy asked. "Hanky-panky? Tickle the pickle? Hide the—"

"Tickle the pickle?" Zin said with a snort. "If that's the best you can do, you really have to start dating. Nobody says that anymore."

"Okay, you should talk, Miss Wannabe Ranger."

"There wasn't any date," I said, mostly to break up the argument. I felt a tiny bit of guilt not admitting the full story. Though we'd been desperately referring to what we had as a non-date, everything about the kiss we'd shared had felt real.

"I see how it is," Poppy said. "I make one date with Hettie, and I miss all the fun."

"Why did you sneak through my window this morning?" I grumbled. "That's a bigger problem."

"No way, José," Poppy said. "We're your cousins and your best girlfriends. We do things like that for each other."

"I'm not hanging around climbing through your bedroom windows."

"That's because we don't have men sleeping over downstairs. Men that we're keeping a secret from our best girlfriends," she said pointedly.

"That's not the only reason we stopped over," Zin said, casting a glance over to Poppy. "There's one more thing. We need some help."

"With what?" I asked. "Is everything okay?"

"It's nothing," Poppy said dismissively. "And Lily knows about the problem anyway. Just deal with it and stop complaining, Zin."

"Deal with what?" I looked between the two. "Someone tell me what's going on here."

"Poppy is hiccupping like crazy," Zin said, wrinkling her nose. "It's loud, and it smells like a rotten fish slept with a chicken and they had rotten fish eggs. It goes on, and on, and on, and she can't stop!"

"It's not that bad," Poppy said, waving a hand in front of her face and stifling an untimely hiccup. "Really, it's minor."

Zin shook her head, and then looked to me with a desperate expression on her face. "Can you please fix her?"

"Is this a side effect of the Vamp Vites running low?" I asked.

"Maybe." Poppy looked sheepish. "I've never had anything like it before. I can't seem to stop."

She hiccupped again, as if emphasizing her point. The smell was so noxious I had to dip my nose into my nightgown and breathe into the freshly laundered fabric to block the scent.

Zin rapidly fanned her face, her eyebrows knitting in disgust. "Do you see what I mean?"

"Wow," I said. "That is definitely a problem."

"Now we know why Poppy doesn't have men sleeping over," Zin said. "She can't even share a house with us. Hettie threatened to kick her out this morning if she couldn't stop hiccupping."

"I've never had this before." Poppy covered her mouth with her hand. "This is weird. Make it stop, Lily."

"Have you ever had low levels of your Vamp Vites before?" I asked. "Are you only taking half of your dosage?"

"I'm down to a quarter dose per day," she said softly. "I don't want to rush you, but I'm starting to get scared. What happens if you can't find the ingredient you need? Are you sure Gus has no idea where the last Mixologist secured it from?"

"No, I asked him twice. He has no clue." I waited a beat. "But there is one person who may know a solution. I'm going to talk to him this morning, but before I do, it's my turn to tell you guys a story."

"You've been holding out on us!" Zin said too loudly. "You and Ranger X are a thing."

"We're not a thing, but we did have dinner together last night. As friends. Except, we had an interesting walk home."

"You kissed!"

I halfheartedly denied it, but the blush on my cheeks gave me away.

Poppy pointed at me. "I knew it!"

Dodging the question, I filled the girls in on everything from seeing Gus conversing with his former classmates, to learning that Gus was a Black Ribbon wizard, to finding a man's body washed up on shore. I left out the kiss, only because the girls already looked shell-shocked at everything that had happened, and I didn't want to add another iron to the fire.

"When you two peeked downstairs, did you find Gus?" I asked, finishing up the story. "I haven't seen him since last night."

Poppy shook her head. "If Gus had been here, things wouldn't have been so odd. It was mostly suspicious that Ranger X was hanging downstairs by himself."

"We thought that you and Ranger X might have requested some alone time." Zin winked. "We couldn't think of any other reason that Gus would stay away. He loves that storeroom."

"I told you, X and I are not a thing," I said. "But if you want to keep teasing me about it, then let me bring up the fact that Gus went on a date with your mother last night." I swiveled to face Poppy and raised my eyebrows. She turned white, and I gave a half smile. "That's what I thought."

"We'll agree to tone down our teasing if you stop mentioning that tidbit," Poppy said, glancing nonchalantly at her nails. "Enough dating talk. Where's Gus?"

CHAPTER 17

"Hey," I said as I made my way down the stairs a few minutes later. "How'd you sleep?"

Ranger X smiled at me over a cup of black coffee, his gaze somewhat tender, compared to the fierce expression he'd worn after discovering the body last night. "I'm fine, I can sleep anywhere. What about you?"

I gave a one-shouldered shrug. "Not awesome, but I'm not sure that awesome could be expected after the day I had."

"I made coffee." Ranger X stood up and moved toward the coffee pot. "Have a seat. Mimsey whirled in here a moment ago shouting about breakfast."

My eyes fell on the table where he'd brought my most favorite mug in from the outdoor bar and had it waiting for me. My heart melted at the thoughtfulness behind the gesture. As he stood and reached for the coffee pot, I waved him off. "Thank you. I can take it from here."

"Let me pour you a cup," he said, sounding so proud of the fact that he'd managed to brew a proper pot of coffee that I found myself sitting and saying thank you without argument. He looked up anxiously as steam rose from the top of my mug. "How is it?"

I took a sip, the coffee brew as dark as the devil and as bitter as a lemon, but I managed a smile. "This is delicious."

"Really? I didn't know how many beans to use," Ranger X said nervously. "Are you sure I didn't go overboard?"

I forced one more sip of the concoction down my throat. "Really brilliant. Thank you."

The smile that bloomed on his lips at my approval made every second of drinking the pile of sludge worth it. "Oh, I'm glad. I know you need your coffee. Gus says so, at least."

Internally, I sighed. Ranger X paid attention to my little quirks. He remembered things people said about me. He made the effort to keep me safe, make me comfortable, and tell me the truth. For a Ranger who could never marry and wasn't interested in a relationship, he would make a darn good boyfriend. Shame.

"Thanks for staying last night," I said. "I really appreciate it. I know... I know you could've gone with your men to look for the murderer, but instead you stayed here."

"I would never have left you like that," he said softly, our eyes locking over the curl of steam reaching for the ceiling. "I'll always be here when you need me."

"I know. It makes all the difference. I wouldn't have gotten any sleep without you down here."

"You look tired."

"I am tired, but two hours of shut-eye is better than nothing." We shared a quiet smile, the late morning more peaceful than usual, as if the wake of the crime had cleared all activity away.

"Eggs?" Mimsey called. "Who wants eggs?"

Ranger X looked to me. "Would you like some?"

"I'm okay," I said. "Still feeling a bit queasy from last night."

"You really need to eat," he said. "You didn't sleep, you probably burned through all of your calories, and you need strength. Have some eggs."

A loud noise sounded overhead before I could agree. It sounded suspiciously like two pairs of footsteps. Ranger X raised an eyebrow first at the ceiling, and then at me.

"That's nothing," I said quickly. "But sure, I'll have some eggs. A lot of eggs."

Still giving me skeptical expressions, he stopped lecturing me about eating after I fixed him with my most innocent stare. When he turned to give Mimsey our orders, I shot a murderous glare through the ceiling, wishing I had the power to freeze my cousins in their tracks. Unfortunately, I didn't know a spell for that.

Poppy and Zin had agreed to wait upstairs in my room until I could clear out the downstairs long enough for them to slip out the front door unnoticed. Turned out, *leaving* through the window was a lot harder than coming in, and neither of them felt particularly keen on explaining to Mimsey why they'd snuck into their cousin's bedroom. However, judging by the sounds of the conveniently timed footsteps above, Poppy still wanted to put in a breakfast order.

"Was Gus planning on coming back last night?" Ranger X asked. "I haven't seen him this morning."

"I don't know. He doesn't keep me abreast of his schedule, believe it or not."

Ranger X laughed. "That doesn't surprise me in the slightest, though it does surprise me that he's not around by now."

Mimsey swept into the room with two plates, one in each hand, dropping them heartily on the table. "Eat," she instructed before sweeping right back out of the room.

"We're keeping things quiet," Ranger X said, dipping his head low and taking a bite of the eggs. His voice was barely audible over the light crashing of the waves. "Only the Rangers know about the murder. The fewer people involved, the better. We don't want to cause a wave of panic to spread through the islanders."

"Because he was a Black Ribbon wizard?"

"That's one part of it."

"After all this time, I spoke with two Black Ribbon wizards in the same day. Can that be a coincidence?"

Ranger X took another bite of eggs. "I don't particularly believe in coincidences."

"Me neither."

"But that doesn't mean it's a bad coincidence. We don't know that Gus is involved with things, let alone the wrong side of things, and we shouldn't jump to hasty conclusions."

"Then where is he?" I leaned forward, my shoulders pressing against the table, my voice a hiss. "If he's the only other Black Ribbon wizard, shouldn't he be here helping us figure this out? Why did he disappear?"

"I can't answer those questions right now, but I'm having my men look into it as we speak."

"Eat, you two." Mimsey poked her head into the storeroom. "Too much whispering and not enough egg swallowing."

I forked an egg for show, but as soon as Mimsey resumed her cooking in the other room, I set it back down. "We don't have time to sit here eating eggs."

"We don't know anything is wrong," Ranger X said firmly. "Gus may waltz in at any moment. If he doesn't, we'll just trace his last steps…"

Ranger X trailed off as we met each other's gaze, both of us realizing we had Gus's last steps cooking eggs right next door. At once, we both called out "Mimsey!"

"What is it?" Mimsey appeared again in the doorway. "You almost made me burn the toast, and we all know Gus hates burnt toast. Where is that man, by the way?"

Ranger X and I shared a quick glance before I turned back to my aunt. "He's not with you?"

Her face turned the shade of a blooming rose. "Me? What? Never," she spluttered. "What do you think I am, a hooligan? I don't let men sleep over on first dates."

Ranger X and I shifted awkwardly in our seats while Mimsey eyed us judgmentally.

"Is there something you're not telling me?" A bit of egg splattered in our direction as Mimsey thrust the spatula at us. "Are you two playing the dating game?"

Ranger X rose from his seat, the motion intimidating due to the sheer size of his body. "Mimsey, we need to know what happened with Gus last night. He didn't stay over?"

"No," she said, a genuinely confused look on her face. "He dropped me off at home plenty early, like a gentleman. I went home and watched the rest of a show with my daughter. Although, I think he mentioned something about catching up with an old friend afterward when I invited him in. He declined, and I didn't ask too much about it. I was rather excited to get some alone time with my daughter. I love family, but sometimes there are a lot of them around, and it was a nice quiet evening for the two of us."

I swallowed hard. "Do you know which old friend he was meeting?"

She shook her head. "He said it was a quick nightcap. Maybe at the B&B? Or maybe he was headed to Sea Salt, I don't know." Mimsey laughed. "I did ask why he wasn't going to bring his friend to the bungalow for a drink to give you some business, but he said he didn't want to bother you."

"I'll bet he didn't," I muttered. Gus wouldn't have bothered me, but Harpin's presence would have. Plus, Gus showing up to a meeting in his black robes would've raised some questions he wanted left secret. "So you haven't seen him?"

Mimsey shook her head. "Ranger X saw me arrive here a few minutes ago. I got straight to cookin', I didn't even think to check around for that ol' grump." Even as she called Gus a grump, her face turned a girlish pink and her eyes sparkled. "I thought he was just in a mood and was organizing the storeroom or something."

"We haven't seen him," I said. Then I clarified. "None of us have seen him this morning."

Mimsey rested a hand on her hip. "Hmm, now that is strange. Maybe his meeting with his friend went late and he slept in?"

"When's the last time Gus slept in?" I said. "He's always

puttering around here until the wee hours of the morning, and he's still the first one up."

Mimsey frowned. "You're right. I don't know then. That's strange."

Ranger X stood. "It's time for me to get going."

"Is something wrong?" Despite Mimsey's attempt at keeping a straight face, a layer of fear danced underneath. "X, what's going on?"

"I'm sure Gus had an event with his friend that he didn't tell either of you. Maybe they got breakfast this morning or something." Ranger X gave Mimsey a quick salute. "Don't worry, Miss Magnolia, we're just going to check on him. Neighborly duties."

"Fine, good. Good," she said, distractedly tucking the spatula behind her ear like a pencil. Her fingers fidgeted with one another. "You'll find him then?"

"You have my word," he said. "Lily, can you walk me out?"

I followed Ranger X out the front door, down the steps, and onto the beach where my toes formed little caves in the already warmed sand.

"Are you going to be okay?" He turned toward me, one of his hands resting on my waist as he looked into my eyes. "Do you want me to stay? Just say the word, and I won't go anywhere."

I flashed him my strongest smile. "Go. Find Gus. I have to take care of a few things here, and then maybe I'll see if Mimsey can watch Magic & Mixology. I have to meet with Liam to see if he knows where the ingredient for Poppy's Vamp Vites can be purchased."

"Be careful."

"I will," I whispered, my hand coming to rest on his chest, the firmness of his muscles strong and comforting under the soft pads of my fingertips. "You too."

Ranger X took a few steps down the path, and I watched him go. Just before he reached the main beach path, he turned around and winked.

I tilted my head to the side. "What's so funny?"

"Tell your cousins they can come out from hiding now," he said. "I left them some eggs."

My mouth hung open. "You knew this whole time?"

"Tell Poppy that if she swears like a sailor while she's trying to climb your trellis, she's never going to be sneaky."

"What about Zin?"

"Zin..." He winked again. "She did good."

CHAPTER 18

TWENTY MINUTES LATER, I'D USHERED Poppy and Zin safely out of the house, though their absence didn't last long. As soon as they hit the beach, they turned right around and knocked on the door.

"Hello," I said, trying to keep a straight face as my cousins stood on my front steps without ever having left. "How are you ladies this morning?"

Stifling smiles, they came into the storeroom and got right to work on the eggs.

"Nice of you to show up, girls," Mimsey said. "Save some food for your cousin! She is shrinking. Lily, don't you like my eggs?"

"I love your eggs," I said in the most serious tone I could muster. "But I have to run an errand. Would you three be able to hold down the fort for an hour by chance?"

"Oh, run along. Trinket's got the supply store under control today, and frankly I'd rather be here." Mimsey hiked herself onto a bar stool and spread out to catch as much sun as possible on her white-as-marshmallow skin. It was a stark contrast to the blinding green muumuu floating around her plump figure. "I'm working on my tan, anyway. Don't you think Gus would find me extra attractive with a tan?"

"Ew, Mom," Poppy said. "No romance talk while I'm eating breakfast."

Zin winked. "I think your mom would look lovely with a tan."

Poppy reached over and forked an egg from Zin's plate. Zin

leapt to pull it back, but she missed, and Poppy caught the whole thing in her mouth.

I snuck out with a wave and a quiet goodbye, figuring that sooner rather than later was the best time to make my exit. Otherwise, I risked caking my hair in flying egg yolks.

The walk across The Isle was quick. I had no clue whether or not Liam would be at the B&B, but I didn't know any place he'd be instead, nor did I have anyone to ask. Best to start at the beginning. Thankfully, the beginning was also the end of my short journey.

"Lily!" Liam rose from a seat at the coffee house just outside of the B&B. It could hardly be called a house, however. Born of a small wooden shack, the cafe's only seating consisted of a few rickety tables plunked outside, and the only employee was a nervous young man who was so twitchy I wondered if he wasn't high on espresso fumes. Liam waved. "How are you, dear? Let Sylvester know your order."

I nodded to the twitchy espresso man called Sylvester. "One cappuccino, please."

"Come, join me." Liam pulled out a chair next to his. "What brings you around so soon?"

I waited to dive into my story until the cappuccino arrived a minute later, the frothy beverage delivering the jolt of caffeine I needed. Ranger X's gesture had been nice, but the pot of coffee he'd made had been as undrinkable as a tub of gasoline. As I sipped, Liam watched me carefully.

"It's good?"

"The best," I said, glancing around. When it was clear that nobody was within listening distance, I bit my lip and struggled with where to start my request. There was no good place, so I dove right in. "I hear you have the ability to obtain, uh…" I hesitated. "Hard-to-find materials."

Liam's face didn't register surprise, though one corner of his mouth quirked upwards. "I may, or I may have a friend who can help, depending on your needs."

"This is private?"

"All of my business is private. Completely."

"I'm looking for Dust of the Devil."

Liam sat back. "Powerful. Dust of the Devil is a very volatile ingredient. May I ask what you plan to use it for?"

"Did the last Mixologist ever ask you how to find it?" I didn't want to lay all my cards on the table before Liam gave me a peek into his hand. "From your reaction, it sounds like you've heard of it."

"I've heard of it, though I've never sold it."

My heart sank. "So my grandfather didn't come to you for help?"

"I didn't say that." Liam crossed his arms over his chest, sizing me up for a long moment. Eventually, a ray of understanding crossed his face. "This is for your friend. The vampire."

I shifted but didn't answer either way.

"I'd forgotten about that. He only asked me for it once, many years ago."

"If you don't sell it, do you know who does?"

"It's not a who..." Liam paused for an excruciatingly long moment. "It's a where."

"Where?"

Liam nodded. "The plant is self-sustaining. As I mentioned, it has volatile tendencies, so I refuse to transport it, as do most other traders." My face must have sunk in dismay because he raised a finger. "Don't look so blue, Lily-bell. Fortunately for you, it grows right here on The Isle."

"No way," I breathed out. "Really? I've been looking everywhere, and it's right under my nose?"

"Not so much," he said carefully. "It's dangerous to use, and it's dangerous to harvest. It lies within The Forest."

I swallowed. "Can you lead me to it?"

Liam laughed softly. "My job does not require my hands to get dirty, and I like it that way. Some say I'm a pansy, but I don't mind. I'd rather be a pansy than an idiot. I'm sorry, I don't venture into The Forest."

"But how will I find it?"

"Are you sure you want to?"

I thought of Poppy's worried expression when she'd told me she was only taking a quarter of her necessary dosage. "I need it. Whatever it takes."

"Fine. Give me your napkin."

Chapter 19

Under the branches of a tree in bloom—
To the left of the biggest, yellow mushroom.
There, you'll locate a desired find—
Take only enough; leave plenty behind.

I SPENT A FEW MINUTES IN silence analyzing the riddle Liam had left on the napkin. "What's wrong with good, old-fashioned directions?" I grumbled. "This means nothing to me."

"Because you've never been to The Forest," Liam said. "The Forest is a mystical place full of wonderful, dangerous things. Within The Forest's boundaries, things have a tendency to move and flow with nature. There, directions are not a fixed entity, merely a directional tool."

"So no map?" I asked longingly.

"Sorry, but no. The Forest is in a constant state of flow, and it has adapted to be like this for a reason. It protects and guides those with purpose, while discouraging those who wander aimlessly."

"Sounds easy to get lost."

"It is."

"How can I not get lost?" I swallowed. "Trail of breadcrumbs?"

"I wish it were so easy," he said. "And I wish there was a house made of candy at the end of the trail."

I laughed. Liam's presence, even during stressful times, was easy and pleasant to be around. "That would be ideal."

"Are you going alone into The Forest?" After my laughter died down, his expression turned somber. "Even with directions, it is a place rife with creatures that go bump in the night."

"I'll hopefully go during the daylight," I said with another laugh, this one sounding noticeably forced. Liam didn't seem amused, so I moved on. "I'm going to swing by today. I can't endanger anyone else."

"This is for a friend, yes? The friend will not go with you?"

"I don't plan on telling her that I'm going at all," I said. "She'd go with me in a heartbeat, and that's exactly what I'm worried about. I'm not risking either of my cousins' lives in there."

Liam nodded, his eyes not fooled. "And what about those who aren't your cousins?"

We were both thinking of Ranger X. "He's busy today. I won't bother him."

"I imagine he'd like to be bothered if he knew you were going alone into The Forest."

"Well, there's a lot going on right now." I looked into my cappuccino, wishing it refilled itself. Almost as if he'd read my mind, Sylvester swept over, his dark, greasy hair swinging in front of his twitchy face as he swiped my empty cup and replaced it with a new one. "It shouldn't take long to gather a bit of the ingredient, right? I only need a small dose to start."

"Yes, but it's your first time attempting the harvest."

"Did the last Mixologist bring company into The Forest?"

Liam remained silent. "That was different. He—"

I narrowed my eyes at him. "Don't you dare say it was because he was a man."

"I was going to say because the last person to go inside The Forest wasn't the real Mixologist," Liam said, clearing his throat. "With only one Mixologist, we—the islanders, I mean—value your life highly."

"Everyone's life is valued the same," I said evenly. "I am not special."

Liam gave me a sad sort of smile. "My dear, you are young. I admire your optimism, but we must agree to disagree. Most islanders would give their life for yours. Myself included."

The thought made me uncomfortable. "Have you seen Gus today?"

The change of subject was an obvious one, but luckily Liam was a gentleman and went with it. "I have not. Is he missing?"

I nodded. "How'd you know?"

"My dear, if you ask where someone is... typically you can't find them."

I flushed with an embarrassed smile. "Sorry if I came off a bit snappish. There's a lot going on, not that it's any excuse."

Liam reached over and squeezed my hand. "I assume X is on the case?"

I nodded.

"Then don't worry about Gus," he said. "Gus will be found. Don't forget, both he and Ranger X are impressive creatures. You need to focus on yourself. If you are truly going into The Forest today, you need to concentrate on getting in and getting out—alive."

"You're not going to try and stop me from going?" I asked curiously.

"What's the point?" He sat back and took a dainty sip of his cappuccino. "If I fight you on it, you'll just go anyway. I see the way you talk about your cousins. You'd do anything for your family, and a word of caution from me isn't going to change that."

"You talk about family like you understand it."

He gave a tight smile. "More than you know."

"I thought your parents died when you were young. Is there more to the story?" I asked. The more I spoke with Liam, the more I realized he was a complicated man built from many layers. I'd barely scratched the surface of getting to know him. I understood now why Ranger X was hesitant to arrest him, regardless of whether he walked the line between legal and illegal.

"In my line of work, I do the question asking, my dear." The glint of sadness left Liam's face. "You have a beautiful family, and I can see they love you as much as you love them. If you are going into The Forest then by all means, I'd rather have you be safe than stupid, and it'd be stupid of me to try and talk you out of it. Humans and wizards alike need to make their own mistakes and learn from them. I'd just rather have you be alive afterward in order to learn."

"Then tell me what I need to know."

CHAPTER 20

ANOTHER HOUR AND TWO CAPPUCCINOS later, Liam had given me the pep talk of a lifetime. He'd explained that anything slithering with a red body was not harmful at all. In fact, those snakes could be used for healing powers.

However, the innocent-looking rabbits with the violet eyes—those, I needed to watch out for. One glimpse of violet eyes, and I'd almost certainly be dead in seconds. Trees with seven-sided leaves needed to be given a ten-foot radius, or they'd lure me in with their spell and lull me into a dream-like state of sleep, leaving me vulnerable for all of the other creepy crawlies lurking just beyond the darkness. And that was just the introduction.

My head swimming with knowledge, Liam and I bid farewell when our final cappuccinos were drained. I feared sitting with him any longer would bring on a wave of emotions I didn't want cropping up as I set off into The Forest. Between the excessive amounts of caffeine wiring my nervous system and the impending doom of disappearing into the darkness, I was already shaking.

Instead of heading toward the Lower Bridge, the safest, most well-traveled route back to the West Isle, I took the beach path north. Intentionally, I took the scenic route, which wound its way around the shore of the East Isle. I needed some time to calm down and think. My hands shook with nerves while all of Liam's information whizzed around like a sack of bouncy balls let loose in my skull.

As I walked, the sand glittered under the sun and the waves

made for a soothing background track. The advice from Liam began to sink in as I ran over his words again and again. By the time I reached the Upper Bridge, I was feeling nervous, but ready. As ready as I could ever hope to be for my first venture alone into The Forest.

Unlike the Lower Bridge, the Upper Bridge was not scenic. There were no vibrant orange goldfish dancing, or dolphins and sharks circling as friends. Here, the water was dark and barren, as if even the fish had decided it wasn't safe. The sunlight shone on only half of the bridge. The path in front of me lay buried in shadow.

The coolness hit my shoulders, and I shivered the second I crossed from light to darkness. Simultaneously, a loud splash rang out to my left and I leapt to the opposite side of the bridge, watching in horror as a large, ugly fish that resembled the love child of a semi-truck and a pug—with fins—leapt from the water and snatched a butterfly from the air. My heart pounded, and I raced toward The Forest without looking back. If I didn't continue now, I'd never go at all.

A few steps into The Forest and the immersion into darkness was complete. This was a different world than the airy, vacationy portion of The Isle. The sun failed to battle its way through the thick tree branches, and the fresh lake air might as well have been miles away.

Inside The Forest's grasp the air was cool and heavy, damp with the weight of moss and dew. It was stifling. I struggled to take a deep breath as I hurriedly glanced around to make sure there were no seven-sided leaves nearby.

It took a few seconds, but eventually my eyes adjusted to the dark, my breathing adapted to the thickness of the air, and I took a step forward. The hefty layer of growth over The Forest floor muted my footsteps, giving off the eerie sensation that I didn't really exist at all.

It didn't take long before I could no longer see the bridge. Panic rose in my chest, and for a moment, I was sure I couldn't take another step. Then, like a flashlight in the darkness, I remembered Liam's words. Going into The Forest takes purpose. I forced myself to think about Poppy. Focus on the missing ingredient. Recall the instructions to harvest Dust of the Devil.

I repeated these steps over and over again to myself.

Under the branches of the trees in bloom...

Everything around me was green or black. Leaves and moss grew everywhere except for the air, and the open spaces were seas of darkness.

Then I noticed the scent. It started subtly, as if it'd begun seeping into my consciousness without my realizing it. I sniffed, and the smell grew stronger. The more I focused, the stronger and stronger it became, guiding my feet forward as if someone else had control of them. Before I knew it, I'd gone deeper into The Forest, and my surroundings began to change.

I focused on that scent like it was the light at the end of a deep, dark tunnel. Continuing forward, I paused only when a crack in the distance or a rustle underfoot broke through my concentration. The seconds morphed into minutes as time itself turned into an elusive entity. Like Liam's directions, I sensed that minutes and seconds and hours were but a fickle thing inside The Forest. Time moved lightning quick one second and as slow as molasses the next.

My feet slowed of their own accord, and I couldn't help but believe these trees were rife with magic. When I focused on the scent, it grew stronger. If for any reason my mind began to wander, I found myself stopping more frequently, looking around, starting down the wrong path. When I refocused, the scent pulled me along like a trail of breadcrumbs.

"Here you are," I murmured. "The mushroom!"

I bent down, scanning the monstrous plant. It grew to my knee in height, while the top was wide enough to be an umbrella for a dwarf. I stared at it, soaking in every aspect of the plant. It was like no mushroom I'd seen before. It looked like it belonged in Alice and Wonderland with its yellow and red and blue and purple color-scheme.

I leaned further forward, examining the tie-dyed pattern, until something stung me on the nose so hard I stumbled back several feet and landed in a pile of soft moss. "Ow!"

"Get away!" A teensy tiny thing—likely a sprite or a fairy—shook a fist at me from her perch on my knee. "Leave my home alone. I don't go stomping into your house and peeking in your bedroom windows!"

"I'm—I'm really sorry," I said, enthralled by her tiny features. From the blond pixie haircut to the floral green dress, she resembled Tinkerbell with a bit more sex appeal. This fairy had big red lips and, from the looks of it, she was smoking something that looked like a cigarette, though it didn't smell like tobacco.

"Darn straight you're sorry! This is my shroom."

"Can you tell me where I might find the blooming tree?"

She scowled then pointed. "Open your eyes!"

"My eyes are..." I said, trailing off as the fairy fluttered over and poked me right in the center of my chin. Before I could swat her away, she was already back on her mushroom, hands planted on her hips. "Sometimes it amazes me how long you non-Forest dwelling folks live. If I was as unobservant as you, I'd be dead in a second."

"This is beautiful." I was too busy taking in the sight before me to respond to her sarcasm. The tree in question was laden with hundreds of thousands of blossoms the color of a blood moon. Orange swirled into red as flowers as big as a sunbonnet flapped with the slightest hint of a breeze.

"Beautiful?" The fairy's voice held a note of curiosity. "Yes, it's beautiful."

"Why do you sound so hesitant?"

"Because it's also deadly."

"Deadly?" I swallowed. Liam hadn't mentioned anything about the flower being deadly. "Are you sure?"

"You don't believe me? Go take a flower and we'll see just how deadly it is."

I took a few steps toward the tree's blooms and inclined my head toward it, breathing in the faint scent washing off the huge petals. "It smells nice."

"From a distance, maybe."

"What happens if I go closer?"

"Try it."

"You look far too giddy for me to want to try that."

"You're smarter than you look," the fairy said with a frown. "You don't wanna die?"

"No, not really. Plus, you've lived here longer than I have, so it'd be stupid of me not to listen. Will it kill me?"

She pouted. "It could."

"Which part of this is Dust of the Devil?"

The fairy flew over and landed on my shoulder. Apparently, we were now friends.

"They really are gorgeous." She stared into the branches of the enormous, colorful tree, her mouth parted slightly in awe. "Have you heard the story behind them?"

I shook my head. "I'm here to help a friend. It's not for me."

A spark of recognition flashed across her face. "You're the new one."

"The new what?"

"The new Mixologist."

"That's me. Did you know the last one?"

She pointed a haughty finger over at the large mushroom a few paces back. "Of course I knew him! His first time here he trampled my shroom. Do you know how long it took me to re-grow my home? I suppose I was due for a remodel anyway, but honestly. He had huge feet and they just stomped all over my roof."

"How often did he come?"

"I think I scared him away the first time," she said thoughtfully. "There was a while he didn't come back to visit me. I was nicer the second time. After that, he came back more often."

"Why can't we grow these closer to the bungalow?" I reached for a flower, but the fairy pinched the skin of my shoulder so hard I yelped and leapt backwards. "What was that for?"

"I just saved your life."

I rubbed the skin on my shoulder, a red welt appearing where she'd pinched me. "That hurt."

"At least you can still feel hurt. If you touch the petal, your skin will burn. If you hold on long enough, you'll die."

I blinked. "How am I supposed to gather it, then?"

"Have patience," the fairy said in a dazed tone of voice. "That's the biggest mistake you outsiders make when you come into The Forest. You grab, grab, grab, and you take, take, take. Maybe if you stopped for a second and smelled the foliage, you'd understand. Patience can save your life."

I stood still. As the fairy sank into some sort of dreamlike trance, her eyes grew large. She stared into the flowers, focusing on three spokes poking out from the center disk. "It's beautiful."

Reaching out, I pinched the fairy around the waist and drew her back. I gave her the tiniest shake as I set her safely on her shroom a few feet back, planting myself on a nearby log. "Are you okay?"

She shook herself. "I haven't been that close in a while."

"Did I save your life? Why'd you go all dreamy on me?"

"No," she said with a scowl. After a long beat, she reconsidered. "Thanks for bringing me out."

"What is in those flowers that's so powerful?"

"They're called Dust of the Devil for a reason," she said. "A long time ago, a witch from the East Isle came into The Forest and she saw the beauty in these flowers. She became entranced by them, staring straight in their centers for hours upon end until finally, she tried to gather them up and bring a bouquet home."

"Did her skin burn?"

"Many times. That's the thing about these flowers. They draw you back over and over again. Even when her fingers had layers of blisters on them, she came back for more."

"Like an addiction."

"Yes." The fairy glanced toward the tree with reverence. "After enough failures, however, she got it right. She figured out how to harvest some of the flowers without getting burned."

"What'd she do with them?"

"She treated them like any old flowers and made the blossoms into a bouquet. Selfishly. She took all of the blooms—every single one—and the tree withered and died. Turns out, the tree needs its flowers as much as the flowers need the tree; there is no one or the other, they are symbiotic."

"Is this the same tree?"

"Yes, but it took hundreds of years for it to return! You see, the more blooms there are on a tree, the faster they populate. To grow that first bloom takes hundreds of years. The second takes half that time, the third a quarter of the time and so on. A tree this full has been growing for thousands of years."

The reverence in her gaze made a bit more sense now. The sheer age of this tree gave it an aura of wisdom that commanded respect. "That's the second part of the riddle," I whispered. "Do not take it all."

"I'm here to guard it." The fairy crossed her arms. "If you can give me a good enough reason why you need a bloom, then I'll show you how to harvest it."

"You never did finish your story."

"Oh, that witch… that dreadful witch, she put her bouquet on display at her kitchen table. But what she underestimated about the Dust of the Devil was its strength. She thought she'd killed the blooms by removing them from the tree, but let me tell you this:

The Devil's Dust doesn't go down without a fight. As the flowers wilt, they release a poisonous gas."

"If they're going to die, they're taking their destroyer with them."

"Exactly. To steal these blooms is to make a deal with the devil. You'll get a brief flash of beauty and glamour—all of the islanders crowded by this witch's house to see her wares. Day and night, visitors flocked to her living room. But in the end, all of the guests were gone, and the witch was left to suffer the consequences. The blooms in that bouquet didn't just go down fighting, they went down with a war."

I shuddered, trying not to visualize any of it. "I take it she didn't survive?"

"Let's just say I wouldn't make a bouquet anytime soon."

"If I take just a few, is that also a deal with the devil?"

"Everything in The Forest has consequences. Taking something you don't understand is dangerous. These plants haven't survived thousands of years because they're weak. Many are stronger than you."

"What would my consequences be of taking the Dust of the Devil?"

"It depends on your intentions."

I explained about Poppy's dilemma and how the side effects of not having access to Vamp Vites was wreaking havoc on everyone around her. That soon, her supply would dwindle to nothing.

"You're like him."

"Who?"

"The last Mixologist," she said. "He was a good man."

"The fill-in? The guy who worked here for the last two years?"

Her eyebrows knitted in thought. "No, the one before. The real deal."

"You knew my grandfather," I said, sucking in a breath. "What was he like?"

"Kind. Respectful. If he wanted to rule The Forest, we would have let him. He didn't want to, and that's exactly why he would've been the best for the job," she said, sighing with dismay. "We miss him, but we don't have time to talk now. Darkness is on the horizon, and you don't want to be caught out here at night."

"I can take care of myself."

"I don't think you're stupid, lady, but it would be pretty stupid of you to stay here."

"Then how do we do this?"

After some careful consideration and a long period of deliberation, the fairy nodded and led me back toward the tree. Very carefully, she demonstrated how to harvest the Dust of the Devil. It was simple really, but it'd be impossible to guess the process without a teacher. After she'd shown me three times on three different blossoms, she nodded for me to try on my own.

With a gentle touch and the bending of leaves in a certain pattern, I was able to extract the dust from the very center of the flower without injuring myself on the first try. I took just a little from three or four different flowers—enough to last me a month, according to the fairy. If all went well, I could take a bit more next time.

"This is incredible." Glancing down into my open palm, I let my eyes rest on the powder lying there. Red mixed with black in a shiny substance that looked like diamonds shattered to the consistency of fine sugar. My eyes locked hard and wouldn't let go. "This is magic."

"Put it in here." Sharply, the fairy directed my attention to a small container that looked like it'd formerly been an acorn. "Don't look at it for the entire walk back. When you do use it, use only the tiniest pinch at first. Close the container right away, or it'll suck you in and drive you mad."

I dusted the powder from my palm into the container and snapped it shut. "Thank you for your help, Miss..."

"Ferrah," she said. "Got the name from my momma."

"It's lovely. Thank you for letting me have a glimpse of the Devil's Dust."

"Think of it like the sea," she called as I turned to leave. "You need to respect it, study it, and be prepared for the worst. Even a stormy sea can capture the best of sailors."

"But the best of sailors know when not to go out onto the sea."

Ferrah saluted me. "You're ready, Mixologist. Thank you for your services."

Chapter 21

I WAS STILL GLOWING THIRTY MINUTES later from the fairy's compliments and the success of a completed mission. I was proud that I hadn't had to lean on Gus, or really involve him in the slightest. A bit of independence put a nice spring in my step. I whistled a low tune as The Forest grew steadily darker. If I was remembering correctly, I should be at the bridge in a minute or two.

However, a minute or two stretched into ten or twenty, and the darkness set in hard and fast. There was nothing subtle about night within The Forest's walls. The blackness smothered everything inside of the branches and opened up the door for creatures of the night.

The happy glow from the success of safely gathering the Dust of the Devil faded rapidly as I stumbled further into the darkness. The light at the end of the tunnel should have appeared by now. Normal watches didn't work on The Isle, but according to my inner clock I should have been halfway across the bridge and well on my way home. Even worse, none of my surroundings looked familiar.

Liam's words floated through my head: Have a goal when entering The Forest.

My heart sank. As I'd been floating on cloud nine and whistling my way back, I'd forgotten the most integral part of this entire trip. To remember why I'd come. I swore quietly, kicking myself for my forgetfulness. Now, the success of navigating The Forest alone, solving the riddle, and befriending a fairy was all overshadowed by one large, looming problem: None of it mattered if I couldn't find my way out.

A bird trilled in the distance, jolting me to attention. Hidden beings lurked behind every corner, and I realized with startling clarity that I had no way to differentiate between the deadly and the friendly. If it weren't for the fairy's generosity, I might already be dead.

Slowing my walk, I came to a standstill in the middle of a small clearing, the patch of clear grass surrounded by trees. Underbrush snaked out from the edges of the darkness, their tangled masses snarling over the grassy forest floor. I held my breath and listened.

At first, there were no sounds except for the whoosh of leaves brushing against one another, peppered with the staccato snap of twigs in the distance as creatures prowled outside of my line of sight. A dull thwacking repeated itself over and over again, nearly driving me insane until I found the source just on the outskirts of the clearing—a branch knocking against its tree trunk.

My shoulders relaxed for a moment as I watched the branch in its rhythmic song, relieved that the sound wasn't coming from something alive. However, my spine stiffened as something beyond the edge of the clearing caught my attention. I took a few steps closer.

As I reached the edge of the grassy patch, the object that'd caught my eye shone brighter. Except it wasn't an object per say, but the subtle glow of light. Squinting, I couldn't make out anything except for a dull, bluish aura—like that of a lava lamp. It neither illuminated The Forest nor provided a clear path. It merely existed.

Like a moth to a flame, I took a hesitant step outside of the clearing. My gut told me to turn back, since this could easily be a trap of some sort to draw me out of the open space and into the gnarly depths of the trees. But the fact of the matter was that I was utterly, completely lost.

If I didn't find a way out of here soon, I had no doubt that this night would be a tough one. At best, I'd survive a night in The Forest, curled up in a ball and terrified out of my mind. At worst, I wouldn't see morning. My only chance was to find help, and to find help, I needed to follow the light.

I stopped every few feet to listen, but there were no sounds at all now. It was quiet, too quiet. Another step brought me right up to the edge of a small island circled by a tiny babbling brook. It wasn't an island in the traditional sense. Instead, it reminded me of a castle surrounded by a moat. This moat sparkled, however, glistening with the subtle shimmer of magic.

Someone—a wizard—had been here. It might have been days, or weeks, or even months—but not longer than that. The sizzle of magic was fresh enough in the air that this spell couldn't be over a few months old. After a time, even the strongest of spells dimmed, and this one was still going strong.

I reached out a hand, tentatively feeling for any barrier or trigger, but there was nothing. My hand passed easily over the space above the water without ill effect. The temperature was much cooler. Cool enough that the skin on my arm broke out with goose bumps. When I retracted it to my side, it returned to normal.

The island in the middle of the water was small, about the same size as the clearing I'd just left. However, a thick fog shrouded the moat and prevented me from seeing past the water. It was from the center of the fog that the blue glowed brightest. I'd have to cross the stream to see what lay inside.

My gut told me to walk away, but my mind said differently. I wanted to step over the moat and into the fog, to find whatever was causing the light to glow blue. There was a chance I wouldn't make it, but...

I jumped over the fog and cleared the stream without much effort. I landed on the island, my body passing through the outer layer of fog and freezing my skin for one flash of time. When I landed on the ground in a crouched position, my hands up in a kung fu stance, all was quiet.

My skin returned to normal temperature, and the fog had all but disappeared. It'd moved to the outskirts of the small island once more. Instead of giving off a sense of foreboding, it now felt like a protective outer layer. Turning my gaze inward, I inhaled a deep breath. I'd discovered the source of the blue light.

I'd also found *The Magic of Mixology.*

CHAPTER 22

MY HEART RACED AS I rushed forward to scoop up my lifeline to the Mixology world. Just before my fingers touched the cover of the book, however, I paused and surveyed the surroundings. The grass here was lighter, a dulled, pale green compared to the rest of The Forest. Golden letters glinted up from the cover of the book, the words *The Magic of Mixology* spelled out in gorgeous penmanship. It'd been weeks since the spellbook had been taken from me—weeks filled with stress and unanswered questions. My hope of ever finding the book had been rapidly fading.

But now it lay before me. Perfectly intact and relatively untouched, the cover was closed, though a leaf poking out from the top of the pages made me think someone had flipped through it recently and saved a spell with nature's bookmark. I wanted to pick it up, hold it close to my chest and never let go, but I was too wary of a booby trap. There was magic nearby, I could feel it.

"What are you doing here?" I whispered aloud. "Who took you from me?"

I forced my eyes away from the spellbook and focused on the rest of the small island. On the far side, a few steps past the book, sat a small jar the size of Pooh Bear's honey pot. Underneath it, a small blue fire crackled, which was the source of the glow I'd seen from a distance.

Peeking into the miniature cauldron, I held my breath as a purple-blue liquid frothed and bubbled inside. A small ray of steam twirled up from the surface, and I took a step back, hesitant to inhale unknown fumes that were likely brewed by a thief.

I quickly scanned the rest of the grassy knoll, but there wasn't anything else out of place. A few sticks littered the ground while rocks the size of my fist created an embankment of sorts down to the bubbling brook. All of it appeared to be native to The Forest.

Returning to the book, I cautiously flipped the pages open to the leaf-marked spot. When nothing happened immediately, I scooched closer and read over the page, holding my breath until I reached the very end.

"That is not good," I said to myself. "Not good at all..."

Most of the words in this book had been carefully scripted in ink made from gold. The thin, twirly words had a timeless feel that easily had me believing they'd been written centuries ago by the original Mixologist. However on this page, the spell was handwritten in what looked like plain black ink. The writing was neat, drawn with the thick-to-thin swirls of a calligraphy pen and the smooth flow of a steady hand. Even so, it was new. So new that the page was devoid of normal wear and tear.

It wasn't the newness of the spell, or the lack of wear and tear on the page. The name of the spell is what gave me pause: Vitamins for Vampires.

After inspecting the list of ingredients, there was no doubt in my mind that this was the potion that'd been created for Poppy. At the very bottom of the list sat the mystery ingredient I had in my pocket. Dust of the Devil had been highlighted and circled with a red pen, and in the margins of the spell someone had written a note.

Swap for Hog's Vein.

The writing was different from that on the rest of the page. Likely, a new hand had recently penned this note, judging by the unfaded coloring. *Swap Hog's Vein?* This could easily be Gus's writing, but it also could belong to a chicken. The note had been scratched out and the handwriting was difficult to read. Gus normally wrote with painstaking clarity on the permanent labels, but I'd seen him jot down notes here and there for himself, and those resembled the handwriting of all men in the world—chicken scratch.

I sat back and crossed my legs, reading over the spell a few more times before letting my mind drift off into space. I stared at nothing in particular, running through a list of potential reasons the spellbook had ended up in The Forest. Why had the thief set up shop here? Sure it was secluded, but there had to be safer places to brew a potion. As for the Vamp Vites—that wasn't a particularly harmful mixture. The worst it'd do is upset a non-vamp's stomach for a few minutes. It was hardly dangerous, and it certainly wasn't deadly according to Gus.

Thinking of my mentor—who was back in the real world—made me remember that I was stuck in The Forest with no way out. I needed to get back. I scooped up *The Magic of Mixology* in my arms and gave one last look at the cauldron. From the pictures in the spellbook, this potion was a halfway-brewed vitamin for Poppy. According to the description, the potion bubbled blue and simmered purple. It wasn't until the Dust of the Devil was added that the potion assumed it's final, blood-red shade.

I'd leave the potion for now. If I found my way out of The Forest, Ranger X and I could come back. I wouldn't remember the directions, but he might be able to find the way. The first priority was to get out of here. The second was to talk to Ranger X, which was necessary to accomplish the third point: Find Gus.

Liam's words danced in my head once more as I leapt across the small stream around the teensy island. The flash of cold bit at my skin, but it was gone before I could shiver. *Have a goal*, my brain told me over and over again. I focused on the vision of the Upper Bridge, of talking to Ranger X and of weaving my way through The Forest with ease.

After a few hesitant steps, I found myself gaining confidence and picking up the pace. I couldn't have written directions on paper or explained them to a friend. But somehow, I knew the way out.

Whether it came from inside of me or from The Forest itself, I couldn't say. One step after another drew me in a curvy path, twisting and turning through the trees. The breeze acted as a whisper in my ear, guiding me away from the heart of the darkness.

I stumbled once. I was nearing the entrance, my body could feel it. However, as I turned to look at what I'd tripped over, all movement ceased and any thought of an end goal vanished. There, in the middle of the walkway, lay a cane. Gus's cane.

"There you are, pretty girl," a man's voice spoke in front of me. "You just about made it out of here. *Brava*, darling, *brava*."

"What do you want from me?" I asked, clutching the spellbook to my chest and willing my voice not to crack. "What'd you do to Gus?"

"Turn your pretty head around and follow me," he said, gesturing at my hands. Ribbons shot from his fingers, binding my wrists together as the book fell to the ground. He picked it up, stroking the cover with mild affection. "Come along now, come along. We have some fun waiting for you."

CHAPTER 23

THOUGH IT FELT LIKE I'D been walking for ages, I must not have gone very far at all. In a matter of minutes, we arrived back at the cauldron.

"What do you want from me?" I held my wrists out, the thin bindings straining against my skin. "These really aren't necessary."

"It won't be much longer." Thomas hummed a little ditty as he peeked into the cauldron, balancing the spellbook in his other hand. "It's almost ready."

"That looks like a potion invented to treat my cousin's blood-intolerance issues. It's not dangerous."

"Not yet." Thomas reached a long, thin stick into the potion and gave it a few swirls. He tapped the side of the cauldron to shake off the excess drops before facing me. "While we're waiting, entertain me. Tell me how you found out about everything."

I hesitated, but Thomas was looking over with an expression in his eye that told me he wasn't feeling generous. I cleared my throat, figuring it best to keep talking before his patience waned. "I overheard you talking with Gus and Harpin, but it didn't sound like the three of you were getting along."

At this, Thomas threw his head back and laughed, a clipped, calculated sound. His black cloak danced in the wind, the orange ribbon around his hood signifying his status not as a beginner, but also not as a master. "Many people work together without being friends."

"What were you working on?"

"Some people think they can change the world for the better." He shook his head, his eyes holding amusement that made my nerves rattle from my head to my toes. "It's funny. Naive, rather, especially when it's coming from a man of your grandfather's age."

"It's never too late to change the world."

"Even if your mentor, or whatever you call him, managed to bring about change for the better, what would that get him?"

I waited in silence.

"It'd get him nothing," Thomas finished. "Because he wouldn't be here to enjoy it. What's the point? Why not let someone else worry about it?"

My teeth ground against one another, and I wished my eyes could burn holes in this man's skull.

He sighed. "Then again, I suppose that's exactly why I'm here. Leaving the job for others to finish is *never* a good idea. I might as well do everything myself."

"What job?" My heart started thumping. "Are you with The Faction?"

"That's the whole problem with The Faction," he said, a flare of anger passing quickly across his face. "We started out small. Tight. Adaptable. Now, they've turned into a corporation. Meetings and budgets and rules and yada, yada, yada. I wouldn't be surprised if they started handing out medical benefits and a 401k."

"So you don't belong to The Faction anymore?"

"It's complicated." He shifted his weight from one foot to the next, his robes curling with the effort. "You wouldn't understand."

"Try me."

He hesitated, his forehead wrinkled in thought. "I brought a solution to the leaders, a solution that would end all of their problems, and do you know what they told me?"

I shook my head.

"They said they'd think about it. *Think* about it! I was their most loyal member, and after giving years of my life to them, they come back with… they'll *think* about it?"

"Maybe there were better options," I suggested reasonably. "That doesn't mean *no*."

"My plan would have worked," he said shortly. "You know nothing about the way. we work. They forced me to go out on my own."

"What was the plan?" I had a second thought that caused my stomach to flip flop. "Is Harpin working with you? Does he have Gus?"

"Harpin, Harpin, Harpin… he'll appreciate what I'm doing. Gus, not so much. He never liked me, that old man, but he had no choice except to work with me."

"Why not?"

"Have you heard of The Core?"

I blinked at the change of subject. "No."

"*Hmm*, I'm not surprised Gus didn't share his little secret with you."

"What is The Core?"

"A small group of wizards only. Cretan graduates mostly. At the moment, only five of us know of The Core's existence."

"Let me guess, you, Gus, and Harpin." I counted aloud. "I heard the three of you talking about some project on the path last night in front of that old ice cream hut."

"Ah, yes. Well, Gus was the second member to join the group. The three of us and Turin. Then, there's the leader, but he is unnamed. Nobody knows who he is, or what he's called, or where he's located. This leader handpicked a few members to join. Think of The Core as a resistance sort of group. A small cell that is flexible and able to pivot quickly in order to fight against The Faction."

"Gus's entry makes sense," I said. "But Harpin? Who let you and Harpin into the group?"

"I got in because of my background. Anyone entering The

Core must ingest the Truth Seeker potion and answer a series of questions under its influence."

"How did you pass the Truth Seeker test?"

"They asked me if I used to work for The Faction, and I said yes. They asked if I continued to work for The Faction, and I said no. Therefore, the leader of The Core deemed me invaluable. You see, I have contacts inside The Faction. I know things, and I have information that nobody on the outside could ever hope to learn."

"That doesn't answer my question."

"They forgot to touch on one crucial point. Although I don't work for The Faction, that doesn't mean I don't sympathize with their cause. I work for myself now. When they asked if I was joining The Core to fight The Faction, I said yes. It wasn't a lie. I *am* fighting them, but not in the way The Core had hoped."

I tried to recall the scene from last night, but my memory was choppy at best. "Why was Gus supposed to have information on me? Why did he need to prove himself?"

"Gus stole your little book," he said. "The leader gave him a test to see if he could keep a secret from you. As you weren't invited to be a part of the group, you weren't allowed to know any of the information. It was a test of his loyalty."

"He stole *The Magic of Mixology* to prove something," I said, more to myself than anyone else. It made sense. Gus had always had the means to do it. All I'd been missing was the motive. "He would've given it back."

"Maybe." Thomas shrugged. "Until I knocked him out early this morning. I needed that spellbook, and it was just my luck that Gus had lifted it from your safe."

"What did you do to him?"

"Unfortunately, Gus returned home too quickly after our meeting, and so he left me no choice but to immobilize him."

"Where is he? Why are you carrying out this plan? The Faction will never take you back."

"This isn't about The Faction anymore," he said. "Consider it a labor of love. The Faction doesn't realize the significance of what I'm doing yet, but someday they'll understand. Someday, they'll remember my name in stories."

He was crazy. Insane. My eyes flicked over toward the potion, and I struggled to find a way to keep him talking. "I thought you'd have selected a more dangerous potion if you wanted to make a splash in history."

"Oh, this potion is plenty dangerous when one swaps out a pinch of Dust of the Devil with a pinch of Hog's Vein."

My limbs froze. I hadn't put it together in the heat of the moment, but suddenly it all made sense. The ingredients used in Vamp Vites crossed over to make another potion—a deadly poison.

"Maybe Gus mentioned it?" Thomas peered down at me. "Hog's Vein can be a brutal killer."

"I don't focus on ingredients that hurt people."

"That's a shame. You might've recognized what was going on here if you'd paid more attention. Let me educate you." He paced in a slow circle around the bubbling cauldron before clasping his hands behind his back. "Hog's Vein changes the polarity of a spell. When swapped for half of the most difficult ingredient in any potion, it takes the healing natures of that spell and funnels them into one of destruction."

"Still, you can't possibly get everyone on The Isle to drink a mysterious potion. Even if you somehow managed to test it on one person—nobody would pick up the goblet after the first person died."

"It doesn't need to be ingested." He moved to the mini cauldron and sat down next to it. Wafting a hand over the steaming curl of smoke on the top, he inhaled deeply. "The danger is airborne. This potion is not yet ready, but I've brewed a trial run, and I'm confident it will work."

"How could you do that if you don't have Dust of the Devil?"

"I used a substitute ingredient that is not nearly as potent, but far easier to obtain. That batch was my practice run, and it worked. In fact, if you've been paying attention, you'll notice that a certain friend of yours has been suffering from bouts of nausea."

"Poppy? That's her withdrawal from the vitamins."

"Hmm. Vampires have highly increased senses, particularly hearing and smell. Therefore, your cousin would be impacted by even a pale imitation of the real thing..." he trailed off, glancing lovingly at the potion.

A chill ran down my spine. I had no antidote in the bungalow for an attack like this one. The simmering, purple color of the potion told me he hadn't yet added Hog's Vein, but a pinch of the final ingredient would give off a poisonous scent so strong Poppy wouldn't be the only one looking for help.

I frowned as he sniffed the mixture eagerly. "What's the point of it all?"

His eyes were still focused on the curling steam. "The point? I started out by pledging my life to The Faction. I swore to help them, dedicated my life's work to the cause." He stood up, eyes sharply pointed in my direction. "Even after I'd given them my soul, they let me down."

"I'm sure you're hurt, but there has to be a different way."

He glanced forlornly back at the bubbling potion. "This should get their attention."

"There are other ways to get their attention! We can come up with something together. I will help you if it means protecting the islanders. You have my word."

"I'll ask for your opinion if I want it," he snarled. "The only reason you're still alive is that Hog's Vein is hard to come by. So is Dust of the Devil, but you managed to secure plenty of that, so my needs shouldn't be an issue."

"I'm not helping you poison people. You heard my offer."

"You will help."

"Or what, you'll kill me?"

He slid a sideways glance in my direction before crossing his arms. "You don't believe I would?"

Something hitched in his voice, and I couldn't tell if it was excitement or fear. That something took a second to sink in, but when it did, I knew with certainty that the man had killed before. "You murdered the Black Ribbon wizard."

"Turin Jalop," he said. "Good wizard, from what I hear. I didn't have much personal experience with him until it was too late. As I said before, he was the fourth member of The Core. Ironically, out of five of us, two were double agents. While he'd infiltrated The Faction, I'd come from The Faction and infiltrated The Core. Fair is fair, I suppose."

"Why would you kill him? Don't you want the strongest wizards working with you? They can't be helpful if they're dead."

"But they're even less helpful if they're traitors," he snarled. "Turin was a long-time member of The Faction. Imagine my surprise when I found him sending messages back and forth with your mentor."

"Gus and Turin worked together before The Core?"

"Apparently their Black Ribbon bond was stronger than Turin's loyalty to The Faction, though I'm not convinced he was ever loyal."

I sat back in stunned silence, gathering my thoughts.

"You don't believe Gus was in on anything?" Thomas sneered. "You think your old man just puttered around the shop all day?"

"I'm not surprised," I said, realizing that was the truth. "Gus is many things, but a coward is not one of them. If he was working with Turin or against The Faction, it was because he believed in the cause. My loyalties are with him."

"I was afraid you'd say that," Thomas said slowly. "Which is why Gus is currently out of commission. I figured your death might not be enough of a bargaining chip. Unfortunately, I need you to work with me, so I created a backup plan. His name is Gus, and if you don't find me that Hog's Vein before tomorrow, then his death will be on your hands."

"I'll need to talk to a few people," I said, clearing my throat. There was no good way out of the situation, and my only option was to go along with the plan and stall as long as possible. "I didn't find Dust of the Devil on my own."

"I'm sorry, that's not allowed either." Thomas twisted his lips into a mock-apologetic grimace. "You and I are searching right here in The Forest. I have a timer set on Gus's location, and if I don't check in with a friend in time, it will open up a Suffocating Spell. The air will flow, leaving Gus thirty minutes to breathe before..."

He trailed off, the implication enough.

I opened my mouth to argue, but Thomas held up a hand.

"I wouldn't do that," he said carefully as he waved a hand in front of my body. The ribbons vanished from around my wrists. "You want to argue? I'll sit here and talk to you all day long, but that doesn't help either of us. Do you want your friend alive? Give me what I need."

CHAPTER 24

THIRTY MINUTES OF STUMBLING THROUGH the underbrush had gotten me nowhere except lost. Thomas followed close behind, his gaze piercing enough to bore deep holes into the back of my skull as I ducked under bushes and shimmied up tree trunks.

I needed to put on a good enough show to stay alive. The second Thomas sensed I was useless, I had no doubt he'd get rid of me for good. Not to mention Gus.

For Gus's sake, I ran through every plant name I'd learned since stepping foot on The Isle. Herbs and flowers, foods and drinks—none of it relevant. All I could recall about Hog's Vein was its "common" name. On the street, folks referred to it as the Switcheroo—named for its ability to turn a spell from good to bad in a heartbeat. For this reason, it wasn't kept in our storerooms. There was too much potential for accidental misuse.

Because the ingredient was not kept in stock, my knowledge of it was limited. I knew it grew in The Forest, thanks to Thomas, but that was about it. *The Magic of Mixology*, my beloved spellbook, had been left behind near the miniature cauldron.

Pausing for a breath as I stepped over a fallen log, I pictured the page of the book featuring Hog's Vein. Only a paragraph was featured there, along with a picture. The image of Hog's Vein was of a dainty little flower, contrary to its name. With long, skinny stems and teensy yellow flowers, it looked like a miniature daffodil.

"Are you going to stand up there all day?" Thomas shifted his weight from one foot to the other. "Time's a ticking, you know. For Gus, that's bad news. For you, that's bad news. For me? I can stand here all day."

"I was thinking," I growled. "I have never seen Hog's Vein in person, let alone gathered it in the wild."

"What were you thinking about?"

"I'm trying to recall a page from *The Magic of Mixology*! I'm sure you've read it—after all, you stole the book. If there's one thing that I'd hate more than having the book stolen in the first place, it'd have to be having the book stolen and knowing the person didn't appreciate it. At least do your due diligence and read the thing."

Thomas had the grace to blush. "Quiet."

"You haven't even read it."

"Tell me what it says!"

"I can't remember," I said dryly. "I just recall the picture."

He gave a derisive snort. "Those who live in glass houses—"

"There!" I pointed before he could finish his saying. "That yellow flower, do you see it?"

His gaze darted across the expanse of underbrush to where I pointed. He must have seen the photo in the book too, since his eyes widened at the sight. "You've found it."

I beat him to the small patch of flowers growing in the shade of a large, beautiful weeping willow. As soon as I bent over, I sensed something was wrong. "Wait," I said hesitantly. "These look correct, but I don't think they are."

"What are you talking about?" He kneeled next to the flowers and gently touched the stem of one. "These are perfect. In full bloom, just like I need."

"No." I shook my head, confident something wasn't right. I just couldn't put my finger on what. "Don't touch it."

"You're tricking me. You want me to believe this isn't right. I haven't had time to read the whole book, but I looked at the page on Hog's Vein. This is it."

"No, no, no," I murmured now to myself more than anyone else. "There's something wrong."

"Get out the vial. We're picking some."

I reached into my pocket, pretending to dig around for the vial, stalling for time as I fumbled with the fabric. What is it about those flowers? I closed my eyes, struggling to recall the text on the page next to the images of the tiny, sweet-looking flowers dressed to kill. "Wait!"

It was too late. He'd plucked one of the blossoms. I watched with horror as he held it up to his nose and took a sniff. "These smell nice."

Resting my fingers on the thin stems of the flowers, I focused on the details of the plant and let my hands dance up and down the long, twisty vines. Aloud, I muttered the phrase from the pages of the Mixology spellbook:

Daffodils and flowers gold—
Each one born from a matching mold.
On the stems you'll find the key—
A vein throughout guides you to me.

"These flowers don't have veins," I said slowly. "These are Trappers."

"What's a Trapper?" snarled Thomas, throwing down the flowers. "Did you do this on purpose?"

"No!" I shook my head. "Of course not. It was an accident."

"Why should I believe you?" He looked down at his hand, which was turning red from contact with the Trappers. "What have you done?"

"There's an antidote," I said breathlessly. "We need to get back to the bungalow. I can save you. I know the antidote," I lied. There was an antidote, but I didn't know it by heart. I was confident I could figure it out with the help of my spellbook, however. But that was only if—a very big if—we got back in time. "Let me help you. We have to hurry."

CHAPTER 25

"LOOK WHAT YOU'VE DONE!"

I winced as Thomas held his arm out for me to examine. His fingers had turned red first, but that redness had seeped up through his forearm and touched his elbow. In its place, a dark purplish shade had taken over, the skin stretching as the swelling began. "I warned you. If you hadn't touched it, this would never have happened."

"You led me to believe it was Hog's Vein."

"It looked like it from a distance, but that's the point of a Trapper!" I stepped forward and lightly held his palm in my hands. It was warm to the touch, and if we didn't get him to a place where I could whip up an antidote quickly, he wouldn't survive. The swelling alone would wreak havoc on his nervous system, if it hadn't already.

"How did you not know this was a Trapper?"

"The point of a Trapper is to mimic other plants. It's not a clever name," I said. "It's an obvious, practical one. The plant 'traps' unprepared users into choosing it over their intended target. The Forest is brimming with dangerous plants, you know that. This is one of many."

He flinched in pain. "Why didn't you touch it?"

"Patience saves lives," I said, parroting the fairy's advice. "If you look closely, you can see a difference." I pointed toward the stems on the small plant. "Imitation is the sincerest form of flattery, but even a Trapper can't imitate another plant perfectly. Hog's Vein is named for the tiny blue vein running through its stem. If you look closely, these Trappers don't have veins."

Thomas didn't look convinced, so I chanted the rhyme that'd tipped me off in the first place.

"If you'd read the book, you'd have seen that clue beside the picture," I explained. "I almost didn't catch it, but when you reached out, something jarred in my mind."

"How convenient." His face pinched in pain, his eyes widening as he looked down. "It's spreading."

I pulled his arm closer to me, my fingers following the red and purple as it crept past his elbow. "We have to hurry. The chances of sparing someone's life after the Trapper's venom has spread past one extremity is low."

"It's nearly up to my shoulder!"

"We need to move fast," I said, pulling him along. "How do we get out of here?"

"Why should I trust you?" He yanked his arm from mine.

"If I wanted to kill you," I said harshly, "I'd just sit down and watch you die."

Our gaze met in a fiery battle of wills. This time, his crumbled first. "To the left. Follow that path, and then turn right every time you see a Lily of the Valley."

I guided him down a path formed from overhanging tree branches and a lack of brush beneath our feet. Now that I was looking for Lily of the Valley, the path seemed to appear before my eyes, almost as if someone had flicked on a flashlight and pointed the way forward. One cluster of little white flowers appeared after the next, and each time we hung a right, a new batch of scenery appeared. No more traipsing in circles and dancing between the trees. My feet were sure, though Thomas stumbled behind me now and again.

"Stop looking at your arm," I said. "If you keep falling we'll never make it."

He stopped walking completely. "We aren't going to make it anyway. Look."

I whirled around, the sight of his infected arm now grotesque. It lay useless against his side, thick as a club and purple as an eggplant. "I'm going to lose my arm."

"Maybe," I said. "But that doesn't mean you have to lose your life."

"I'm not afraid to die," he said. "For the cause."

"What cause? Your only chance of help is me. We are deep within these trees." I raised my arms to show the thick woods surrounding us. "I don't care how loudly you fall, there is no one around to hear it. Except me. If you think I'm going to spread the 'word' of your cause, you're wrong."

"How'll you explain my body?"

"I won't have to. I can't possibly carry you out of here, and by the time I get back..." I let the sentence hang, and a cluster of hoots and calls from the animals walking over The Forest floor cemented my point. "There won't be much to explain."

"I prefer to die."

"I'm not letting you," I said. "I can't do it."

"Why?"

I chewed on the thought a moment, not quite sure myself. Thomas wanted us dead, and he wanted to die. So why was I fighting so hard to keep him alive? "Did you open *The Magic of Mixology?*"

"Of course I did."

"Did you read anything beyond the page on how to brew your poison?"

His silence gave me the answer.

"Well, if you had, you would've seen an inscription." I folded my arms over my chest. "On the first page of the spellbook there is one line. Two words only. It's written in the hand of the first Mixologist. I imagine you can't guess what it is?"

A subtle shake of his head prompted me to continue.

"*Do Good.*" I took a step closer, my eyes not leaving his face. "That's it. Simple. I don't like you, but I have my own cause I'm working for, and I won't abandon it, even now. Contrary to what you may think, we do have something in common."

Thomas gave a wry sort of laugh. It bordered on apologetic, though it was cut with a heavy layer of mirth. "No, we don't."

"Belief," I said firmly. "Faith in a system. You believe in something that is beyond us all. Beyond the human touch. Beyond ordinary life. You believe in an idea and a way of life, just like I do. The only difference is that yours is a broken, vicious dream, and mine is simple."

Thomas snorted. "Just wait until someone lets you down. It's only a matter of time, Lily. You've been on The Isle for a few short weeks and your optimism is sickening. Sickeningly sweet, like a vial of Lilac Sugar."

"Better sweet than sour."

"That's not how it works. Everyone has their breaking point. For me, that point has come and gone. You'll see someday. Someone will hurt you badly enough that even you, Miss Lily, won't be able to forgive."

"There's a difference between forgiving and forgetting," I said. "To forgive is to take the high road. To forget is to be foolish. If you forgive someone just one more time than they betray you, the bitterness stays away."

Thomas's gaze turned softer, almost resigned, as he glanced down at his arm. "Maybe. I almost wish I could live just to watch you, to see if this life gets to you—if the terrors of this earth seep into your mind and disillusion your dreams. Maybe, just maybe, you'll be able to fight it. For how long?" He shrugged. "You're resilient. Maybe you'll make it to your death. Then again, maybe you'll have an early death like me. We are similar, you know."

His words shook me back to reality. "You're not dying. I'm not letting you. Come on."

Waving my hand for him to follow, I spotted the next bunch of Lilies of the Valley and swung a hard right. However, when I turned to see if Thomas was behind me, there was only an empty path. An empty path flanked by a familiar flower—a healing flower.

"Thomas! I found something!" I cried out as I sprinted toward huge, thick leaves of aloe.

The plants on this island were different, though some of them went by the same name as the human world. These leaves were large, filled with healing salve, and a quick spell murmured by an even the most inexperienced witch or wizard would invoke the soothing qualities of the plant.

"Come here!" I stood up, lugging the leaf in my arms like a stuffed animal. "I've found something."

Whipping around the corner, I came to a screeching halt. Thomas still sat on the log. Cradling his arm over his legs like a child, he didn't glance up at my shouts.

He turned his gaze up to me, his eyes first resting on the aloe in my arms. "That won't save my life. If I'm lucky, it'll stave off the infection until you can brew an antidote. Then what? You call your boyfriend and have him drag me off to jail?"

I ignored the boyfriend comment. "You tried to kill me. You stole my property. What do you expect?" I stepped forward, at the same time cracking open the aloe leaf and smoothing balm over my hands as I muttered a simple spell.

As soon as I finished the chant, my hands began to glow as if surrounded by halos. The spell turned the thick sap from the plant into a healing glove. I lightly pressed my warm fingers to Thomas's arm. He flinched when my skin touched his, but some of the pain seeped immediately from his face, and he stopped resisting. Instead, he closed his eyes and let me apply the salve.

I started at the top, at the place where his shoulder met his body, and applied it in a circle to stop the advance of the infection.

Once I had a barrier against the infection spreading to the rest of his body, I stood up. "You won't die."

"The rest of my arm," he spluttered. "Apply it!"

"Let Gus go." I nodded toward the Comm Device circling his wrist. I recognized its similarity to the one Ranger X had given me a while back. Unfortunately, it was on my dresser at home. "Let Gus go, and I'll apply the rest of the Aloe."

Fury flashed in his eyes. "And you think I'm the monster?"

I struggled to keep my face passive. "Just let Gus go. I'm not asking for anything unreasonable. Think about it, Thomas. Who'll continue your work after you're gone? Not Gus. Not Harpin. From what it sounds like, you don't have anyone."

Thomas bowed his head, as if my words were a surprise sucker punch to his gut. The wheels turned in his brain, and I could almost hear the gears clicking as the notion sunk into his skull. Then, without looking up, he raised the Comm Device to his lips and activated it with a breath as he spoke quietly. "Let Gus go."

I licked my lips. "How do I know it's done?"

In an answer, Thomas held up his wrist. A moment later, it crackled with a response. "Are you sure?"

"Let him go, and then get out of there. Vanish," Thomas said, "and make sure I never see you again."

A long pause followed. Then there was a blink of a red light, a crackle of static, and the voice came back. "It's done."

Thomas looked up. "Are you happy?"

My heart ached with hope. There was no way to be absolutely certain Gus was free, but I was a woman of my word, and I stepped forward and laid my hands on Thomas's arm. The healing began immediately, and the relief in his sigh shook the leaves of the trees overhead. It took longer than normal due to the advanced stage of the infection.

Ten minutes later, sweating and breathing heavily, I stepped back. "It's done. You'll have that bruise for a week, but it should fade. You may experience a slightly numbed sensitivity in the nerves of your fingers, but with a bit of luck, that'll return to normal as well. You'll still need to take the antidote within twenty-four hours, or your symptoms will come right back. Come with me to the bungalow."

"I'll have to have someone else prepare it," he said slowly, turning his arm over before his eyes. Light streaks of blue wove around his arm where his veins had swelled. He flexed his fingers. "It's a shame about the sensitivity."

I reached into my pocket for the ring of pepper spray around my keychain. Sometimes, non-magical weapons worked wonders on wizards. They didn't expect it, and their counter-curses didn't work against it. "The sensitivity should return shortly."

"Not shortly enough." He looked up, his smile twisted. "Because the time has come for you to die, and I only wish I could feel it."

I raised the pepper spray and turned to run, but he was faster. Before I could move, he propelled himself off the log toward me, his hands clasped around my throat. He squeezed tight, so tight that my breath vanished and all I could do was lock eyes with him as his voice turned into a sing-song chant. "Good-bye, Lily."

CHAPTER 26

THE BLACKNESS CAME SWIFTLY. My senses shut down, the last buzzes and scuffles from The Forest spiraling into a muted cacophony at the base of my skull. The lack of oxygen burned my lungs, and I thrashed like a drowning victim.

No amount of arm flailing and leg kicking spurred Thomas into letting go. If anything, he gripped tighter, pushed harder, and smiled brighter the more I struggled until...

Until I couldn't struggle any longer.

The orchestra banging deep in my brain finished its song, the last notes of the melody faded to nothingness. As the curtain fell before my eyes, I sank deeper into the blackness, welcoming it, begging for it to come faster. I fought hard to remember what had brought me here in the first place, but even that pivotal information eluded me. As my body stilled, I had nothing.

"Lily..."

Through the blackness, my name sounded from a voice that was neither alive nor dead. The word wasn't spoken aloud, but neither was it whispered or thought or dreamt. It merely was.

"Open your eyes."

It was an uphill battle to peel my eyelids open, but I managed it after a few failed attempts. My thoughts were a confused mess, and I couldn't say whether I was alive or dead or floating somewhere in between. "Where am I?"

I thought I spoke the words, but my lips didn't move. None of my body moved. I stared straight upwards, but instead of seeing the face of the man who'd killed me, I saw only white.

White all around—the sort of white that made me feel walled in from all sides. Captive, but free, all at once. This new place was full of contradictions: it had no name, but it existed. I was awake, but not alive. I heard voices, but nobody was speaking.

"Look at me, please. I have limited time."

The voice grew clearer. I tried to squint, but my eyes wouldn't move. Anything I tried resulted in frustration. My limbs were frozen, all the way from my eyelids to my toes.

"How can I look?" The words were accompanied by a slight echo. "Why don't my lips move? I can't look. I can't move at all."

"Listen to my voice. Listen to your name. Do you know who I am, Lily?"

The careful way he said my name shook life into my mind, and a flood of memories came rushing back. Ranger X's lips hot on mine as we kissed under the moon. Gus's careful precision as he guided me through The Elixir potion. The man with the black hood and black ribbon floating onto shore.

"You drank The Elixir," I said with finality. The gravelly tone in the man's voice had disappeared after his death, as if the only thing keeping it there had been the weight of the world on his shoulders. When he spoke now, it was with the lightness of a child and the experience of a grandfather. I found myself trusting him inherently. "Your name is Turin."

As soon as I said his name, the outline of his body solidified. He appeared before me like a mirage, and I remembered Ranger X's warning that names had power.

"Yes, it's true," Turin said. "Names are powerful things. They attach you to something—or someone—who is real. Listen, Lily."

His use of my name jolted me awake again. My vision had begun to blur, the light flashing into a rainbow of disorientation.

I gasped for air, my lungs constricting. "Am I dead?"

"You are not alive," he said carefully. "Listen to me. I took The Elixir to help you. I'd already been poisoned when I requested it—"

"By Thomas?" I asked. "Did Thomas kill you?"

"It doesn't matter now. What matters is that I was already gone. By taking The Elixir, I exchanged a few minutes of life for a few minutes to help you, and that's why I'm here now."

"You shouldn't have done—" My voice was raspy, and I couldn't finish my thought.

"I wanted to. I needed to—I must give you one last thing."

"I can't move," I whispered, the whiteness morphing into a blinding flash of light. "I can't..."

"When you wake, clench your palm. I've set something in your fist, a piece of your past that will help with your future. I'm sorry, I wish that I could save you, but I don't have that power. I'll be gone as soon as you wake, and you'll be left to save yourself. When I touch your forehead you will have three breaths to make your wish. One, two..."

"Wait!" I cried, just as he said the word three.

All at once the pain came crashing back, a wave as large as the one that'd welcomed me onto The Isle, but far more intense. Ice shot through my veins, slicing my insides, burning through my limbs. My breaths were stifled, but the hands around my neck had let go. As I forced my eyes open, I saw the back of Thomas. He was walking away, but at the sound of my desperate gulp of air, he whirled around. The shock on his face told me that he'd thought I was dead.

Breath number one. The count had begun.

I clenched my fist tight, the smoothness of the item jogging my memory to that moment on the beach. The salty air whipping across my face as Ranger X's fingers twisted into my hair. The warmth of his kiss washed over me and desire filled my stomach, giving me the strength to concentrate.

Breath number two.

Thomas started toward me.

Angel's Breath. I tried not to breathe, floundering as I reached through blackness to remember his words that night. Angel's Breath allows for one wish... It hit me, Turin's instructions and Ranger X's voice all at once.

Fury turned Thomas's face into an ugly mask as he lunged for me, his arm outstretched. As his fingers clasped my wrist he looked down, his eyes locking on my clenched palm as he swiped at my clothes and tore at my limbs. He let out a howl as he realized what was in my palm, but not before I closed my eyes, made a wish, and took my last breath.

CHAPTER 27

THE SOUNDS OF THE FOREST played quietly in the back of my skull. Unlike the harsh screech and dizzying swirls of sounds that'd ushered in unconsciousness, the chirps of birds and rustle of leaves tinkled a soothing background track as I regained awareness.

My eyelids lay heavily closed, my breathing even. Though I was aware of my consciousness, I had no desire to open my eyes. A part of me thought I was dead. I hoped against hope that wasn't true, but another part of me was too scared to check.

Instead, I focused on the feel of my chest rising and falling. I noticed the air exhaling between my lips and the pounding of my heart against my ribcage. As I lay still and focused on the sounds and movements around me, another noise joined the mix.

Snoring.

When I'd been alive, I had never snored. I wasn't about to start now, especially if I was dead.

More likely, someone was in the room with me.

Opening my eyes, I saw white. Except this time, the white wasn't an absence of darkness nor a flash of brilliance. It was just the ceiling.

I swept my gaze over the surroundings: I lay in a bed. A familiar bed, though it wasn't mine. Logs lined the walls, the fresh, woodsy scent bringing me back to cabin days on the lake.

The bare kitchen to my right was unmistakable. My eyes dropped to the figure sprawled over an armchair in the corner of the room, a new addition since I'd last been hauled into Ranger X's hut. Maybe someday I'd end up here for a reason other than trouble. One could dream.

I hardly noticed my own breath hitch as I took in Ranger X's ragged appearance. He wore a suit fit for a wedding, which led me to believe he'd come straight from the office. The neckline was open, his tie swung loose over his shoulder. The dark, thick shock of hair on his head had been ruffled one too many times and stood up in boyish disarray.

Even in sleep, his expression gave off a concerned look, as if he were concentrating on something important that I could never understand. His chest rose and fell in regular motions, and I imagined it matched the strong beat of his heart, a beat I longed to hear again as I rested my head on his chest.

While analyzing Ranger X's body, I hadn't noticed his eyes open. He cleared his throat, and drew my attention away from where I'd been staring, at the open patch of shirt dipping just a bit too low to be professional.

My face warmed as I jerked my eyes off his chest and back to his face. I relaxed almost immediately under the soft glimmer of his expression, his dark eyes glistening with sleep. "Hi."

"Hi," I murmured. There was so much more to be said, but no good place to start.

Thankfully, Ranger X took over. Kicking his feet to the ground, he pulled himself into a standing position and crossed his arms over his chest. "How are you feeling?"

I raised a hand to my forehead. "I'm okay, I think. Very confused."

Ranger X's face went slack with surprise, and then he laughed. "I'd imagine so."

"Why are you sleeping over there?" I offered a shy smile, patting the bed next to me. "I mean, we've already had a non-date. We might as well have a non-sleepover. You'll crick your neck sleeping in the chair like that."

"I didn't want to leave, and I don't make a habit of climbing into bed with unconscious ladies who prefer getting in trouble to asking for help."

"Come here." I patted the bed again. For some inexplicable reason, I wanted him close. I needed to touch someone solid. Feel something real. "Can you hold my hand?"

Two steps brought him across the room, his long legs carrying him with a grace I envied. Despite his mass, he moved without a trace of footsteps. With careful precision he seated himself on the bed next to me, cautious not to ruffle the mattress. He raised a tentative hand and combed it through the tips of my hair sprawled loosely across the pillow. "Is this better?"

I looked into his eyes, complex as multi-faceted diamonds, and I nodded. "Thank you."

"Do you hurt anywhere?"

I shook my head quickly at his concerned gaze. "I'm fine. A little sore maybe."

"You've got scratches on your arms."

"Probably the branches from The Forest," I said, my lies bringing forth the last images of Thomas clawing at my arms. "What happened?"

Ranger X's expression hardened. He didn't believe me. "I was wondering the same thing."

Clearing my throat, I gathered up the last of my willpower and explained in great detail the events leading up to my foray into the dangerous wilderness. His eyebrows knitted in concern when I described Dust of the Devil, and he nodded in approval after I explained the trick to the Trappers. His eyes burned black when I mentioned Thomas, and a shade of sadness passed by at Turin's parting words.

When I finished, his hand stilled, a thin lock of my hair twisted around his fingers. "Why didn't you ask for my help?"

"There wasn't time. I knew you wouldn't let me go alone, and I needed to do this for Poppy. You were busy looking for Gus, and if it weren't for Thomas, I would have succeeded just fine without you."

"That wasn't smart."

"Sometimes risks are worth taking."

His eyes scanned mine, but I didn't relent. It was easy to meet him eye-to-eye when I had nothing to hide. So when he looked away, the hairs on the back of my neck rose.

"What aren't you telling me?"

"There's one piece of this puzzle that I'm missing," he said. "What brought—"

He didn't have time to finish his question because at that moment, Poppy threw the door open and burst into the room, followed closely by Zin.

"We were waiting outside like Ranger X asked," Poppy trilled. "But when I heard you talking I just couldn't wait any longer. How are you, dear?"

My cheek squished against Poppy's chest as she wrapped me tight in a hug. "Fwine," I mumbled against her skin. "Cwan't breathe."

X gently pulled her back. "She's been suffocated enough today without your help."

"Oh, right." Her eyes turned with worry toward my neck. "How are you?"

"I'm fine," I said for what felt like the ninetieth time. My hand subconsciously flew to my neck as she and Zin continued to stare. "What's wrong?"

Poppy winced. "It's just… you have a bit of…"

Zin pulled a small mirror from inside her pocket and stepped forward. Without a word, she opened up the compact and showed me the image.

My breath burned, the inside of my throat still raw, as I took in the angry red marks streaking up my neck. Purplish bruises the shape of small coins dotted the sides of my neck where Thomas's thumbs had pressed, and my arms were rife with scratches—both human and otherwise. I finally managed a forced smile. "It looks worse than it is."

"The wounds will heal," Ranger X said, fighting to keep his face stony. "I've used so much salve since you stumbled onto this island I'm going to have to start ordering it in bulk."

"How did I get here?" I gingerly rubbed my neck. "What happened to Thomas?"

At my last question, all three of the others exchanged glances that told me I didn't want to know the answer. Finally, Ranger X broke the silence. "It was Zin. She found you and took care of Thomas. If she hadn't gotten there in time, things might have turned out quite differently."

Poppy nodded in agreement. "It was incredible. I was with Zin when it happened. She just shifted into the most beautiful animal I'd ever seen. We don't have a word for them on The Isle, but Ranger X said you call them jaguars on the mainland."

"Those are much more intimidating than a turtle or mosquito." I got a laugh out of Poppy and a smirk from Ranger X, but Zin looked less than amused. "I'm sorry, I shouldn't joke. How did you know I was in trouble?"

"Animal instincts?" Poppy grinned. "Cat's intuition?"

The color left Zin's already pale face. She was light-skinned on a normal day, but now she bordered on ashy. The deathly pallor of her skin was offset drastically by the sharp bob of her jet-black hair and her dark mascara and lipstick. "Can I have a word with you, Lily? Alone?"

Poppy gave a sniff and opened her mouth to protest, but Ranger X beat her to it. He rested his fingers lightly on her elbow and tilted his head toward the door.

"I have to speak to you anyway, Poppy," he said softly. "May I?"

Looking slightly appeased, she nodded. "I suppose. At least someone wants me around."

Once they'd left, Zin stood stiffly with her arms crossed.

"Thank you for saving my life," I said after a long moment of silence.

Zin squinted in my direction. "What happened?"

"What are you talking about? I was going to ask you that very same thing. The last thing I remember is Thomas's hands around my neck before I went unconscious. I only came to a few minutes ago. I don't remember anything in between."

My cousin didn't look convinced. "Why'd you do it?"

"Go into The Forest? I was looking for Dust of the Devil so I could finish Poppy's Vamp Vites. I'm sorry I didn't mention it sooner—"

"No," she said. "Why'd you bring me in to help?"

I gave a confused shake of my head. "You're speaking gibberish. I just told you the last thing I remember is passing out."

"There're rumors circling The Isle right this very moment." Zin paced around the outskirts of the room. "Rumors about me."

I smiled. "About your heroics? You deserve them. I'll put the rumors to rest and make them facts."

Zin studied the ground, still not amused. I fell back on the pillow, closed my eyes, and waited for her next move. I had a creeping suspicion what those rumors might be, but I wanted her to come out and say it first.

"They say I'll be announced as a Ranger Candidate in the next cycle," she blurted. "The next cycle is only weeks away."

My eyes shot open. "That's incredible!" I surveyed her tense expression, which showed no signs of pleasure at the news. "Why the long face?"

"Do I deserve it?"

"Tell me what happened in The Forest."

"You really don't remember?"

I shook my head.

Zin blew out a breath. "I was with Poppy when it happened. Someone, or something... I don't know how to describe it." Her eyebrows knitted together in concentration as she recounted the story. "We were in the middle of a conversation and it was as if someone were tugging at my arm and telling me to run… Run fast."

I waited patiently as she paced a few more laps around the room.

"It wasn't a person. It wasn't a ghost or a spirit—at least, not one that I could see. Poppy says she didn't see or hear anything. She looked at me like I was insane to even ask about strange voices." Zin's gaze locked on mine. "Am I insane, or do you know what I mean?"

"How can you think you're insane when you saved my life? Maybe it was intuition. There are plenty of explanations."

"There aren't," Zin said forcefully. "There aren't a lot of explanations. Whatever, or whoever it was, told me to run to you. I had no clue where you were, what you were doing, why you were there, but I did it anyway. I've never shifted into a jaguar form before but it suddenly felt so natural, as if I were putting on an old winter jacket after a summer in the closet."

"Is it your final form?" I raised my shoulders. "I don't know what that feels like. Maybe you can talk to another shifter."

"I won't know until I can shift in and out easily," she said. "It's impossible to know from a single instance, but from what others say, this might be it."

"That's not a bad final form," I said with a small smile. "They're beautiful creatures and very intense. Just like you."

Zin paused, digesting the compliment before continuing. "The rumors of my Candidacy came from inside of Ranger Headquarters. Poppy told me."

"I've always said you deserve to be a Ranger. Just as much as the next man."

"That's my issue with this whole thing." Zin rounded on me, her finger poised on her lip in thought. Her smooth movement reminded me of the jaguar she'd become hours before, and I had a sudden flashback to a moment in The Forest. I'd swam in and out of an unconscious haze, drawn to reality by the threatening growl of the large, sleek forest cat. At the time, I hadn't known it was Zin. As the memory replayed in my mind, I recognized the similarities as she'd leapt for Thomas, claws outstretched...

"What did you do?" Zin's voice jerked me from the memory. "How did you call me to you? Something led me to The Forest, and I want to know what."

I blinked away the images of Thomas, his screams as he fell off of me. "I don't know."

Zin narrowed her eyes at me.

I swallowed, trying to avoid the question. I didn't know what had brought Zin to The Forest, but I did know that I'd held the stone of Angel's Breath in my palm, and I'd wished for one final thing as I'd taken my last breath. "I didn't call you to The Forest."

"Then who did? Or what?"

When I didn't respond, she glided toward the edge of the bed, her arms and legs moving in combined grace. Her eyes glinted with a shimmer of gold, as if the jaguar hadn't fully left her body, as if a part of it had taken hold within Zin and stayed. Her new confidence, the way she moved, that watchful gleam in her eye—all of it was more pronounced than it had ever been before.

"Tell me what you know," she said quietly. "This is important."

"It doesn't change anything," I said. "You still deserve to become a Ranger."

"Do I?" she asked icily. "Do I deserve it? Or is it a fluke that will eventually get someone killed? If they name me a Candidate and I'm not up for the job, it's not just my life at stake, it's everyone's."

"I know that," I said quietly. "It doesn't change my mind."

"A few weeks ago, Ranger X pulled me aside." Zin turned her back to me, staring out the window to where X and Poppy sat at a makeshift picnic table deep in conversation. "He told me what it meant to be a Ranger. Do you know what he said?"

I had a feeling I knew exactly what he'd said, but I felt uncomfortable repeating it, so I shook my head.

Zin looked over her shoulder at me. "He said he had nothing against a female joining the Ranger team. He thought with enough training, there was a chance I could even join the program."

"Of course you could."

"Then he told me he'd never appoint a Ranger who he didn't trust a hundred percent to save the life of someone he loved. And that is the ultimate criteria."

"Ranger X doesn't love anyone," I said hoarsely. "It's against the rules."

"That's what I told him." Zin turned the rest of the way to face me. "He just blinked. Then he said the times are changing. I don't know what that means."

"I'm sure he meant that he'd never seriously considered a woman becoming a part of the Ranger program before. You're paving the way for women across The Isle."

"I'm not so sure that's what he was getting at," she said. "I can tell when someone is lying. Call it… animal instincts."

Her joke caught me off guard, and I gave an awkward laugh.

"When he talked about loving someone, he wasn't exaggerating. He wasn't lying, and he wasn't stretching the truth. There's only one person on this island he's ever looked at through eyes not focused on work."

"What does this conversation have to do with anything?"

"If I become a Ranger, and I can't protect you because I'm not fit for the job…" she shook her head. "I couldn't live with myself. Ranger X would probably kill me, and that'd be a welcome punishment. So I need you to tell me what happened."

"Zin, it's not like that."

Finally slowing her pacing, she crossed the room and sat on the edge of the bed. "I want to become a Ranger more than anything in this world, except one thing. I want the safety of my family and friends first. If I don't deserve to be a Ranger, I need to know now. The next cycle is in three weeks, and the rumors are swirling loud and clear. I'd rather put them to rest before they grow legs and have me believing in something that's not true."

I sat up in bed, my neck muscles screaming with the effort. I ignored the pain and shifted against the pillows behind my back. "If I know one thing, it's that you deserve this more than anyone in the world. You work the hardest. You care the most. Your morals are the strongest. If the rumors are swirling, I'll be the one to put them to rest—with the facts. The fact is that you deserve to become a Candidate."

"Not if this was a fluke," she said, shifting her weight. The discomfort showed in her face as a pinkish-tinge lightened her cheeks. "Did you or did you not bring me there?"

Even after Turin had visited me in that lucid dream, I hadn't believed that I could survive for longer than three breaths despite his promises. It was too late. Thomas had taken too much of my life away, and he would only squeeze harder once he saw me breathing again.

My pulse raced at the memories, and my hand caressed my neck where ghost fingers still pressed against my windpipe. I hadn't used my wish to save myself. I'd wished that Zin would find the strength to become a Ranger. On the verge of death, it'd been the only thing to cross my mind, but now I struggled with how to explain that to her.

"I didn't bring you there," I said firmly. "Any actions you made were yours alone. I'll be honest, Zin, I don't entirely know what happened, and that's the truth." It *was* the truth. I had never expected she'd come racing to my rescue. "The only thing missing right now is confidence in yourself. Ranger X has appointed many men over the years into these positions. He knows what he's looking for, and if he says he wants you on his team, nobody will argue with that. Anyone who says otherwise is speaking from jealousy or envy. If you're the best for the job, then you deserve it."

"How can I deserve a job when I can't explain what happened?"

"You've prepared for months. Years, even. If you hadn't, you'd never have been able to save my life, even if someone had guided you into The Forest and handed you a map on a silver platter. The only thing preventing you from accepting the Candidacy is the belief that you can do it."

"You believe I can do it?"

A smile curved my lips upward, and I reached for her hands. "More than anything."

She stood up, pressing a hand to her forehead in shock. "I can't believe it. I can't believe it! Ranger X mentioned when I came in here that he wanted to talk to me about the next cycle." Her black eyes now tinged with gold locked on mine. "I can't believe it's happening."

"Go talk to him," I said, nodding outside where Ranger X and Poppy were shamelessly staring at us through the window. Based on the tilt of Poppy's head, she was trying to eavesdrop. "It sounds like we've got a lot to celebrate."

CHAPTER 28

L ATER THAT EVENING, RANGER X and I set out for a walk. Poppy and Zin had spent the rest of the afternoon at the cabin, and together we played card games and chatted about nothing in particular. Poppy prepared food while Zin babbled on and on about her training with Hettie.

The smile on her face only grew as the hours stretched on, and the gold in her eyes didn't fade for a second. We didn't discuss Thomas, or the events of the previous evening. We didn't even bring up Zin's hopes for Ranger status. The four of us were merely content to while away the hours with happy chatter, good food, and a bit of wine.

It wasn't until the night began to creep in, cloaking the sun in darkness, that Ranger X's glances in my direction became more frequent. His eyes would lock on mine with a sudden intenseness before he looked away, back to his hand of cards or at the plate of food in front of him.

Eventually even Poppy noticed the pattern, and without further ado, she cleared her throat and excused herself and Zin. When Zin protested, Poppy elbowed her cousin and gave a very obvious head tilt in my direction. Zin's sharp eyes took in Ranger X in a flash, and before she could argue again, Poppy had dragged her out of the room with promises to return in the morning.

Ranger X's cabin-like home was just inside the edges of The Forest. I shivered as we set out, the dark tree trunks shooting me back to a less than pleasant time. Without asking, Ranger X reached over and took my hand. My fear all but disappeared as he squeezed it, and when he turned his eyes on my face, the rest of my worries vanished. Before I knew it we were on the beach, the full moon providing plenty of light as I kicked my sandals off and dug my toes into the cooling sand.

"You look beautiful tonight." His words broke the quiet lull in the air. Even the backdrop of waves faded to white noise as he cleared his throat. "Then again you always do, but there's something about the moon that brings out your eyes."

I looked up in surprise. "Are you feeling okay?"

He laughed, the sound a low rumble in the night that sounded like nature. His voice blended with the waves and the breeze as if he were part of the outdoors himself. "I'm fine."

"You're usually not so..." I hesitated. "Expressive?"

"Let's just say that I understand what people mean when they argue that sometimes, it takes a tragedy to bring two people together." His eyes softened, the intensity of his expression disarming. Extending a hand, he brushed it through the hair at the base of my neck. I'd showered at his place and left my hair down to dry in natural waves, and as he pulled the locks tight, my eyes fell shut. As he pulled me close, his words floated out on a breath of air. "I'm one of the lucky ones."

"Lucky?"

"Lucky," he repeated roughly. "I can't explain what I felt when I thought you were gone. Zin dragged you here and you were scraped and bleeding and breathless. Your chest was still when I said your name..." He fell silent for a moment. "I said your name, and your eyelids didn't so much as flutter. I thought you were gone."

His lips pressed against my forehead as I leaned into his body and wrapped my arms around his waist. I squeezed. "I'm here. I'm alive, thanks to Zin and you. Don't worry, I'm not going anywhere. I hear I'm pretty hard to get rid of—a few people have tried, and that's the general consensus."

My humor missed the mark, but my arms around his waist were right where they needed to be. Ranger X gripped me tight, his hands grasping my arms as he placed a gentle kiss on my head. When he spoke, he pulled back enough to make eye contact. "Lily, I care so much about you. I think—"

I raised a finger to his lips and pressed it against them. "Not now. Whatever you're going to say, just wait. Think about it before you speak. You're stressed, and emotional, and..." I sighed. "You're a Ranger. You know the rules. You're not allowed to get married, or... or have anything resembling a real relationship."

He began to speak, but I shook my head and he fell silent.

"I'd never come between you and your career. I know how much it means to you. Whatever you say now is influenced by the situation. Your emotions are running high, and you're not thinking with your head."

"I don't think you realize how much you mean to me." He didn't flinch as he said the next line. "I'd give it all up for you in a second, and that became crystal clear when you were lying in my arms next to dead. In that moment, I didn't remember a thing about being a Ranger. My training was all but useless, and my instincts were dull. The only thing I could do was hold you and hope. I was useless. I didn't choose to fall for you, Lily, but it happened somewhere along the way and I'm afraid it's too late to go back."

I couldn't speak. My hands reached for him of their own accord, my fingers running up and down his arms as my mind fought to find the words to say. "I care about you a lot too. More than you know," I said finally. "But I can't interfere with your job."

"You already have. It's dangerous for me to think I can protect you. When Zin brought you back, I should have leapt into business mode, but I didn't. I was helpless. I froze. I have never frozen before, and I've seen friends and family die. I've fought the worst and trained with the best, but at the end of the day... I was crippled by what I feel for you."

I sucked in a few breaths and forced a smile. It was a lot right now. Too much to process at once. "Well, look at it this way: Just because rules are in place, it doesn't mean things can't change. Look at Zin for example. I bet nobody expected to see a female Ranger ten years ago. Why is it so hard to think that a Ranger could balance a career and a serious relationship?"

"Rules are in place for a reason," he said firmly. "To keep people safe."

"Sometimes rules need to be re-evaluated. Once upon a time, women couldn't vote on the mainland. At the time, that rule was there for a reason. Did it need to be re-evaluated?"

He looked down.

"Well?"

"That's different."

"Every rule is different. No circumstance or situation is the same, and that's exactly my point."

"This is a matter of life and death. What if I was the one to find you lying there on The Forest floor?" He turned a pained expression on me. "Do you think I'd be able to stop and think? You weren't breathing. If he'd killed you, there is no way I could've stopped myself from…" He took a shaky breath. "I wouldn't have thought logically. I would've reacted on basic instincts, and my basic instincts would've ended in Thomas dead. I wouldn't have thought twice about it. That is dangerous."

"He was going to kill me," I said quietly. Until now, I'd been hiding my neck. The angry marks made me feel self-conscious and weak, even though it wasn't my fault. However now, I tilted my neck upwards and exposed the lines to Ranger X. "Maybe your instincts should be trusted."

"I am the leader of the Ranger program. I have to live by a code."

"Would any of your Rangers have objected if you'd killed Thomas?"

Ranger X bit the inside of his lip and stared forlornly out into the distance. His code of honor was strong, and I could see his wants and needs and desires all fighting for a place in his heart. The battle stalled, his eyes empty.

"On the mainland we have people who protect the other humans. Firefighters, cops, hundreds of thousands of people risk their lives every day running into burning buildings or standing up to criminals with guns," I said softly. "They're allowed to love. They're allowed to be married, experience life, and be happy. Nobody on this island wants you to sacrifice everything for them. The islanders love you. They won't begrudge your happiness."

"Maybe they don't know what they need."

"Maybe not," I said, my voice cracking as I realized the futility of arguing with him. My heart sank and my shoulders dropped, suddenly lifeless. Even my head felt too heavy to hold high. "Do you know what I think?"

Ranger X had been running his hand along his chin in thought, but he paused at my tone. "What do you think?"

"I think you're scared." My eyes smarted with tears. "I don't know why, but you seem to think you can't have it all, that you can't care for me and care about your work. We've only known each other a few weeks. There's no reason we can't take things slow and see how they go, but if we do, then we have to talk about it. You and I have to work together and try and fight to figure things out."

"But—"

"I care about you, but I can't be your everything," I barreled on. "What will you do if you give up your work? You love being a Ranger. I've seen you working a handful of times and it's written on your face. We can't be two halves of people coming together—that'll only lead to a broken relationship. We need to be two whole people before we can work on us being one together, and I don't think you want to do that."

"Of course I'm scared," he said, his voice as soft as a knife slicing through air. "But we have rules for a reason. If someone gets hurt on my watch, or if my decisions are not solid, or if something happens to you, then what?"

"I want to be with you." I stepped forward, a salty tear coursing down my cheek. "I would love to make a relationship work, or at least try. But what are you going to do, work at the supply store? Ask Harpin for a job stocking tea?"

"What do you want me to say?" He ran a hand across his forehead. "It's an either or situation."

"I want you to be with me, but I want you to be happy, too," I said. "Tell me honestly. If you gave up your Ranger career to be with me, would you be happy?"

His extended pause was all I needed to hear.

"That's what I thought," I said softly. "This situation isn't hopeless, X. Times change. Rules evolve. There is a way for you to keep your career and have a relationship with me if you want it badly enough. I can't force it on you, though. I can argue and fight for it all I want, but at the end of the day, you have to decide what makes you happy."

"Lily…" He drew me to him, his fingers cinching the skin on my hips until it bordered on painful.

I pressed my face to his chest and gripped his shirt as his hold on me loosened. He murmured an apology, encircling his hands around my back, his lips reaching for mine.

He held me tight, the two of us wrapped in an embrace as the cold water danced over our ankles. My skin prickled with goose bumps, but my face warmed under his kiss. His tongue slipped into my mouth as his hand raked over my bare back—gentle, but possessive. The summer dress I wore flowed down to my feet. It was strapless, for which I was grateful as his hands ran over my shoulders and sent shivers down my spine.

I whispered his name carefully, but the word was swept away by an even deeper sound from his throat.

When he said my name back, I jolted back to attention and stepped away from him.

"No," I said, my entire body trembling. "I don't even know your real name. Anything else isn't fair for either of us. Figure out what you want, and then come and talk to me."

The rest of the tears began to fall then, so I turned away and ducked my bruised neck. I was vulnerable enough without showing my scars to the world. With my head down, sandals in hand, I shuffled across the sand and away from Ranger X. He called after me once, and I ignored it. The second time he said my name, I started to jog. The third time, I ran as fast as I could in the opposite direction.

His voice carried over the sand and his eyes watched me go, but his feet didn't follow.

CHAPTER 29

Three weeks later

"I TOLD YOU TO START GETTING ready earlier, Mom," Poppy said. "We're going to be late."

"Oh, dear, relax," Mimsey said, her tone as scattered as her curly locks. She ran her hands over an armchair-patterned dress that looked like it should be covering a bean bag instead of a human, but Mimsey somehow rocked the look anyway. Sweeping another hand through her locks, she muttered something about her glasses.

"Here, Mom," Poppy said, leaning over and handing her mom the thick-rimmed glasses hanging from a necklace made from bright pieces of sea glass. "They're always around your neck."

"It's been so long since I've had an excuse to dress up. It's not my fault I can't remember how this works." Mimsey gave a faux-glare at her daughter. "It's not like any of you children are getting married. If I had a wedding to go to, maybe things would be different."

"Yeah, yeah, we've heard it. Come on, Zin is waiting. Trinket is going to tear you a new one if we show up late to the ceremony."

"Trinket can tear herself a brand spankin' new—"

"Mom!" Poppy roared. "Put your glasses on, and let's go!"

I hid a smirk and followed the bickering mother-daughter duo. Despite their banter back and forth, they walked side by side. Poppy carefully intertwined her arm through her mother's, the two of them balancing off one another as they navigated the rocky beach path in their high heels.

I, too, was dressed up, but I'd opted for wedge sandals which gave me the height without the trouble of a stiletto. Mimsey and Poppy didn't factor practicality into their outfits. What they did factor in, however, was color. Walking together, the pair looked like a fruit basket tie-dyed in Kool-Aid.

Mimsey's dress was sky blue and bright yellow, while Poppy flaunted a long, flowy muumuu in bright red decorated with green and yellow flowers. She looked stunning, the dress brushing softly over her curves, complimenting her dazzling personality and bright smile. Her cheeks were flushed from walking, and her eyes were bright with excitement.

I'd gone with a much more toned-down look. My dark hair was pulled in a chignon at the nape of my neck, mostly so I wouldn't have to battle flyaways from the lake breeze. My closet had populated with a variety of dress options after I'd learned the appropriate spell, and I'd selected a navy-blue dress that wrapped tight around my body with simple, tank-top sleeves. It ended just above my knees, and I'd added a white shawl. Poppy told me I looked like a sexy sailor. Mimsey told me I looked like a politician. I'd settle for looking presentable.

"Turn here," Mimsey said, guiding us past the supply store to the edge of The Forest. "I hear them setting up. We're just in time for the opening anthem."

The three of us shuffled into an arena that I'd never before seen. In fact, the inside was so large, I wondered if it hadn't been enhanced by magic. There was no other explanation for how I'd missed the basketball court-sized space plopped in the middle of The Isle. Seats rose high on either side, putting the nosebleed section at American football games to shame. Luckily, as we were Guests of Honor, we didn't have to go far. Trinket waved us over, her face pinched in annoyance.

"Told you she wouldn't be happy," Poppy muttered. "Do you think she saved us a seat?"

"My sister's never happy," Mimsey said. "There are three spots next to her, I see them."

We shuffled into the saved seats just in front of Trinket and six of her seven children. The seventh child, Zin, was nowhere to be seen. However, when I snatched a program off the empty chair a row ahead, I found her face staring back at me.

Zin, along with nine others, had been selected to join the Ranger Initiation Program. Today, she'd be given the gear and the blessing of the islanders as she started the rigorous training program. Though it was a cause for celebration and much honor, she had a long way to go before she became an official Ranger. According to Poppy, less than fifty percent of the starting class finished the program. From there, only one or two Candidates were hired to work for Ranger HQ.

Even so, this was a big step forward—not only for Zin, but for the entire Ranger culture. Whispers circled the arena as everyone watched and waited to glimpse the first ever female Candidate.

I couldn't have been more proud.

"There she is!" Mimsey clapped her hands wildly, and then stood up and whistled so loud the entire stadium quieted. "Sorry, sorry," she murmured as Poppy tugged on her arm. "Sorry, it's just so exciting—that's my niece down there!"

Despite Poppy's efforts to calm her mother down, none of us could wipe smiles off our faces.

However, mine dimmed as Ranger X walked onstage, looking handsome as ever in a tailored suit. The confidence and grace surrounding him was second to none, and this time, the audience quieted on its own.

"Islanders," he called out. "Welcome."

A few last-minute arrivals squeezed their way into seats. After everyone settled down and all eyes focused on the stage, Ranger X looked up at the crowd and scanned the audience collectively.

I wondered whether or not he knew I was in the stadium. He'd probably assumed I'd be watching—a safe assumption since *everyone* on The Isle was here. Plus, Zin was my cousin. There was no way I'd miss the event. Oddly enough, however, his eyes skipped over our section and skimmed the rest of the faces as he made a full sweep of the arena.

"This is a year of changes," he said, before spiraling off into a long introduction that detailed the long, strenuous process the Candidates would have to endure before becoming a Ranger. "The chances that more than two of these Candidates standing before you today make it to the final challenge—securing a position at Ranger HQ—are slim. But we applaud their effort. It's not easy to become a Candidate, and the going will only become more difficult. When you see one of these faces on the streets this week, thank them. They are here to protect all of you."

Another speech followed, detailing the rise of The Faction and the dangers that hid in our midst. Word of the attack against me had spread, and paranoia had seeped into the minds of some of the islanders. Children were called to bed early, and parents looked over their shoulders and locked their doors. Luckily there'd been no further incidents, but it was only a matter of time now. Chatter about the unity and strength of The Faction was loud and clear, and even the most skeptical of islanders were forced to pay attention.

I'd zoned out toward the end of the speech, not recognizing many of the names as Ranger X began to announce the Candidates one by one. When there was only one name left, Poppy elbowed me. "Look, she's up!"

"I started this speech by saying this was a year of changes. Now and again, we must revisit the rules we have in place and ask ourselves why they are there." He looked up, his gaze eerily falling on mine for a long moment before he blinked and scanned the rest of the crowd. "Our policy against female Rangers is one of them. It ceases to exist as of today. The strongest, the smartest, and the most deserving individuals will join our program. With that said, I am pleased to announce our first ever female Candidate. She has landed here through hard work, perseverance, and bravery. Above all, her selflessness has saved a life. I am honored to present Zinnia Dixie as a Candidate for the Ranger program."

The applause was thunderous. Tears streamed down Mimsey's cheeks, and even Trinket dabbed her eyes with a beautifully embroidered hanky. Zin's siblings went as wild as orangutans on cotton candy, and the rest of the audience was no different. Ranger X had to signal upwards of four times before the islanders quieted down. "These next weeks will be difficult ones for the Candidates, but I believe that I speak for all of us when I say we're looking forward to it. Without further ado… let the training begin."

CHAPTER 30

"I HAD NO IDEA BECOMING A Candidate was such an honor," I murmured to Poppy as we descended the stairs from the arena amid a sea of excited bodies. "I mean, I knew it was difficult and honorable, but this is like a reality TV show. The Candidates are celebrities."

"It's the highest honor," she said, looking over her shoulder in search of Zin. "I'm so proud of her."

"Me too," I said. "Will we get to watch the training?"

"You'll be able to watch some of them via live broadcast, though there are a few private sessions." She winked. "It's an exciting time."

"By the way, I forgot to give you this. I finished it up this morning." From my oversized purse, I pulled out a sealed bottle of her Vamp Vites. "I tried it myself, and it seems to be working fine."

"Oh, thank you," she gushed. "I ran out of the temporary supply earlier today. I was going to check with you, but with everything going on, I forgot. You are a lifesaver."

Before I could wave off her thank-you, a shadow appeared by my shoulder. "May I have a word?"

I looked up to find Ranger X's large frame standing over me, his outfit impeccable despite the warmth of the sun this afternoon. I glanced to Poppy, who nodded back with wide eyes. "Okay," I said. "But I need to find Zin."

"I'll be quick," he said in a clipped tone. "I promise."

"Take your time!" Poppy yelled after us as we walked away. "Zin will understand—I promise."

I hid a small smile as we walked away, our shoulders not quite touching. We hadn't spoken much in the past weeks.

Once we were a safe distance away, he peered through dark lashes at me, his gaze a complicated one. "Zin's really something. You should be proud of your cousin."

"I am." I nodded. "I'm really happy for her."

As we walked away from the arena toward the bungalow, we passed the same spot he'd kissed me on the night we'd discussed the complicated thing between us.

"I talked with my Rangers," he said abruptly. "We sat down and reviewed our best practices and rules. All of them."

"I suppose you had to, what with Zin becoming a Candidate."

"All of the rules. Not just that one."

"Mmm."

He turned to face me. "I wanted to make sure I wasn't changing the rules for selfish reasons. We're a team at Ranger HQ, and that wouldn't be fair."

"That's very noble of you. Then again, I wouldn't expect anything less."

"We decided to open up the rules regarding relationships," he said. "It's on a trial basis right now. Turns out, most of the Rangers have a—shall we say—special sort of friend on the side anyway. It was unanimous."

I cleared my throat. "That's great. I'm sure it'll make a lot of ladies happy."

"Will it make you happy?" He looked out of the corner of his eye at me as we reached the front of the bungalow. "Because that's the only lady I care about."

"It does make me happy," I said slowly. "But it's also just a rule. A note scratched on a piece of paper. What would really make me happy is if you threw the rule book away and told me how you feel."

Ranger X's expression briefly flashed discomfort. Then he nodded. "Fair enough. Here's what I want: I want to get to know you. Last time we talked, I was upset. I was angry, too emotional, and I shouldn't have used that time to talk about us. But I've thought about it a lot, and I want to take things slow. I want to take you on a real date with a real kiss."

"And your career?"

"I plan on staying on as Leader of the Rangers for as long as I'm able," he said with a mischievous sort of grin. "Someone has to watch over Zin as she learns the ropes."

"I like this plan," I said. "If you're happy with it."

"I'll be happy if you'll have dinner with me tonight."

I bit my lip. "We're celebrating Zin's accomplishment. It's not the best time, I'm really sorry."

"Another night, then," he said. "No problem."

"No," I said suddenly. "Come with me tonight. The others would love it."

Ranger X pulled me into a hug, dipping me low, dusting a kiss against my lips. "I'll be there."

"No, you won't," a voice called from behind us. We both straightened up so fast I got dizzy. "Not if you keep kissin' like that. I'm tellin' Mimsey on y'all if you don't stop makin' out in front of the bungalow. It's unprofessional."

"Don't be a snitch, Gus," I called to the old man tapping about on the porch with his cane. "Or I'm going to tell Mimsey you don't like her toast. I see you hiding it under your plate."

Gus fell silent, and I knew we had a deal.

"Get inside," he growled finally. "We've got work to do. Your antidote for the poison is finished. It'll burn if you don't untangle your lips from that hooligan's face."

Ranger X spluttered. "Hooligan?"

"Yer a hooligan!" Gus pointed his cane at him. "Stop distracting my girl from her studies."

At Gus's words, my heart melted a bit. "I've gotta go," I said to

X. "I've been working on a potion to combat the poison Thomas was brewing, just in case we ever need it."

Ranger X grinned. "He already thinks I'm a hooligan. Might as well live up to my reputation."

Right in front of Gus, he kissed me on the lips and twirled me in a circle. He made the show a little extra long until Gus started cursing a blue streak. It was too distracting to ignore, so we broke apart with broad grins.

"So, what's it called?" Ranger X asked as I made my way up to the bungalow a few moments later. "The antidote. Just in case I ever need it."

I glanced inside the storeroom, smiling at *The Magic of Mixology* which, thanks to Zin, had been retrieved from The Forest and placed back in its safe. Still smiling, I turned back and took a bow. "Witchy Sour, comin' right up."

EPILOGUE

Later that Evening

I MADE MY WAY THROUGH THE Twist dressed, as Hettie had instructed, in a black robe that covered my face and swished around my ankles. The hour was late, the moon creeping toward the sky as flowers the size of my kitchen table bloomed to either side of the path.

A few minutes later, swatting at a swarm of zingers—the magical nickname for mosquitos—I stumbled out of The Twist and into the well-manicured yard that Hettie called her lawn. Squinting, I realized that I wasn't alone.

A second person dressed in all black robes stood at the front door. Just as I hesitated, trying to recognize his or her figure, the door swung open and a hand beckoned the stranger inside. The door closed just as quickly as it'd opened.

I hurried forward, hoping that Hettie hadn't assumed it was me under that robe. I crossed my fingers, wishing the other guest to be friend, not foe.

I jogged down the cobblestone path and cleared the bridge over Hettie's decorative, bubbling brook in an instant. I was at the front door with my hand raised hardly twenty seconds after the first figure had disappeared inside.

Hettie had called me here tonight for one reason.

She'd promised me answers.

After my tussle with Thomas in The Forest, I'd been left with some burning questions. Gus and Ranger X didn't seem particularly chatty when I brought them up, and Poppy and Zin were either clueless, or they were great at pretending to know nothing.

"What are you doing? *Knocking?*" The door swung open, and Hettie's eyes danced across the lawn. "What didn't you understand when I told you to be *discreet?*"

"There was someone here before me—" I stopped abruptly at Hettie's obvious stare. "Oh, you were expecting someone else, too."

"Yes," she grumped. "Come in now before the entire world sees you."

"Nobody can get through The Twist unless you ring them in," I said, stepping into the echoing hall that looked out of place from the cottage-esque exterior. I lowered my hood. "Well, and West Isle Witches, but nobody followed me."

"I'm glad to see you can obey some instructions." Hettie closed the door firmly behind me, and I scanned the hallway, looking for a tiger. I was pretty sure it didn't exist, but I'd gotten into the habit of checking, just in case. Better safe than sorry, especially when it came to Hettie's tricks. "Come out to the porch. It's charmed to keep all sound inside so we won't be overheard."

I followed Hettie to the rear of the house where a full-sized wraparound porch spanned the length of the back wall. "Who else are we waiting for?"

"You're both here." Hettie gestured to the porch.

"Gus?" I moved forward as he pulled his hood back from his face. "What are you doing here?"

"This is my meeting, not his." Hettie clapped her hands. "Attention on me, *por favor.*"

Feeling more confused than ever, I took a seat in a rickety old rocking chair and gave Gus a curious side-eye as I waited for Hettie to clear her throat.

"Lily, I asked you here tonight because I think it's time you learned a few answers to those questions you've been annoying everyone with lately," Hettie said. "You know, the ones about your history, and all of that jazz."

"Annoying everyone?" I said faintly.

Gus gave a subtle roll of his eyes and a shake of his head. If I read his look right, he was telling me not to argue.

"Wonderful," I said instead. "Answers?"

"When we brought you back to The Isle a few months ago," Hettie said, "we wanted you to learn and grow and adjust organically to the culture. We knew it'd be a shock after spending most of your life in the human realm. We would have brought you over sooner, but unfortunately due to the curse, that wasn't possible. We couldn't find you. It took years and years to crack that curse."

"Mimsey and Trinket have mentioned that before," I said. "Who cursed me?"

"Your own mother cursed you," Hettie said. "She made it impossible for us to find you for twenty-five years."

"What?" I cleared my throat. "Why would she do that?"

"She wanted you to live to see your twenty-sixth birthday." Hettie's pace slowed, her eyes darkening as she remembered. "I can't say that I blame her."

I shook my head, still not understanding.

"She knew you had the Mixology gene, or suspected it, at least. I think we all did on some level when you were born. There's something about you, Lily. A power that seeps from your pores. Even as a baby..."

She trailed off, and then cleared her throat. "I'm sorry. Your mother is my daughter, and sometimes..." Hettie stopped to gather her breath. "She *was* my daughter, I should say. Almost a year after you were born, your mother slipped into the dark of night and brought you to the mainland. You see, The Faction realized you had been born. The next Mixologist had arrived, and for them, that was dangerous."

I looked over at Gus, but he was too busy staring at his hands, listening, to look back.

"If your mother had stayed on The Isle with you, we would have trained you from birth. You would have worked hard, you would have been pushed to learn and understand and do great things, even as a child. And, most importantly, you would've had a target on your back."

"Your mother came to me," Gus interrupted. "The night she left for the mainland, she came to me with you as a babe, cradled in her arms. I'll never forget it." He shook his head. "Her eyes... they were on fire. I've never seen such a look before. She loved you, Lily, a lot."

"Why did she take me away?" I asked. "I like it here. I would've liked it here, even if it was dangerous."

"It was more than dangerous." Gus folded his hands in his lap, continuing to stare at his fingernails. "You wouldn't have survived. The Faction would've targeted you before you became an adult, before you realized your full powers, and they would have eliminated you. When your mother came to me asking for my opinion, I gave it to her. She asked if it would be selfish of her to steal you away, to curse you so that nobody could find you until you were old enough to understand the risks yourself, and I told her *no*. I didn't think it was selfish then, and I don't think so now."

"My mother cursed me herself..." I still couldn't *understand* it. Not completely.

"I advised her to do it," Gus said. "And I stand by my words. I helped her escape that night, though we couldn't tell anyone else. I'm still sorry that your mother couldn't say goodbye, but it was just too risky. If someone suspected, if someone interfered with the curse, all would have been lost."

"What happened to her?" I swallowed. "Is she... alive?"

Gus blinked, once and then twice, before continuing. "The Faction realized what was happening as soon as she reached the mainland. They got to her, but it was too late for them to find you—the curse had already been enabled. Your mother was not as fortunate."

"And my dad?"

"Lily, the man you grew up with is not your father," Hettie said. "He was a decoy."

I shook my head. "Excuse me?"

"Ainsley." Hettie stepped forward. "You know the name?"

"Are you talking about my assistant from Lions Marketing?"

Hettie laughed. An actual chuckle. "I suppose."

"What about her?"

"She is so much more than a marketing assistant," Hettie said. "She is a Guardian."

"I don't understand."

"MAGIC, Inc. is the name of our central governing body on the mainland. It stands for Magic and Guardians Investigative Committee. Ainsley works as a Guardian, and that means it's her job to watch high-risk targets."

"That's impossible," I said. "She only worked with me for a short time."

"She's been around," Hettie said. "We learned of her after your twenty-fifth birthday. The curse was also a protective charm, and it meant that Ainsley was bound to you for the length of the curse—twenty-five years—and it was her duty to protect you from any and all harm."

"That's impossible," I said again. "She's not old enough to have been around that long."

"Aging as a witch is much slower than aging as a human." Hettie's face turned mildly amused. "In Ainsley's world, she's only been watching over you for two years. She got the job on her twenty-first birthday, a young little pipsqueak. She just turned twenty-three."

I frowned. "But what about Poppy and Zin? Are they my age?"

Hettie nodded. "The slow aging only begins as an adult.

Children grow at the same rate as human children. It's only once witches hit adulthood and full power—sometime between the ages of twenty and thirty—that the aging process slows. You, Poppy, and Zin are all just beginning the process, but Ainsley started early. Probably on her twentieth birthday, if I had to guess."

"Back to Ainsley..." I said. "So, she has been watching over me my entire life?"

Hettie nodded. "Did a good job of it, too."

"She's magic," I said flatly. "She knew about magic this whole time."

Hettie nodded again. "More than you, I'd say."

I frowned, trying to process. "Does that mean I can see her again if she already knows about this world?"

My grandmother waved a hand. "Of course you can. But let's focus for now. Time for parties later."

"Let me get this straight. The man I always thought was my father was a decoy. Who was he?"

"A Companion." Hettie winced. "A shifter from the mainland who was tasked to protect you." She gave me an apologetic expression. "I hear he wasn't the most friendly soul. Sorry about that. But he turns into a bear, and I hear he's pretty ferocious. You couldn't see that part, of course."

At this point, my mouth just hung open, and I gave up trying to make sense of anything. "Then who is my real father?"

Hettie shook her head. "I can't answer that for you. I don't know. Your mother never told us."

I blinked. "Excuse me?"

"We don't have time for that story today," Hettie said. "I'm sorry, you can talk to your aunts about that some other time, though they don't know anything either."

I moved on, even though my head was spinning. "The curse broke when I turned twenty-five."

"It broke just after your twenty-sixth birthday, and that's

when we came for you," Hettie said. "Well, Mimsey and Trinket at least, since I was feeling lazy and didn't want to make the trek to the mainland."

"How thoughtful."

Hettie ignored me. "In retrospect, the curse was the best gift your mother could have left you with, even if it was the most frustrating thing in the world for a quarter century. We looked for you, we searched and searched and searched but we couldn't find you."

"Neither could The Faction," Gus said. "And now, we have you here. A powerful Mixologist. We need you now more than ever, and it's thanks to your mother that we have you here today. The curse saved your life."

Staring at the two of them through eyes as wide as dinner plates, I shook my head. "I thought I came here for answers. I have more questions than ever."

"We need to talk about what happened with Thomas," Gus said quietly. "I owe you some explanations."

"You?" I turned to him. "What haven't you told me?"

"I stole *The Magic of Mixology*," Gus said, beginning with something I already knew. "I had to do it to prove my loyalty to The Core."

"The Core," I said quietly. "The group of five people formed to fight The Faction."

Gus nodded. "The Core was made up of me, Harpin, Turin, Thomas... and the leader."

"Do you know the leader?" I asked, looking between the two. "Do you?" I asked Hettie.

"Nobody does." Gus shook his head. "I explained to Hettie about The Core only because she needed to know, and now you do, too. But it must be kept secret. Turin and Thomas are gone now, but The Core must remain."

"Turin. I saw him," I said quietly. "He came to me before Thomas…"

"I know," Gus interrupted. "Turin could see what was happening. He suspected Thomas. When he sensed the end was near…"

The room fell silent.

"Turin took The Elixir to protect you," Gus said. "Thomas was after him already. He may have already been poisoned by Thomas. Taking The Elixir gave him one last chance to help."

"He was poisoned," I whispered. "He saved my life."

"It's what he wanted, Lily." Gus got to his feet and took a few steps over. He rested a hand on my shoulder. "All of us who joined The Core vowed to give our lives to serve."

"Why is Harpin allowed into The Core?" I asked, pulling my head out of my hands. "He's terrible."

Gus's breath caught. "I don't disagree with you, but the leader chose Harpin."

"The leader also chose Thomas."

"No," Gus said. "We thought the leader chose Thomas, but really, Thomas tricked his way into the group. We didn't realize it until it was too late. By then, Thomas had already inflicted too much damage. He even took my cane, probably to frame me, and left it in The Forest." Gus's fists shook with rage. "If you hadn't found him, he would've killed me and set me up to take the fall for the deadly potion. Thomas would've escaped."

"And Zin, does she have a role in any of this?" I looked to my grandmother.

"Zin has her own path to follow," she said. "And it is not the same as yours. In fact, it is of the utmost importance that you not tell her, nor Ranger X, about The Core."

I frowned. "But you know about it, and I know too. Plus, there's Gus, Harpin, and the leader. Don't we want more people on our side?"

"Rangers are loyal first and foremost to other Rangers,"

Hettie explained. "The Core is loyal to The Core. Do you see our issues? Should Zin become a Ranger, we may have our differences, however slight."

"Aren't we fighting for the same thing?"

Hettie conceded my point with a tilt of her head. "Still, there are instances where our tactics may differ. I need your word, Lily."

I hesitated, and then blew out a breath of air. "Fine. I won't say anything. Why are you allowed to know but not them?"

Hettie smiled, her eyes both sad and amused, all at once. "I am The Core."

Gus's mouth parted in surprise, but his eyes didn't reflect the same emotion. His face had the content look of someone who'd known this ending was inevitable.

I didn't feel the same way. "What are you talking about?"

"Your grandfather entrusted me with the care of you, with the care of The Isle, and with the care of our people," she said. "It is from him—my husband—that you've inherited the genealogy that allows you to become the Mixologist."

A thousand questions entered my mind, but I refrained from asking any of them.

"Before he died, he made me promise to carry on in his footsteps." Hettie's wild personality had softened into the frame of a tired, elderly woman. "I may appear old, I may look frail, and I may dress like a popstar because I'm glamorous. But glamorous old ladies can still be badass, Lily."

"If this is all so secretive, then why are you telling me about it?" I wanted to hear more about my grandfather, but now was not the time. Those stories would have to come later.

"Because we need you to join The Core," Hettie said. "Without you, we are nothing. Please consider it. The risks are high, and the cost severe. If I could give you a way out, I would. The truth is that we need you, and your grandfather would agree."

I looked to Gus, but he raised his eyebrows in question, also waiting for my response.

"Whatever you need," I said. "Of course."

Hettie stood up, straightened the tiara that'd slipped off of her gray hair, and hiked up the rhinestone-studded sweater around her shoulders. "Good," she said. "Then let's get started. I have a target on my head, and I want it off."

I blanched. "What sort of target?"

"A target to the tune of ten million coins," Hettie said without flinching. "Someone from within The Faction is silencing the leading voices of the resistance one by one. Apparently, I'm up next on the black list. Let's put an end to this, shall we?"

The End

THANK YOU, ISLANDERS!

Dear Islanders,

Thank you for reading *Witchy Sour*! If you enjoyed it, please stay tuned for the story to continue in book three! Lily and Ranger X wouldn't be here without you.

Sincerely,
Gina

Books By Gina LaManna

Here is a list of other books by Gina
LaManna: http://bit.ly/GinaLaManna.

Magic & Mixology Mysteries:
Hex on the Beach
Witchy Sour

Reading Order for Lacey Luzzi:
Lacey Luzzi: Scooped
Lacey Luzzi: Sprinkled
Lacey Luzzi: Sparkled
Lacey Luzzi: Salted
Lacey Luzzi: Sauced
Lacey Luzzi: S'mored
Lacey Luzzi: Spooked
Lacey Luzzi: Seasoned
Lacey Luzzi: Spiced

The Little Things Mystery Series:
One Little Wish
Two Little Lies

Misty Newman:
Teased to Death
Short Story in Killer Beach Reads

Chick Lit:
Girl Tripping

Gina also writes books for kids under the
Pen Name Libby LaManna:

Mini Pie the Spy!
Mini Pie the Christmas Spy!

WEBSITES AND SOCIAL MEDIA:

Find out more about the author and upcoming books online at www.ginalamanna.com or:

Email: gina.m.lamanna@gmail.com
Twitter: @Gina_LaManna
Facebook: facebook.com/GinaLaMannaAuthor
Website: www.ginalamanna.com

About the Author:

Originally from St. Paul, Minnesota, Gina LaManna began writing with the intention of making others smile. At the moment, she lives in Los Angeles and spends her days writing short stories, long stories, and all sizes in-between stories. She publishes under a variety of pen names, including a children's mystery series titled Mini Pie the Spy!

In her spare time, Gina has been known to run the occasional marathon, accidentally set fire to her own bathroom, and survive days on end eating only sprinkles, cappuccino foam and ice cream. She enjoys spending time with her family and friends most of all.

Made in the USA
Middletown, DE
27 May 2020